She didn't want to meet a new man. The one she'd already met was driving her crazy...

Dee scanned the rest of the crowd. "Sure do wish Alex Whitlow had come."

"You better not be trying to match me up with a rock star."

Dee put on her expression of doe-eyed innocence. "He's been married forever. Where Alex goes, his Suze goes. I was just wishing they'd come. We went to 40-Watt to hear his band Saturday night. Would've called, but knew you wouldn't go. Anyhoo, Alex has a buddy visiting from Los Angeles. Lordy, Kay, that man is so handsome he'd make you squint. And...drum roll...he's single."

"Does 'so handsome you'd have to squint' mean he's dark like Tom Cruise and Tommy Lyndon?"

"Um-hum." Dee massaged her tired feet. "That's why you and I never fought over boyfriends. You can have the blonds with big ole goofy grins."

For all Dee's seeming frivolity, she was astute at reading people. She gave Kathryn's hand a meaningful squeeze. "If you should meet Alex's friend, be nice. That's all I'm saying. Alex called earlier, asking where you live."

"Me? Why?"

"I dunno. The caterer showed up, and I didn't have time to ask."

"My, my." Tommy flopped into the chair beside his wife. "I'd like to be a fly on the wall over here."

"Gal-pal gab," Dee said. She rolled her eyes toward Kathryn, who had drifted far away again.

Joe Butler's voice rang in Kathryn's mind: *Movies and musicians make good bedfellows.* She knew exactly who was visiting Alex Whitlow.

Grieving the loss of her husband and child, she just wants to be left alone...

On the brink of severe depression, Kathryn Tribble abandons her New York editing career and seeks sanctuary in rural Georgia where she grew up. But one of her major clients, celebrity author Joe Butler, pursues her, insisting she edit his first fiction novel. Kathryn reluctantly agrees, but is devastated when the manuscript seems to be mined from her very own misfortune. Instead of finding the peace she longs for, Kathryn is once again pushed to the brink.

Hiding a sham marriage and caring for his seriously ill daughter, he wants much more from her than editing skills...

Descending from Hollywood royalty, Joe's first book was a biography of his family, but Kathryn recognized he has a rare talent and challenged him to write fiction. Doing so, he transforms the raw courage he sees, in her efforts to reclaim her life, into what promises to be a blockbuster heroine. His hard work backfires when Kathryn refuses to have anything more to do with the book—or with him. Heartsick at the pain he's unintentionally caused her, Joe abandons the project. However, his megastar cousin, Colton Bennett, is determined to make it into a movie. Even worse, Colton becomes infatuated with Kathryn, convinced that, in his world of make believe, he can anchor himself to reality by making her his wife.

Mired in grief and pain, these three troubled people face a hard choice—to walk away and risk losing everything that matters, or to act on the heart.

KUDOS for *Act on the Heart*

In *Act on the Heart* by Genie Smith Bernstein, Kathryn Tribble is a burned-out New York editor. Grieving the loss of her husband to the war in the Middle East and her baby to a miscarriage, she leaves her job and heads for rural Georgia to find some peace and healing. But her major client, celebrity author Joe Butler, follows her to Georgia, demanding that she edit his new novel. Since Kathryn was the one who recognized his talent and encouraged him to write fiction, she feels obligated. However, when she reads the manuscript, she is horrified. It seems to be a thinly disguised, unauthorized biography of her. Despite his obvious talent and the blockbuster potential of the novel, she refuses to have anything more to do with the book or with Joe, and begins seeing Joe's cousin, Colton—a serious mistake for everyone concerned. Bernstein really has a way with words. Her voice is unique and refreshing, very down to earth. Her characters are well-developed and feel very real. This is a story that will tug on your heartstrings. ~ *Taylor Jones, Reviewer*

Act on the Heart by Genie Smith Bernstein is a heartwarming story of a young woman who's devastated by the recent loss of her husband to war and her unborn child through a miscarriage, and who is trying to start over by leaving her big city life with its heartbreaking memories and returning to her roots. Our heroine, Kathryn, leaves her high-profile job as a New York editor and heads for rural Georgia and a deceased relative's small cottage, where she hopes the peace and quiet will allow her broken heart to heal. Enter our hero, Joe Butler and his movie-star cousin Colton Bennett. Joe was one of Kathryn's clients in New York and he is determined to have Kathryn edit his new novel. Colton is just determined to have Kathryn. Period. But all she wants is to be left alone, and she is totally caught off guard when she somehow ends up in a love triangle with these two dynamic men. Somehow, her healing time in her little rural sanctuary is causing her more problems than if she had stayed in New York. Add in Colton's psychotic fan who now sees Kathryn as her number one threat, and just about anything can happen. The characters are both charming and realistic. You can't help rooting for Kathryn as she tries to put her life back together after her tragic losses. *Act on the Heart* is about starting over and trusting once again, even though your head tells your heart it's not worth the risk. ~ *Regan Murphy, Reviewer*

Act on the Heart

Genie Smith Bernstein

A Black Opal Books Publication

GENRE: CONTEMPORARY ROMANCE/ROMANTIC SUSPENSE

This is a work of fiction. Names, places, characters and incidents are either the product of the author's imagination or are used fictitiously, and any resemblance to any actual persons, living or dead, businesses, organizations, events or locales is entirely coincidental. All trademarks, service marks, registered trademarks, and registered service marks are the property of their respective owners and are used herein for identification purposes only. The publisher does not have any control over or assume any responsibility for author or third-party websites or their contents.

ACT ON THE HEART
Copyright © 2015 by Genie Bernstein
Cover Design by Jackson Cover Designs
All cover art copyright © 2015
Act on the Heart painting, *Reflections on a Summer Porch*, by Esther Farley
All Rights Reserved
Print ISBN: 978-1-626944-22-0

First Publication: AUGUST 2015

Published by Black Opal Books **http://www.blackopalbooks.com**

DEDICATION

To my Husband and Family
I love you one and all!

Prologue

Deep in a Georgia Forest, 1944:

Her note had said "tree at three." Charlie arrived early. He took out his penknife and dug away more of the bark, deepening the heart he had carved on the forest giant when he was merely a lad. A lad in love.

His coonhound heard her first and bayed in welcome. Putting away his knife, the young man felt his chest swell with anticipation. He turned, eagerly waiting for his love to step into the clearing formed by, and ruled by, their rare double-trunk oak. Cold winter sunlight glinted off the brass on the uniform she wore, tiny bolts of lightning too bright and painful for him to look upon.

Aghast, he ran to enfold her in his arms. "Why?"

"You know why," she said, pulling away, straightening her new cap.

"Be—because of me?"

"Because of us."

"This isn't right."

"It's the only right thing to do." She looked up into

the branches of the majestic white oak, its meadow their meeting place throughout their years of innocence, and beyond. "One of us must go, and you can't. Not with your—" She placed a hand on his chest, over his heart with the faulty valve, damage from when she'd almost lost him to rheumatic fever.

He heard the catch in her voice, but he recognized the set of her jaw, the resolve deeply embedded in her quiet brown eyes. "WAC's is the army. Where will you go—be sent?"

"I'm not sure. England, maybe France. I asked for France. I've always wanted to go there."

The weight of her words crushed him to tears. "Yes, but with me. We were going together." He grabbed her to his chest, holding on desperately as his world dissolved. "I love you, Tildy," he choked. "I'll die without you."

She took his hand and held him at arm's length. "We have too much love, Charlie. It will ruin our family if I stay."

Chapter 1

Kathryn Tribble arrived at work, fighting for air and holding back tears. She bolted off the elevator on the seventieth floor and added claustrophobia to her list of ailments. With a false smile plastered on her face, she negotiated the maze of cubicles between the lobby and her office, intent on not catching the eye of anyone on the editorial staff. She'd almost drowned yesterday in the stream of happy family Memorial Day tales from Monday's holiday. One more and she would scream.

She had promised herself she wouldn't call home, but as soon as she safely closed her door, she dropped her briefcase on the desk, pressed speed dial, and switched on the speaker. Slumped in her chair, she closed her eyes and imagined the hollow ringing in her empty apartment—one, two, three, four—until Sam's recorded baritone issued forth and embraced her.

"Hello, friend." He considered everyone his friend. "Kitty and I can't come to the phone right now." Kitty.

Sam's nickname for her. "Leave a number, and we'll get back to you."

Well, he didn't, did he? A roadside bomb in Afghanistan saw to that. Kathryn cut off the call before the jarring sound of the beep.

Nobody here named Kitty, she thought, rising to stand without purpose in the middle of her high-powered, high-rise domain. She had achieved her goal of becoming a copyeditor in a New York publishing house by the time she was thirty. Well, her thirtieth birthday, along with what should have been her baby's birthdate had rolled past in May. Now she was facing June with nothing motivating her except a desire to burst out the door, sprint for the dreaded elevator, and never look back.

Phyllis, exuberant maven of Omni Publishing and Kathryn's editorial assistant, barged in from the outer office. She wore a look of thunder behind her Swarovski-studded bifocals. "Oy! Colton Bennett is not showing up for this meeting either." She snatched a file off the desk. "It'll be his manager again, the cousin, Joe Butler."

Kathryn snapped her work smile into place. "Well, after all, Cousin Joe is the author. No reason to expect demi-god Colton. He'll have his own biography someday, but this one is focused on their grandparents, Hollywood royals who helped shape the movie industry. The media's macabre interest in their tragedy never wanes."

"True," Phyllis said. "Colton and Joe will go to their graves known as The Bennett Orphans."

Opening her briefcase, Kathryn pulled out galley copies of two other manuscripts she had worked on at home. "You've met more celebrities at Omni than you can shake a stick at, Phyl. What's so special about Colton Bennett?"

Phyllis pressed a hand to her chest in pretense of a swoon. "He is the spitting image of his grandfather. Not

ACKNOWLEDGEMENTS

I hope everyone has as much joy reading this book as I had writing it. As I pause to reflect on my many encouragers, not only in writing but in my life as a whole, I am truly humbled.

More thanks than I can express go to:

My husband Irwin, our six children, and their beloved spouses, plus each of our amazing grandchildren. You are everything.

God, for directing my thoughts and giving me siblings— Esther Farley, Roy Smith, and Patrice Underkofler. You keep me grounded. Special thanks to Esther for painting the world I imagined, and to sister-in-law, Phyllis Nardone, whose name brought a character to life.

Harriette Austin for fostering a community of writers devoted to one another far beyond the craft. Charles and Beverly Conner for the inimitable Harriette Austin Writers Conferences. Groups of writers consistently providing thoughtful critiques, wisdom, and advice: White Car Gang, Wednesday OCAF, Southern Scribes—Chris Antenen, Teresa Bacon, Patricia Bell-Scott, Alan Black, Dac Crossley, Paige Mercer Cummings, Marie Davis, Judy Iakovou, Larry McDougald, Donna McGinty, Jim Murdock, Janice Pulliam, Bob Smith, Diane Trap, Billie Wilson, and many more.

Old Birds Coffee Group for accepting me and freely sharing their wealth of life experiences—Billie Wilson, Connee Flynn, Janine Aronson. In absentia, Janice Pulliam and Diane Rounds. In spirit, Betty Reuter.

Two sets of lifelong cheerleaders for hearing my confessions and keeping my secrets. I count on you.

Keepers—Susan Calhoun, Tricia Fuller, Reena Garrett, Judy Gilbert, Julia Hardy, Joan McMullen, Holly Parker, Ann Rhoads.

Gal Pals—Liz Justus, Sandra Popham, Kristen Corbin.

Pat Worley's Truthseekers Sunday School Class for soothing my spirit. I need you.

Kim Wentworth for remedying my grammar and syntax, and for adding depth to this story.

Janine Aronson, whose life defines courage and inspired the book's title.

Lizz Bernstein for lighting a spark that made me declare, "I'm a Writer."

I love and appreciate every single one of you,

Genie.

only was I a card-carrying member of the William Bennett Fan Club, but Colton's autograph would elevate my stock considerably with my granddaughters."

"Well, what time are we expecting his wretched cousin?"

"Three o'clock. But I wouldn't go so far as to call Joe Butler wretched. Not with those shoulders on him."

"We'd be beautiful, too, if we lived their lives." Kathryn repositioned the placket of her skirt, a reflex acquired since her zippers had started to travel around her shrinking waist. She sat down again and took up Joe Butler's manuscript, fanning out the first chapter on the desk in front of her. "I'm glad you scheduled him for afternoon. I want to make one more pass through this."

Phyllis turned to leave, but stopped at the door and glanced back. "If you're working though lunch again, there's a pastrami in the fridge."

As she continued to pore over the written words, Kathryn could feel Phyllis studying her. The woman disapproved of what she called Kathryn's "bookworm mode."

An observation Kathryn was hard-pressed to dispute, with reading glasses perched on her nose and her brown hair dragged into a thoughtless ponytail.

Phyllis walked back across the room. "Plan on keeping up this pace forever, do you?"

Kathryn leaned back in her chair and tossed her pencil on the desk. "Zach says it's not a good time for me to take leave."

Phyllis snorted and her face hardened into a hawkish frown. "Our mighty leader thinks it's a better time for you to have a nervous breakdown, does he? That helps Omni's bottom line how?" She tapped a fuchsia nail on the desktop. "Listen, if I hadn't taken time off when I lost my Tony on 9/11—Bellevue, here I come. And you, the double whammy. Don't fool yourself. Miscarriage takes a toll."

"Maybe after this project."

"Or the next?" Phyllis's eyes lit on the galleys Kathryn had taken home. "Ruin your health. See what good that does." She marched out, almost slamming the door.

Kathryn took half her ponytail in each hand and gave a quick sideways tug to tighten the band before she picked up her pencil and resumed puzzling over Joe Butler's manuscript. He had a knack for making the truth read like a juicy novel, but she objected to backstory beginnings. How was she going to convince him to move part of his first chapter to a later point in the book? Also problematic was Colton Bennett being known in his family as Benny. But there was no getting around that. She read the first page for the umpteenth time:

> *Harriette 'Pet' Bennett opened her drapes and stepped onto the sun-drenched balcony. She drank in her favorite view. One might suppose that to be the dazzling Pacific beyond the palms in her rock garden, but one would suppose wrong. Looking down at the pool, she gazed upon her grandsons, her "beautiful boys." Up popped Benny, tawny and tan, laughing, with his upraised fist clutching an object retrieved from the depths. Joey broke the surface, dark and sleek as a seal, lunging on top of his cousin, wrestling over the morning's designated treasure. Under they went again, a scramble of elbows and knees, nine-year-old mermen, barely aware of the sharks lurking in the shadows of their lives.*

Kathryn could feel the sunshine and the grandmother's angst. What surprised her was not that the author had captured it, but that he sensed it in the first place. Pet Bennett and her husband William, Phyllis's old heartthrob, had sacrificed their twin daughters to those sharks trolling the waters of celebrity. On their twentieth birthday the Bennett beauties left the world the same way they came into it—together. Joe Butler's manuscript did not gloss over their tragic lives. Colton's mom was a saucy ingénue who'd never assigned her son's paternity to anyone and was thought not to have known it herself. Joe's mother, the hard-drinking sister, had eloped with a Texas oil tycoon. On a drunken jaunt to Las Vegas when the boys were mere babies, she'd driven her husband, twin, and herself into a fiery grave.

Succumbing to the Hollywood mystique, Kathryn read the end of the scene:

> *Pet called down from her balcony, "Last one up here is a rotten egg."*
>
> *Two wet heads swiveled to look up at her. Benny and Joey whooped and splashed their way to the side of the pool. Clambering out, the little hooligans raced into the house, dripping wet, yelling through the rotunda and up the stairs. Joey cut through Pet's dressing room and Benny bounced across her bed, to land simultaneously in her open arms.*

Kathryn hesitated a moment and then marked a swift edit. She combined the pages of the manuscript into a stack and aligned them with the lip of her desk. Rising to slip her thin arms into her suit jacket, she turned to look out over the city below. The glass wall appeared to waver. The office closed in, forcing her to breathe all the way down to the bottom of her lungs. She touched her forehead to the cool pane, an anchor to cold reality.

Vertigo was her new companion, this feeling of standing on a precipice, struggling to remain upright, while terrified she would lose her balance, fall, and keep falling. In her previous experience, grief was a state of mind, a sort of acceptance of loss over time, as with her father's heart failure and her mother's cancer. The six months since November, when Sam died, proved it to be physical. She existed in a void, assailed by myriad ailments. By an effort of will, she returned to her desk. Stomach roiling at the thought of Phyllis's pastrami, Kathryn bent her knees and sank into the chair.

Promptly at three, Phyllis shepherded Hollywood hotshot Joe Butler into Kathryn's office. They shook hands, and he declined her offer of a soda or coffee. As Phyllis was leaving, Kathryn pulled her aside. "You're right, Phyl. Go ahead and transfer my active files to Zach."

Phyllis's head jerked around, sending the chain that dangled from her eyeglasses into a wild swing. Her mouth was shaped in a perfect O as Kathryn closed the door.

Joe took an armchair facing her across the desk. With his rugged good looks and air of understated polish, he could easily have been mistaken for an actor. Tall and lean with an athletic tan, he was only four years older than Kathryn, but his universe was light-years away. She would have found him intimidating anywhere except on her own turf. He had the aristocratic features of the Bennetts but, instead of their trademark lavender eyes, his were dark with hints of purple. In contrast to Colton's famous blond locks, Joe's hair was almost black and cut neatly at a point where it curled naturally.

No coat, no jewelry, no briefcase, not even a ball-point pen. Kathryn liked the man's unfettered style. Charcoal slacks, tailored and tapered, complemented his summer-weight pullover. No doubt Phyllis had noticed how well the green cashmere emphasized his shoulders. This celebrated Bennett orphan could have coasted through life without producing his cousin's movies, much less stepping out on his own as an author. Kathryn considered that more impressive than his pedigree.

"Expecting Colton?" he asked, apparently alert to Phyllis's disappointment.

His clipped manner of speaking had bothered Kathryn when they first met, but she had to admit his economy of words kept his writing clean. "I wasn't," she said, "but if you want a friend for life, you might send Phyl his autograph for her granddaughters."

Joe chuckled. "Done." He propped a foot on the opposite knee and seemed at ease.

They had met only twice before, so Kathryn was pleased that their monthly phone calls had forged a balanced author/editor relationship. When they last sat down in person, ten months ago, she had looked much better. Since then her fanny and cleavage had basically disappeared. Now she didn't fill out her suits any better than a coat hanger. Wearing makeup was too much effort. Hopefully the freckles dotted across the bridge of her nose allowed her to get away with the fresh-scrubbed look. She shifted to the edge of her seat, propped her elbows on the desk, and interlaced her fingers. "Are you glad you wrote this book?"

"Pulling no punches today." He settled back into his chair. "Have to say I am. De-bunks a few media-perpetuated myths."

"You're the only person who could have written it, that's for sure. There are fascinating details in here no one else could know. Except Colton, of course."

"Same memories." He grimaced. "Good and bad."

"You've taken your family out of the tabloids and made them real. Not an easy feat."

"Saying it'll sell?"

"Absolutely. You have a built-in market. Rather than accept your grandfather's death, his fans shifted their adoration to you and Colton. And now Colton has his own legion of fans who will buy it. Plus—and I wish I could convince you of this—you have an engaging writing style."

He shrugged slightly. "Don't think of myself in terms of style."

"You should. Seriously. Have you considered my suggestion about writing fiction?"

He averted his eyes. "Playing around with it. An espionage theme."

She smiled. "I'm pleased to hear that. Getting started is the hardest part."

"Far cry from tinkering with Colton's movie scripts. Don't know if it's any good."

"Every author, no matter how successful, has that same doubt. Go for it. Bring out a mystery on the heels of this biography, capitalize on its momentum."

He rubbed the side of his nose, considering.

"Omni pays me to recognize talent, Joe. It's not to anyone's benefit for me, as they say, to blow smoke up your skirt. Your writing is first-rate." Catching his eye, she raised an eyebrow. "Publish under a pen name."

He dropped his foot back to the floor and sat forward, his head cocked to one side. "Not many people get my need to control the media."

She held up his Bennett manuscript. "I've read the book, remember? Speaking of which, in the first chapter, you're still a bit heavy on back story."

He shifted in the chair and withdrew a flash drive

from his pants pocket. "After you pointed that out, I revised."

"Oh," she said, surprised to find him so accommodating. "Hang on to that for now. You can give it to my boss, Zach Tolliver. He'll be taking you to publication. I'm handing you over to him a bit early, but he'd direct the marketing anyway."

A heavy-browed frown bespoke Joe's annoyance. "You've improved my manuscript ten-fold," he said. "I'm not interested in being tossed upstairs."

"It has nothing to do with your book," she assured him. She had not forgotten that he specifically asked for her, based on Brokaw's recommendation. "I would have told you sooner, but I only decided after lunch. I'm taking personal leave."

His frown deepened. "Personal?"

The disgruntled way he spoke the word and the look that accompanied it made her uncomfortable. Perhaps he had correctly assessed her ponytail as a signal of hair badly in need of styling and noticed her naked nails begging for a manicure, but surely he did not think her so shallow she would drop everything to swan off to a spa.

"When are you coming back?" he asked.

His gruff tone caused her to lift her chin. "I don't know for sure that I will. Be back, that is."

"Jeez." Seeming to take in her overall appearance, he leaned forward, his features softening. "Don't mean to pry, but I hope you aren't sick."

She twisted the wedding band on her thumb, the only finger it now fit, and took a deep breath. "I lost my husband last November. I've never really taken time to decide where I go from here. I don't know if that makes sense to you."

He raised an eyebrow and nodded. "Work is my avoidance technique, too. But it doesn't solve anything."

She stopped fiddling with the ring. "I owe you an explanation."

"You don't owe me."

She was conscious of him silently watching as she let her eyes roam across the room to a quilt hung as tapestry art on the wall. She had designed it for Sam, pieced together symbols of her husband's life and stitched the outline of his laughing face over squares as vibrant and happy as he. Bringing it to the office had been a mistake. It only made her ache for all the good that was gone from her life. She felt light-headed and knew the color must have left her face.

Bringing her gaze back to Joe, she said, "You may have heard about him. Sam Tribble, one of the photojournalists killed in Afghanistan. I'm supposed to…" She pushed away the thought of the little chest filled with Sam's ashes on her closet shelf at home. "…I don't know, move on?"

"I do remember. On the news. Sorry I didn't make the connection. I'm familiar with that lost feeling, when death comes without warning. My grandmother's stroke affected me the same way."

His empathy and softened tone brought Kathryn close to tears, but she blinked them away. She moistened her lips and managed the semblance of a smile.

"How soon you leaving?" he asked.

"Five minutes after you walk out the door."

"You decided all this today? After lunch?"

"Operative word—decided." Kathryn stood, her posture straight.

Slowly, as though reluctant to leave, Joe followed her across the room. "Where to, may I ask?"

"The best place to start a rewrite, back to the beginning."

"From the absence of G's on the ends of your words

sometimes, I'm guessing South. Let me be the first to wish you luck." He gave her hand a friendly clasp and reached for the door. "Five minutes begins now," he said with a farewell wink.

Chapter 2

The acrid odor of burned bacon assailed Joe as soon as he emerged from his wing of the house. He crossed the rotunda and propped open French doors to let in the brisk September breeze off the Pacific. Walking outside past the pool, he saw the sliding doors to the kitchen already welcoming cleansing air. Barefoot, he padded across the threshold and slid into his side of the breakfast nook. At the cooking island, Colton's Barbie from the previous night hovered over Joe's trusty stock pot, scraping its bottom with a metal spatula. Joe's left eye squinted. Nails on a chalkboard.

He sat down and picked out *The Hollywood Reporter* from several trade papers on the table. *The Reporter* seemed skimpy as he thumbed to a review of his cousin's latest romantic comedy. With nominations being bantered about, Joe felt justified in holding the movie's release for the pre-Oscar wave. Damnation! How could he concentrate with that exhaust fan revving like a turbine? He peered over the top of the paper at the starlet. Her platinum hair was as messy as the water-spotted emerald silk teddy she almost wore. Those things inevitably revealed showgirl legs up the yin-yang and more implants than anyone cared to see. He yawned noisily.

Barbie startled with a mincing, "Eek!" She punched off the exhaust fan with an acrylic talon. "You sneaked up on me."

Joe poured a mug of black coffee and hunkered down to read a second review.

"Look at this mess," the blonde whined. She hefted the pot and dumped a stringy conglomeration meant to be bacon into a bowl lined with the missing section of Joe's newspaper. "Criminy! Looks like you could have at least one stupid skillet."

"Ken dolls don't come with kitchen sets, Barbie."

"Don't call me that." She flounced over to the refrigerator. "I'm Barb."

As in wire, thought Joe as he texted Daniel to hurry with the car. Head of security, Daniel was well-versed in this particular drill. Joe rose and went through the house to retrieve Barb's cocktail dress, a scrap of gold fabric on the floor outside Colton's bedroom. Before walking back to the kitchen, he took a spa robe from the towel closet and veered into his study for the envelope he kept at the ready.

Barb pertly sidestepped him when she saw her dress. "I'm going for a swim," she said.

Joe shook his head and took a stance in front of the sliding doors.

"Where's Colton?" She snatched the dress out of Joe's hand and headed for the rotunda where she came to a halt in front of Daniel, solid as a brick wall, blocking the door to Colton's wing of the house.

Joe walked up behind her and draped the terry robe across her shoulders. "Go with grace, or go without."

She turned on the venom. "You can't treat me like this! I have pictures!"

Daniel produced her cell phone, and Joe said, "Had. They're gone."

"You can't do that! I'll call *People Magazine*. Tell them what an ass you are."

Joe laughed and handed her the envelope. "Old news."

Daniel opened the front door and Barb, clutching her payoff, huffed out to the limo.

Scowling toward Colton's door, Joe turned, slung a towel around his neck, and stuffed a leash in his pocket. Attuned to his movements, an energetic boxer appeared at his side. "Good girl, Yankee, let's go." The dog raced out the back door, veered around the pool, and headed for the beach. Joe followed her down the rocky path through Grandmother Pet's garden. He jogged to the northern-most boundary of Bennetthurst, his grandparents' fabled estate, where he turned and jogged back. Yankee lingered for a romp with the guard. She rejoined Joe as he rounded out his first mile. They sprinted past the mansion to the south gate. Over the years, Joe, with Yankee and her pre-decessors, and Colton before last summer's assault, had worn their beach track down to bedrock.

Joe had resented giving up his cousin's camaraderie but he soon found out solo jogs energized his writing. Freewheeling down the beach, he would work out plot points and plumb the depths of his characters. But this morning he had astute Kathryn Tribble on his mind. With the rough draft of his first mystery novel almost finished, he longed for her elegant touch.

Zach Tolliver was a hack editor compared to her. The Omni executive was also a bully. After Joe made the requisite round of talk shows to promote the Bennett bi-ography, he'd steadfastly refused to let Zach hound him into more personal appearances. The man had called again last night, harping on the subject, but Joe stuck to his mantra: "Only fools swim in chummed waters." He wouldn't have had to tell Kathryn that. His appreciation for her insight had grown steadily over the summer. She had correctly predicted the biography's debut strength, and the surge in sales from Colton's new movie. She had recognized the writer in Joe, long before he did.

Gulls fishing a tidal pool rose up, scolding raucously as he ran. Joe smiled. Zach had sounded much like the gulls when Joe followed Kathryn's advice about adopting a pseudonym for his fiction writing. After the biography release, Omni put Joe's mystery novel on a fast track to further capitalize on Bennett fame. But he decided his heroine, Kitty Quinn, southern belle turned spy, must sink or swim on her own merit. He chose the pen name Janine Bruce and would happily send an actress to book signings and promotions.

He slowed to a walk and then came to a full stop, heaving air out over the Pacific. The sun danced along the breakers. Try as he might, he couldn't imagine how Kathryn managed to turn her back on everything she'd accomplished. For him to change his life that radically would be like standing on the edge of his world, stepping off into thin air. Kitty Quinn, the protagonist of his thriller, wasn't Kathryn, but his story really took off when he made the character into a genteel southern woman hunting down terrorists to avenge her husband's death. Kitty was born of Kathryn's unblinking courage. Rail thin when he saw her back in June, she seemed stressed to the breaking point. And yet, she'd had what it took to begin rewriting her life. Joe wiped his sweaty brow. How did a person do that? That simple question drove him to create Kitty. But what about Kathryn? What real life answers had she found?

Joe whistled Yankee out of the surf and turned his back on the ocean. "Bluuaahh," he shouted and gave a full body shake. No point indulging in questions without answers. He was stuck with Zach the Hack. Trudging inland toward the cliff, he felt a spurt of anger when he passed the spot where Colton had fallen thirteen months ago. Etched in Joe's memory was the utter vulnerability of his cousin, splayed on the beach like a gutted fish. An indelible image of blood on sand.

The idiot photographer had pled innocent of malicious intent and *sworn* he only threw a rock to attract Colton's attention. That hadn't prevented the man from making a mint off pictures of the star with his head gashed open. It hadn't prevented Joe's maniacal counter-attack that horrible day either. He had flashed back to when he and Benny were ten-year-olds. Overzealous fans had accosted them on this same beach. They ripped the boys' clothes and pulled out hunks of their hair. On both occasions, Joe came away bruised and broken, but each time he landed sufficient punches and smashed enough cameras to fend the sharks off his cousin.

"Time, Yankee."

As the dog bounded to him, Joe mentally prepped for the tasks he had to accomplish before his afternoon flight to Atlanta—contract negotiation, security review, ever-churning rumor mill. He toweled the boxer's fawn coat and white underbelly before attaching her leash. Rather than retrace the flagstones up through Pet's garden, he took a private path from the beach to the street. Since he and Colton had a new movie to promote, today was as good as any for the sharks to earn their keep. He didn't begrudge the star's fans occasional shots of his sweaty cousin and their drooly dog. There was no denying the box office value of tabloid exposure. Turning his cap backwards to reveal his face, Joe heeled Yankee around the corner to feed the swarm on the street.

Right on cue, an eagle-eye shouted, "Hey, there's Joe Butler!"

Shutters clicked and cajoling began. "Look here, Joe," a woman called, faking familiarity.

"Give us a smile, man," someone yelled, as if this was a photo shoot.

Joe complied with what his grandfather had called a mule-eating-briars grin, plus thumbs up for good will.

Someone whistled to his dog. "Here, girl. Good puppy."

Yankee made a bee-line for the security shack where Daniel kept her treats.

A former linebacker, Daniel blithely shielded man and dog through the gate, swapping a fresh towel for Yankee's leash. As soon as they were out of the reporters' earshot, Daniel handed over Joe's cell phone. "Phoenix been blowing this thing up."

Irritation flashed in Joe's eyes. "Where is she?"

"She wouldn't say."

Joe draped the towel around his neck and pocketed his phone. He wasn't going to let Phoenix cheat him out of his reward for the solitary jog and media exploit. He savored the cool-down walk along the avenue of palms to the pure crystalline waters of the Aphrodite fountain in front of the mansion. Bennetthurst, besieged by paparazzi far longer than he could remember, was sacred. No one except Colton understood that.

With no personal memory of his mother, pictures of her at home were precious. Joe's favorite was a one-dimensional video clip from the sixties, a grainy snippet of film that cable channels re-ran on the anniversary of the twins' auto crash. Joe's mom, Betty, and Benny's mom, Peggy, were still in their teens when a camera caught them in an all-out water fight. They'd been washing matching convertibles, playing at the feet of this same

marble goddess. Classic Calvin Klein jeans hugged their
slender hips and shiny blonde hair flowed almost to their
waists. The only thing that marred his mother's fresh,
youthful beauty was the caged animal look in her eyes.
At times Joe was certain he glimpsed that same expression in his own eyes.

He and Colton grew up having their every step and
misstep publicized. They were taught to cope, whereas
their mothers had been ill-equipped for the celebrity sta-
tus thrust upon them. William Bennett grieved himself
into an early grave over the shock of losing his girls.
Tight-lipped and fierce, Pet Bennett was left to raise her
grandsons and run the family's production company. She
recognized her late husband's superficiality in young
Colton and schooled him on how it transitioned into sensitivity on camera. His course was set for stardom that
eclipsed his grandfather's. With equal vigor, Pet fostered
Joe's innate fierceness. She groomed him to replace her
as family gatekeeper and head of the company.

Winking at Aphrodite, Joe hurdled up the steps into
the house. Across the rotunda, French doors remained
open and only a hint of burnt bacon clung to the air. A
guard nodded when Joe stepped onto the pool deck and
threw his towel at the hamper.

He leaned against the door jamb and started to dial
Phoenix's number, steeling himself for the confrontation.
The woman was as much responsible for him turning
Bennetthurst into a fortress as the paparazzi were. Ab-
ruptly, he changed his mind and called Wrenn instead.

"Told Granna you'd call." Her smug tone came
across older than her eight and a half years. Having to
struggle for every breath did that, boiled her life down to
its essence.

Joe laughed. "Right you are." The sound of her voice
never failed to delight him.

"The new doctor said I can't go home 'til tomorrow. Will you be here by then?"

"Yep, not enough wild horses out here to keep me away."

"Ready-freddy," she said, suppressing a cough.

Joe imagined the spark of mischief in her lavender eyes. His smile faded as he disconnected and rang Phoenix.

"What's up with the kid?" she cracked, herky-jerky and hyper as ever.

Joe flinched at the way she said *kid* in her phlegmy smoker's voice, as if Wrenn were interchangeable with *bug*. She didn't expect an answer and didn't get one. "So I'm in Atlanta. When can I catch you? At the hospital?"

Joe's jaw clenched. He had never slept with Wrenn's mother, never lived with her a day in his life, never once considered her his wife, but that's what she was. Legally. Had been since he was in college and dumb as dirt. "I'll call you when I get there." He ended the call and stomped toward the kitchen.

He would have played Phoenix differently if she hadn't appeared the summer Pet died. He had been soothing the loss of his grandmother with alcohol. Colton reacted by whoring around. Wacky Phoenix, formerly Julie Patterson, a starry-eyed wannabe from Houston, had rung Colton's bell by auditioning in a bikini. By fall she was pregnant. With the sensitivity of a goat, Colton threw money at her for an abortion and ran off to his next movie location. Joe, in some knee-jerk reaction to do what Pet's Catholic principles would have considered right, stepped in and legitimized Colton's baby.

Back then Joe knew little about mental illness and certainly hadn't recognized Phoenix as delusional. She spent her pregnancy in Houston with her mother, Anna. The poor woman agonized over Phoenix's cocaine use harming the baby she planned to raise. The more Anna and Joe insisted on doctors and rehab, the more convinced Phoenix became that they were keeping Colton from her. She developed a full-blown fixation on Colton that was officially diagnosed as erotomania.

Joe had counted down the days until the baby was born, so that he could annul the marriage. What he hadn't counted on was falling in love with the baby. Born prematurely, she brought a new level of unimaginable good into his life. He named the tiny bird Wrenn and swore on his life never to abandon her the way her crazy mother and irresponsible father had. He couldn't protect her from their genes, though, and her cystic fibrosis was gaining ground. Just last month, Joe had moved Wrenn from Houston to Atlanta and put her in the care of a new team of specialists. How Phoenix already knew about that was worrisome, but it gave him a clue to the source of her information.

Realizing he was holding his breath, Joe exhaled and put away his phone.

Colton schlepped in wearing low-slung sleep pants and no shirt. "Yuck. Is that bacon?"

In answer, Joe dropped the grease-soaked portion of his newspaper into the trash can and slammed the lid shut. He mimicked his cousin's trademark aw-shucks smile before twisting it into a grimace.

"Sorry, Joey." Colton glanced around, "Is Barb…"

"Yep, outta here." Joe slapped the edge of the table with the surviving section of his paper. "Benny, why do you keep doing this?"

Colton plowed manicured fingers through his tawny mane and looked befuddled. "Don't be all—" He left a blank for Joe to fill in his own expletive and then closed the sentence with a shoulder roll. "Everybody expects me to be the playboy I play." He lounged against the counter and affected a theatrical tone. "It's a zoo out there. I need a keeper."

"Need a damn wife," Joe snapped.

Colton clapped him on the back. "Yeah, man. That was really the fix for you, wasn't it?" Turning to pour himself a mug of coffee, Colton jibed over his bare shoulder, "Who would you have me hook up with, Joey, a slut like my mother or a sot like yours?"

Chapter 3

Donna-Ray "Dee" Lyndon, the buxom blonde at the helm of Lyndon Real Estate in Athens, Georgia, ate statistics for breakfast. She cheered on the realtors in her bullpen the same way she championed the football team at the University of Georgia. The one person she couldn't motivate was Kathryn "Kay" Tribble, nee Morton, her best friend from childhood.

Adept at reading his wife, Dee's husband took an evening glass of Merlot to her on the deck off their bedroom. "You're going to have to stop worrying about Kay."

"Easier said than done, Tommy. She stayed holed up in our guest room all summer and now she's moping out there in the boonies. You're the psychiatrist. Don't you think she ought to be better by now? Sam has been dead a year."

"Ten months."

"Be as literal as you like, that's almost a year."

"A year full of anniversaries. It was about this time last year when she realized she was pregnant. She knows I'm here if she needs me, but she hasn't indicated—"

"Indicated-schmindicated." Dee jumped out of her chair. "Kay wouldn't indicate she was on fire if her britches were blazing. Do you know how she turned down my alumni party invitation? In a text. A ding-dang text!"

"She'll know when she's ready for the party scene, hon, especially one of your to-do's. Probably figured—correctly might I add—you'd be throwing guys at her. She's okay. Comes over for your little movie marathons, and y'all go out to dinner."

"If you call omelets at the Waffle House 'going out to dinner.' I will not let her go nuts like old Aunt Tildy. Self-contained, my mother's bridge club called her. For crying out loud, Kay is sitting out there in that old bat's house making quilts just like she did."

"Everybody heals at a different pace. Kay came back to Athens, questioning everything, even her own body. She lost more than Sam and their baby. She lost herself." Tommy set his wine glass on the deck railing and put a sheltering arm around Dee. "Her instincts are right. She's starting over with people and places she trusts. Think of her quilting as artistic expression, a way of piecing her life back together."

Dee leaned her head against his chest. "As usual, I'm in too big of a hurry."

"You live for deadlines and closings. Kay can't get unstuck until she's sure she won't come unglued. A year, two, three, five—it takes as long as it takes. A scrape with clinical depression is a helluva frightening thing."

Dee groaned. "I'm horrible. I called her Matilda and told her she'd better get her butt in circulation."

Tommy rested his chin on his wife's head, so she wouldn't see his grin. "What'd she say to that?"

"Said she hadn't hula-hooped since she was fifteen."

He gave way to a laugh. "She sounds fine to me."

e/∂e/∂

A slight movement in the pines caught Kathryn's eye as she set off on her morning walk. It was the only tell of the motley brown dog lurking there.

"I see you, Silly Goose."

The odd-looking mongrel had earned his equally odd name by shying away from humans. Dappled as the forest floor, he hesitated to relinquish his camouflage.

"Come on, Goose," Kathryn called. "I'm not looking forward to this walk any more than you are. Let's get it over with."

He skirted around her, nostrils flaring.

She had discovered the bleary-eyed bruiser sleeping under the porch of Aunt Tildy's boarded-up cottage when she returned from New York to claim it. The carpenter Dee found to refurbish the place had called Goose a 'sooner,' a dog that could as soon be of one breed as any other. Poor thing had fled during the noisy renovations. Kathryn fled too, sleeping away June and July at Dee and Tommy's.

She had come back to Athens, expecting to reclaim her health and vigor. Instead, a deadening blanket seemed to weigh her down. Every bone in her body was imbued with unrelenting fatigue, akin to what she remembered from early pregnancy but with none of the joy.

In August, she finally moved into the cottage. The neglected little fieldstone structure now sported a welcoming smile in the form of an oak porch across the front. Dee had jumped into the project with both feet, modernizing the interior with built-in bookcases and opening up the floor plan. But neither Dee nor anyone else could refurbish Kathryn. She whiled away most of her days in the new swing hanging from a sturdy rafter on one end of the porch. Sitting quietly, piecing quilt squares, was a far cry from her days in a previous swing in that same location, flying high with Aunt Tildy, pretending it was a P-52.

At some point, Kathryn noticed the dog had reclaimed his spot under the porch. As uncertain of her as she was of him, he paid for his lodging by rattling the floorboards with vicious barks whenever anyone approached the house.

Living alone had not come easy for Kathryn, but she no longer saw herself any other way. Her cottage was invisible from The Lane—as Morton Farm Lane was locally known. Aunt Tildy, actually Kathryn's great-aunt Matilda Morton, had chosen this site particularly for its solitude. Matilda had lived in France for over three decades after her WAC service in World War II. She'd come home at age fifty-two, just in time to assume the role of family eccentric, a title relinquished by the death of Charlie Morton. Crazy Charlie had been only fifty-five when he succumbed to his bad heart. Bad in more ways than one, from what little Kathryn knew about him. As a young man, he'd barely survived a bout of rheumatic fever and had gone on to lead a destructive life of alcoholism and legendary meanness. He was the cousin whose antebellum house still loomed at the corner where The Lane branched off the main road.

Kathryn pushed herself to walk the half-mile dirt-and-gravel driveway that meandered along the tree line from her house to her mailbox. As a child, she had thought of that drive as a pencil line drawn in as an afterthought to connect Aunt Tildy's world—now hers—to the outside.

After seven weeks of walks, Kathryn's stamina had increased, but this particular morning, the first day of fall, found her operating on too little sleep. She'd been plagued by a dream that started with Sam holding their child in Heaven. Knowing that he'd died with their baby in his heart had been a great consolation to Kathryn, but last night's dream took a sinister twist. Sam shielded the baby's face from her, deliberately turned his back, and walked away. She had tried to run after him but her legs wouldn't work. She wanted to call out but couldn't. Awaking hollow and bereft, she'd buried her face in the pillow and fantasized about joining them. The dream haunted her as she walked. Despair clung to her like a wet garment in the rain.

Every vestige of energy went toward putting one foot in front of the other as she forced herself past the mailbox. Absently unfastening and refastening the hasp of the cattle gate to the pasture across The Lane, she strolled downhill and circled the pond before retracing her steps and returning to her porch. She slumped into the swing and stared blindly at the sweep of pines fringing her yard. Green boughs blurred and ran into the gray sky beyond.

"No!" she rebuked the trees. "No-o-o."

Head in her hands, she cried, a shrill keening, a sound she might have produced if someone repeatedly stuck an ice pick into her chest. How could a loving God take away her husband? Why did her baby die? What had she done wrong? Her breakfast rose into her throat. She knelt on the edge of the porch feeling sick and broken. Eventually her stomach stopped lurching and she noticed Goose sitting Sphinx-like beside her.

She shifted from kneeling to sitting with her back supported by a porch post. Goose settled down beside her, laying one big paw and his muzzle on her lap. He closed his eyes when she tentatively stroked his wiry head. How many times, Kathryn wondered, had this dog been abandoned? Yet he was willing to trust again.

ɛɔɛɔ

Joe's company Gulfstream deposited him in Atlanta in the wee hours of September twenty-first. Rather than go to Wrenn's Ranch, as Wrenn had named their new home in an equestrian community outside Atlanta, he took a taxi from the airport to his condo. Little more than a suite, the place provided the private space he needed from time to time. At least he'd thought it was private. He'd soon know, based on Phoenix's next move.

By eight in the morning, he was on his way to the hospital. Tightening the slide on his bola tie, he aligned its silver aglets and hurried to the cafeteria. Phoenix was easy to spot trolling the patio outside. He read the signs of a manic phase in the hideous marigold-colored vest and purple leggings she was pimping. They competed for attention with her Crayola-red hair. He might consider her a tragic clown had he not known her better.

Seeing Joe, she tossed her cigarette and sat down at a nearby table. A derisive snort greeted his Stetson. "What'd you do, stop by your condo and change for the kid?"

He wouldn't give her the satisfaction of knowing she was right. It tickled Wrenn when he dressed like a Texan. Imitating his movie star grandfather, who'd switched personas with neckties, Joe wore western garb for her. But Phoenix's comment confirmed his suspicion about her pipeline into his life. He took the chair facing her and refused to be baited. "Don't give a damn, do you?"

She shrugged. The downward dip of her mouth emphasized the fixed grooves of a frown.

"You could at least talk to your mother," Joe said.

Granna, as Wrenn called Anna Patterson, was devoted to her grandchild. She had named her own daughter Julie and raised her with firm, middle class values, only to have her morph into this Phoenix creature.

"She has her little girl." Phoenix spat, "and it's sure as hell not me."

Anger flared inside Joe—disgust reaching all the way back to the day Phoenix delivered Wrenn and then refused to even look at her. "How much do you want?"

Every penny he paid to keep her in some stable mental state was worth it. Phoenix's psychotic father hadn't been much older than she was now when he spiraled out of control and went on a killing spree.

Phoenix withdrew a cigarette from her pack and waved it at him. "Did you really quit?"

"Don't light that damn thing. I'm not taking second hand pollutants to Wrenn."

She passed the cigarette under her nostrils. "You know you still want it." Her lip curled revealing teeth undermined by her lifestyle.

"Put it away." Joe suspected she was more than manic, probably high. Her once knock-out body had lost its bounce, everything about her turning as hard as the double-D's he had most likely paid for. "How much?"

She exhaled the stench of tobacco, coffee, and tooth decay. "I've got, um, expenses—"

"Save it." He couldn't stomach her personal details. Oh, how he longed for an annulment, but psychiatrists warned him a loss of security would likely throw Phoenix into a rampage. It behooved Joe to keep her afraid of him, ever aware of him standing between Wrenn and any threat. This marriage had been Joe's choice and Wrenn was a blessing that trumped any card Phoenix could play.

"Ten thousand." Phoenix blinked her eyes flirtatiously. "Consider it pay for a walk-on in Colton's next film. I won't fly to Paris—nobody is flinging me through the air in a sardine can—but I understand he'll shoot some scenes in Canada. In case you forgot, I went to grade school in Quebec."

Joe coughed back a mirthless laugh. Her reference to his condo had just confirmed she was as useless an actress as she was a mother. Any number of sources could've tipped her off to Colton's movie locations before they were officially announced, even helped her keep up with Joe's schedule, but only one person on God's green earth other than Joe knew about that condo. A pro when it came to prioritizing, Joe would untangle that knot another day.

Jamming his hat on his head, he stood up. "No movie deal and you know it. Money'll be in your account by morning."

He ground his molars. The witch wasn't savvy enough to know his accountants tracked her debit card. Her transactions followed Colton all over the United States. After she turned up as an extra in two of Colton's movies, Joe had gotten a restraining order. If Daniel ever caught her actively stalking again, Joe planned to throw her in jail.

Phoenix's green eyes took on a mutinous expression. "I might—"

Joe propped both hands on the table and loomed over her. "No. You. Won't." He spoke softly, but his tone was pure threat. If she ever threw Wrenn to the sharks, he'd likely strangle her with his bare hands. That was exactly what he let show on his face. As soon as she dropped her gaze, he turned on his heel and headed for the elevator.

This was another trip he would shorthand to Colton as "Atlanta." Except for apprising Daniel of sparse, necessary details, and an occasional mention to Wrenn of an "Uncle Benny" in California, Joe kept her to himself. His mission was to keep her life free of stress, and that included Colton and his attendant publicity. Swinging through the door of Wrenn's hospital room, he saw a bit of worry lift from Anna's brow.

"Bapa!" Wrenn shouted, in what passed for a shout from an eight-year-old battling cystic fibrosis.

He tossed his Stetson on the end of the bed and hunkered down beside the transport chair where she waited. Kissing her soundly on the cheek, he said, "Hey, bird, 'bout ready to blow this joint?"

She giggled, her eyes sparkling cabochons of amethyst. "Guess what I'm ready for."

"Too soon," he said, but he knew there was no denying her their ritual pedicures on the way home.

His negative response caused her to cross her arms in pretense of a pout. "Then I'm not going."

"Oh, yes you are. I'm your wheel man, ma'am." She squealed as he popped a small wheelie out of the room and raced her down the corridor.

Anna grabbed his hat and ran after them.

When they were settled in the car, Wrenn complained, "Granna won't let me have a pony."

"Hear that, Rusty," Joe called to their driver. "Lexus isn't good enough for her."

Typically weighing in on Wrenn's side, Rusty drawled, "Well, she's got a knack with horses and your jumpers are mighty big." Joe had inherited the hardened old codger along with the Twisted B Ranch, his Butler legacy in Texas. Rusty had been loyal beyond reason to the aged uncle who'd lived there, but barely tolerated Joe until Wrenn came along and Joe became less of an absentee owner. Anna cared for Wrenn there until this past August when her doctors recommended a team of specialists in Atlanta. The equestrian community where Joe found their house had been built for the '96 Olympics. Rusty was only supposed to drive the horses cross-country but he was under Wrenn's spell and had thus far stayed on to drive for her and Anna. He was the one who knew about Joe's condo. The only one. If the old sack of salt hadn't been the closest thing Wrenn had to a grandfather, Joe would've fired him on the spot.

Wrenn pressed her advantage. "Ple-e-ease."

Anna shook her head over the child's persistence. "Maybe you should think about a miniature horse, one like we saw on your field trip with the new home-school group."

"No, Granna, they're too small. I like to ride."

Joe reached behind Wrenn and squeezed Anna's arm. She was a rock, but years of home-schooling her granddaughter and round-the-clock breathing treatments had worn her down. "Granna and I will talk about it. Would you promise to let her be in charge?"

"Promise."

"And only go out when Rusty can watch you."

Wrenn snuggled close. "I love you, Bapa."

"I haven't said yes, yet."

She beamed at him. "But you will."

Joe beamed back and hugged her to his side. He pressed his lips against the top of her silky blonde head and relished the faint, herbal scent of her shampoo. That was a fact. And he'd go to the nail salon, too, and get his toenails painted any silly color she chose. That was one activity a dad could do with a girl who sometimes found every breath to be work.

✺✺✺

Relief washed over Phoenix as she cowered behind a retaining wall and listened for the Lexus to drive off. She made a heart-pounding dash back to the safety of her car. Hands shaking, she lit a cigarette and sucked in deep, searing breaths of nicotine to calm down. *That was too freaking close!*

Joe had almost caught her paying off Rusty for giving her the heads-up on the kid's hospital stay. What Joe would do if he knew she had a mole right under his nose didn't bear thinking about. He'd already locked her in a psyche ward once for breaking into Bennetthurst. Well, he might keep her and Colton apart for now, but as soon as the blasted kid kicked the bucket that was gonna change.

All she had to do was to bide her time, and pay that old skinflint for information. He must've lost bigger than usual on whatever he was betting on this week because he'd argued so long it was sheer luck she saw Joe before he saw them. Phoenix snorted, exhaling smoke. "Trick is not to get caught."

She could barely swallow her loathing for Joe, but he was her livelihood. He would cut her off when the kid died, but then she'd be with Colton.

Chapter 4

As the leaves began to slowly change from green to gold, orange, and red, Kathryn gradually turned from seeking an explanation for the loss of Sam and their baby to accepting her fate. She prayed for God to bestow on her the resilience He had given Goose.

One October morning she picked up the phone and called Omni Press. Rather than holding a grudge about her abrupt resignation, Zach Tolliver was primed and ready with an offer. "Why don't you telecommute from Athens? Take Phyl as liaison." He laughed. "Get her off my back."

"I gather she's still playing mother hen?"

"If she had her way, I'd be married with six children by now."

"Watch out, mister, our Phyl has a way of getting her way."

"That's what I'm talking about. Seriously, kiddo, I'm glad to have you exercising your sharp pencil for Omni again."

"Thanks, Zach. I really appreciate that."

"Phyl'll be in touch. Start out with something small and go from there."

Kathryn hung up smiling. Little did Zach know that she planned to start everything small for the rest of her life.

By November thirteenth, the first anniversary of Sam's death, she felt ready for a special hike. She picked up a small wooden chest and set out. Across The Lane from her mailbox, a mile deep into the woods beyond the pasture and pond, lay a clearing she had avoided since her return.

Goose followed as far as the pond where he veered into the rushes.

During the past month, Kathryn's fluid stride from tomboy days had returned. In her teens she had run down that hill countless times—cut-offs, Keds, rolled towel under her arm—for dips in the pond. On the far side of the dam, she passed by a tree of pretty but bitter persimmons. She left them for possums and secured the box under her arm as she helped herself to wild scuppernongs instead. Tromping along an old pulpwood road, she sucked tart juice from the speckled amber grapes and spit out their tough skin and seedy pulp. Pine straw was thick and spongy under her feet and the autumn breeze was rich with woodland aromas. She found her meadow strewn with fat acorns and leaves as big as her hands. In the middle towered a regal white oak. A century ago it had begun as two saplings. The trunks had fused into one, creating a forest giant.

This was Sam's oak, heartwarming and heartbreaking. It bore witness to their early lovemaking, provided the altar of their marriage, and now it would receive his ashes. Instead of memories smothering her, as she had feared, the tree renewed her sense of peace. At Sam's memorial service, his mother's only request had been that

Kathryn disperse his ashes in a place he'd loved. She slowly opened the chest and walked around the clearing, letting them fall where they may. Once the box was empty, she put it down beside the tree and stood reverently beneath its canopy. With her forefinger she traced the heart Sam had carved in the trunk. He'd put it beside another heart carved in another couple's lifetime. Kathryn felt if she could connect with Sam anywhere, this was the place. Spreading her arms, she pressed her body against the trunk and closed her eyes, laying her cheek against the rough bark.

Goose, wet and slobbery, loped across the meadow and shook vigorously.

"Oh, you!" Kathryn jumped away from his cold spray. "Aren't you 'mister mood breaker?'" Using one of Dee's expressions brought her friend to mind. An image of the liveliest person Kathryn knew supplanted any idea of conjuring up the dead. Wincing, Kathryn remembered her texted rejection to Dee's recent football party invitation, *I don't have any "Go Dawgs" left in me.*

Dee had volleyed with, *Find something red and black and get your pom-poms ready!*

Kathryn picked up the box and strolled out of the meadow with a thankful heart for having been blessed with Sam. When she got home, she would call his mother. And then she would call Dee.

♥♥♥

Tommy polished off his last bite of oyster dressing and grinned at Kathryn. "Can my wife cook or what?"

Kathryn tipped her glass to Dee. "Never known her to half-do anything."

Dee swept her hand around the empty seats at the table. "And not a single, single man."

"Something else to be thankful for this Thanksgiving Day," Kathryn said.

Dee lobbed a napkin at her. "I figure, why bother? You'd shoot any man who came within a mile."

Tommy caught Dee's eye. "Have you told her about the library?"

"Oh, Tommy, Kay doesn't care about that."

"Of course, she does. She's a wordsmith." He turned to Kathryn. "The Board of Realtors is sponsoring a library at Dee's Old Mill Village, a multi-use development of that defunct cotton mill down by the Oconee River."

"Contrary to popular belief, real estate isn't sold from a desk," Dee said. "We're repurposing the sales office into a sort of cultural center for the growing Latino community out there. A man is already teaching guitar after school."

"You said something about looking for math and English tutors," Tommy said.

Dee raised an eyebrow at her husband and cocked her head toward Kathryn. "I don't suppose you'd be interested?"

"I might."

Dee hopped up from the table and scrabbled in the depths of her briefcase. "Wow! I have the schedule here somewhere. And...ta da!" She whipped out a DVD. "I also rented a movie."

Tommy groaned. "It'll be a chick flick. I'll clean up the dishes and watch the game in the kitchen."

Dee kissed the bald spot on top of his head. "You're right, my scullery drudge, it's the newest Colton Bennett film. What a hunky-monkey that man is, Kay. I hear Lila what's-her-name—you know, the girl in that nineties sitcom—is the love interest in his next movie. Wouldn't you kill to be in her shoes?"

Kathryn laughed. "You're so star-struck, Dee. I'm

almost afraid to tell you one of the projects I left behind in New York was the Bennett biography featuring hunky-monkey Colton."

Dee's mouth dropped open and Tommy hee-hawed all the way to the kitchen.

᷄᷅᷄᷅

The day after Thanksgiving, dubbed Black Friday for shoppers, Kathryn set off on her walk accompanied by Goose, but he graced her with his presence only as far as the mailbox.

There he picked up a scent and, barely glancing back, loped off down The Lane. When Kathryn's phone chimed, she slipped it out of her jeans pocket, noting Phyllis's number at Omni.

"Kathryn!" boomed Phyllis. "Thank God I got you!"

"Hi, Phyl. I sent you an email about the galleys."

"I got it." Phyllis hesitated and, unlike her usual take-charge self, gave way to a nervous cough. "Do you remember Joe Butler? Colton Bennett's manager, his cousin?"

"Sure."

"He called just now. Asking about you."

Kathryn stopped walking. "What in the world for?"

"He wants you back."

"Back?"

"Omni signed him for a mystery series after the Bennett bio—a three-book, six-figure package. He's lobbying for you to edit the debut novel. It may be a bigger project than you'd counted on, but you're ready. He credits you with turning him into a fiction writer in the first place. Oy, he's got those shoulders."

"Yes, Phyl." Kathryn smiled. "I remember." The man had obviously followed through with autographs for

Phyllis's granddaughters. That woman didn't go to bat for just anyone. "Why does he want me?"

"Who wouldn't rather work with you than Zach?"

"What does Zach say?"

"Couldn't be happier. His schedule is a killer." Phyllis paused. "And—since you've already finished those galleys—oh crap, Kathryn, I gave him your number."

"To Joe? Here?"

"Not your cell, just your house. I should've checked with you first."

"I wish you had. I'm about to start some tutoring and maybe teach English as a Second Language. I'm not sure I'm ready to take on another book project yet." Kathryn chewed on her bottom lip. "I'll think about it. Anyway, he may not even call."

"Not a chance. This man gets what he wants. You could do worse, dear," she said, signing off.

Making her usual loop around the pond, Kathryn shuffled through her memories of Joe. Was his overarching confidence and geniality contrived? Possibly, but there was honesty in his writing that revealed an intuitive man. Phyl was right. If a girl was looking, she could certainly do worse than tall-dark-famous Joe Butler. He had accepted her abrupt decision to leave Omni with more grace than she'd had a right to expect. She wondered if he'd realized what a mess she was. Poor man probably felt like a tennis ball bouncing back to her after she lobbed him to Zach.

In the back of her mind, questions began to form as she took the morning paper out of her box. Would she ever love someone else? Was there a Joe Butler out there for her somewhere? Gathering a bouquet of gold and orange chrysanthemums from the bank, she was beset by a heart-rending thought: *He might leave me. He could die.*

She hurried up the driveway, away from that unbearable thought, and plunged the flower stems into a tub of rainwater. She entered her cottage through the back door, laid the paper on the kitchen table, and headed into the day room to fetch Aunt Tildy's pottery vase. The square lintel arch left when Dee had the kitchen's double doors removed gave an open view into the room. The sofa was a rich shade of paprika bringing out that color in the fieldstone hearth. Yellow mums in Aunt Tildy's crock would be a nice accent to the Asian-print upholstery on the wing chair and ottoman. Kathryn's desk, a Chippendale table, sat against the front wall of the house. It was afire with sunlight streaming through the twelve-pane window it faced.

Kathryn frowned. On her desk, the red message indicator of her answering machine flashed relentlessly. She averted her eyes. Joe Butler had already intruded upon her.

ℭ✄ℭ✄

Joe enjoyed a cozy Thanksgiving at home with Wrenn and Anna. Daniel was riding herd on Colton who was shooting scenes in Paris, leaving Joe blissfully free for three days leading up to the holiday. He took morning gallops on his best horse and wrote the afternoons away. He polished the third draft of his Kitty Quinn manuscript while sitting on the floor with Wrenn stretched out on the sofa behind him re-reading *Harry Potter.* She often wore her little pink inflating-deflating therapy vest during these quiet interludes. The vest was a godsend for clearing her lungs without all the manual chest percussion therapy that was so hard on all of them.

Working with Zach on the previous drafts, or trying to, Joe was more convinced than ever that Kathryn Tribble was the editor for him. Now all he had to do was convince her. A thousand explanations ran through his head at the prospect of introducing Kathryn to Kitty Quinn. Preferring to handle dicey situations face to face, on Friday morning he had finagled Kathryn's number out of the inimitable Phyllis. He left word on Kathryn's machine that he was in Atlanta on business and wanted to meet with her on Saturday. Athens, where she lived, was less than two hours east, home to the University of Georgia and also Alex Whitlow, Joe's favorite musician and old UCLA roommate.

Kathryn's lack of reply on Friday could mean she was out in the fray of post-Thanksgiving sales. Impatient, he left a second message Saturday morning, saying only that he was bringing the mountain to Mohammed. She couldn't possibly refuse working on his manuscript, not after the way she had so unceremoniously dumped him on Zach the Hack.

Heading for Athens, unshackled from his other world of limos and chauffeurs, Joe tossed his ball cap onto the back seat of his personal car, a Lexus similar to the one Rusty drove for Anna and Wrenn. When he was out of town, he kept this one at the Atlanta condo—the condo where Rusty had picked him up a few times before Joe got his car. Better to have Rusty as Phoenix's pipeline than for it to be a shark. The old gambler likely used what she paid him to square his betting losses. Knowing that Rusty's affection for Wrenn was genuine, and he'd never allow Phoenix near her, Joe decided to let the situation ride. Oil could flow both ways in a pipeline.

Sailing through Spaghetti Junction, Joe kissed the city goodbye and unwittingly joined an exodus of flag-flying UGA fans on their way to see their Georgia Bulldogs play in Athens. An old Pontiac, its horn blaring out a tinny version of the "Glory, Glory to Old Georgia" fight song, swerved in front of him. The driver pumped his arm to the music and woof-woofed out the window. Joe jumped when his cell phone rang.

"What's this about the mountain coming to Mohammed?" Kathryn asked.

"Just don't bark at me." His voice sounded harsher than he had intended. "Sorry. Expected a nice drive but there are a million nuts out here headed your way."

"A hundred thousand at least and half of them drunk. The Georgia vs Georgia Tech rivalry is played here today. Where are you exactly?"

"Road called—" A red and black van loomed out of nowhere and cut off Joe's car. "Hey! Crazy dude tried to run me into the median. Um, it's called University Parkway."

"Good grief, you're smack in the middle of football mania. Get off there."

"Intersection coming up—Highway 11—I'm taking it." He wheeled across two lanes and made a break for the exit ramp.

"Good. Stay on that road through the town of Monroe. Keep going and I'll meet you in Social Circle."

"Social what?"

"Circle, itty-bitty town a half hour ahead of you. I'll join you at a restaurant called Blue Willow Inn. Its food is wonderful."

"Says you," he muttered.

"Exactly. I'm Mohammed, remember, you're just the mountain."

Joe smiled. Wrenn was about the only person who ever teased him. It came as a surprise from Kathryn, as refreshing as a splash of cool water.

☙❧☙

The antebellum charm of Blue Willow Inn extended

all the way to teenage greeters who might have sashayed straight out of *Gone With The Wind*. They tripped over their hoop skirts, serving Joe a mug of hot chocolate, and ensconced him in a granny rocker on the veranda to await his lunch companion.

In a fit of giggles, the young hostesses almost trampled Kathryn when she arrived.

She claimed a mug of cocoa and folded a jeans-clad leg beneath her as she slipped into an adjoining rocker.

"Wow," Joe said.

Kathryn instantly regretted her attire. "Well, it's not like you gave me notice." His sudden trip had barely given her time to pull on a sweater and brush her teeth. "Would you rather I'd kept you waiting while I dolled up?"

He tipped his head at her and winked. "I mean—wow—as in terrific."

She anchored a brunette wisp behind her ear, one she had brushed forward as Dee's admonition 'a ponytail is not a hair style' ricocheted through her brain. Tucking the toe of her sneaker under a chair rung, she set the rocker gently in motion. "Better than before, huh?"

"Lots." He touched forefinger to brow in mock salute. "Thanks for the rescue, ma'am."

Kathryn was surprised by his ease and by the pleasure she felt at seeing him again. He had a stronger, more angular profile than she remembered. Trading on her southern accent, she exaggerated his name, "Mah pleasure, Mist-ah But-lah."

He threw his head back and laughed. "Far cry from your man Rhett."

"Let's see." She twisted imaginary whiskers. "You could absolutely work the Gable mustache, but I don't see you pulling off his supercilious grin."

"Thanks—I think." He arched a brow toward the

girls in costume. "I see Prissy is on equal footing with Melanie and Scarlett."

"Yes. The South is a complex place."

Joe rested a calfskin loafer up on the porch railing and gazed across the neatly defined lawn. His dark eyes were intense, taking on a purple cast in the natural light. "Might get used to it. Driving that back road was great. Restful."

She nodded, and they both said, "Bucolic," followed by, "Jinx!"

"Hey." She laughed. "You owe me a Coke."

"I owe you for a whole new career."

"You'd have gotten there eventually."

"Owe you for the push, then. I hear you're pushing people around from home now."

She laughed. "Who you calling pushy?"

One of the young hostesses reappeared to escort them inside. Tantalizing aromas swirled as Joe and Kathryn were seated at a table in the bay window of what was originally a drawing room. A plump matron hailed Kathryn from the doorway. "Where you been keeping yourself, girl?" Evelyn O'Hara's starched white pinafore declared the kitchen her domain. "And who, might I ask, is this fine young man?"

"This is Joe Butler," Kathryn said. "Joe, meet our hostess, Evelyn O'Hara, council-woman, concert violinist, and the best cook in this county."

Evelyn eyed Joe approvingly. "Now, Mister Joe, where did our Kay steal you from?"

Responding in kind, he said, "Straight off a California beach, Miss Evelyn."

"He's here on business," Kathryn interjected. "How're things going with your historical designation?"

"We'll get it. You know it takes longer to crack some nuts than others." Evelyn looked from Kathryn to Joe and back at Kathryn. "It doesn't always have to be business, you know."

Kathryn grinned and stood up. "We're going to check out your buffet."

Evelyn chuckled and made her way back to the kitchen.

Leading Joe to the dining room, Kathryn said, "I should've warned you about that."

"What?"

"That Evelyn would jump on you, as we say in Georgia, 'like a duck on a June bug.'"

"Hear me complaining?" The smile left his eyes as they widened to take in the dining room's antique sideboards. Still festooned for Thanksgiving, they groaned with southern delicacies. "How do you choose?"

"My strategy is to sample dishes I don't make at home. Fried okra, creamed corn, and sweet potato soufflé."

"Nothing comes close to any of this at my home." He gawked at the dessert table. "Is that *real* caramel cake?"

"Evelyn caramelizes the sugar in a cast iron skillet."

Grabbing a plate, he said, "I'm starting there. Bring on the carbs."

Reseated at their table, Joe sipped from a frosty glass of sweet tea and flourished a drumstick of steamy fried chicken in the air. "What you said about the South."

"I appreciate your economical use of words, but you're going to have to give me a bit more than that."

"Complex. One extreme to the other, no middle ground."

"I see. People do tend to choose sides here." She shrugged. "At least you know where you stand."

"True." He nodded. "Friends call you Kay?"

"Mostly." An odd stillness came over Kathryn. More in her heart than in her head, she heard, *Kitty,* the loving way Sam had spoken his special name for her. She held her breath, feeling his ghost pass her. Re-focusing on Joe, she said, "I'm called Kay by those who knew me in grade school. Like Evelyn. Caramel cake is her specialty. She'll be pleased you like it. I must say, you came far enough for it."

"Wanted to thank you in person. Without your confidence, my fiction never would've seen daylight."

"Our meetings at Omni were so sparse I'm surprised I made any impression at all."

"Definitely."

"I'm flattered you want me to edit your manuscript, especially since I left you in a lurch with the biography."

"You had it whipped into shape. I didn't realize how much so until I worked with Zach. Hope you'll help me with *Daylight to Darkness,* that's my working title."

"You could've sent it by courier, you know."

"Thing is—" He hesitated. "I want to talk to you about it, in person."

She held up a cautioning hand. "Not yet. I do a cold read first. Give me a couple of days, let's say until Monday."

"Okay. I'll stay the weekend in Athens. Call my cell when you're done."

"You may have to go back to Atlanta. Athens is covered up with football fans, plus the Alex Whitlow Band is home for a concert."

"I'll find a couch to crash on." He winked. "Movies and musicians make good bedfellows."

Kathryn was flummoxed at having forgotten his celebrity. His face might not be as well-known as his cousin's but their family was recognized all over the world. And yet he was approachable, likeable. Ignoring the stubborn wisp of hair that refused to stay behind her ear, she picked up her fork.

Chapter 5

Once home, Kathryn gave the bright mix of yellow and purple pansies on her porch a reviving splash of water. "I'm back, Goosey Loosey," she called to her under-the-house guardian.

Lighting the gas logs in the day room, she cleared space for Joe's manuscript on her desk. She expected to be well into it by nightfall but, before delving into his fiction, she pulled the Bennett biography off her bookshelf. At the time Phyllis sent the pre-release copy to her, Kathryn had not felt well enough to appreciate it. Now she admired the cover graphics and read the blurbs on the back from major players in the movie industry. Omni had gone all out. She studied various photos chosen for the pictorial section. Joe was undeniably correct in recounting Grandmother Pet's vision of himself and Colton as "her beautiful boys." Even in their leggy days of puberty, they had been stunning. She decided the flawless jacket photo of Colton had been airbrushed and wished they had used the handsome cousin with eyes like purple agates who'd actually penned the tome.

She paged through the front matter, found a credit to

her but none to Zach. Hours later she was still reading. During the editing process, she had gone over the text word by word, but the finished product still cast a spell on her.

Through a series of skilled flashbacks, Joe took his reader back to the Vietnam War when his grandfather lied about his age to get into the air force. William Bennett's job, self-described as "bagging bodies," gave no hint of the fame that lay before him. Once home and working at a friend's Chevy dealership, he charmed Harriette Colton, a soap opera scriptwriter whom he instantly nicknamed Pet, into buying her first car. Although the rest was history, Joe's gradual way of unfolding their love story entranced Kathryn. She rode the highs and lows of their lives and finished the book wondering what it must feel like to be a public figure before birth, to fight for a life that felt real and honest and normal.

Seeing how late it was, she fed Goose and decided to read Joe's new manuscript the next day. Good thing she hadn't promised him feedback until Monday.

Sunday morning dawned cold and dreary. Anticipating a day of reading in lieu of going to church, Kathryn bundled up and took a quick loop around the pond to clear her head. She came back and brewed a pot of tea, taking it to her reading spot, the old-fashioned overstuffed chair. With her legs bolstered by one of its round chintz-covered arms and her head nestled into the opposite wing, she picked up the synopsis. In the midst of skimming the first page she pressed a hand to her chest and sucked in her breath. Reading further brought her upright with her feet on the floor. Joe's protagonist was a Georgia woman working as an editor in New York, whose photo-journalist husband had been killed in Afghanistan. Joe had even named her Kitty. Un-be-lieve-able.

Kathryn saw her personal misfortune laid bare. She dropped the page and held her head in her hands, aware of nothing, not even the roar in her ears. No wonder he had wanted to talk to her in person about this manuscript. What exactly did he plan to say? "Oh, by the way, I've exploited your life—your loss—even your miscarriage." She felt queasy. She had been in such a state last June she couldn't remember precisely what she had told him. She only remembered how understanding he had been, how easy to talk to. Dangerously easy. That's why he showed up yesterday. He had played her!

Her eyes fell on the Bennett bio she'd left on the sofa. She snatched it up, stormed to the kitchen door, and flung it as far out into the back yard as she possibly could. It made a satisfying thud off the side of the fifty-five-gallon drum she used for burning trash.

Arms crossed, she stomped back and slumped onto the sofa. After glaring a hole in the bead-board ceiling for a few minutes, she found herself too furious to sit. On her way to the kitchen, she reached back and grabbed a handful of hair in each hand, yanking them apart to tighten her ponytail. Anger swirled as she paced, slamming cupboard doors and muttering every vile name that fit the man, and many that didn't. Resolving to read Joe's manuscript—every odious page—she nerved herself with a pot of coffee within reach and set about the task.

Tightly written, Joe's plot followed his heroine's quest for vengeance from Afghanistan throughout the Middle East. With compelling dialogue and a strong hook at the end of each chapter, he hit every plot point dead on. It was late afternoon before Kathryn let the final page drift onto the floor. Bestseller. No doubt about it.

Joe's fictitious Kitty Quinn had the strength to avenge her husband's death. She combed the globe, ferreting out terrorists. Sam Tribble was killed and what had his wimpy, real-life Kitty done about it? Not one damn thing! More bereft than she had felt in weeks, she hid her face in the wing of her chair and sobbed.

At sundown, she wandered outside to the front yard and stood beside Aunt Tildy's birdbath. Goose, no doubt sensing her mood, did not venture forth. Miles from the light pollution of the city, night came to Kathryn's woods like the flip of a switch, daylight to darkness. The very title of Joe's book seemed stolen from her.

***

Showered and well-rehearsed in what she would say, on Monday morning Kathryn sliced a peach over a bowl of corn flakes before dialing Joe's cell.

"Joe's phone," a sleepy female voice purred.

Kathryn's eyes widened. None of the words she had planned quite fit this scenario.

"Hello-o?" The woman stifled a yawn. "Who's calling?"

Kathryn recovered her poise. "May I speak with Joe, please?"

"He didn't answer, so he must not be taking calls. Who are you?"

"Kathryn Tribble. Will you give him a message or should I call back and leave it in his voice mail?"

"I'll take it if it's short."

"Very short. Tell him I'm not his editor."

Kathryn stood at the window, eyed the golden leaves on her gingko tree, and finished her cereal. "Okay." She set her bowl down in the sink. "That's that." She went into the day room, replaced the portable phone in its base, reached behind her desk, and unclipped the land line from the wall jack.

Switching her cell phone to silent, she dialed Donna-

Ray. "Hey, Dee, what time is your Garden Club reception this afternoon?"

"Gal pal, I could kiss you full on the mouth! Get yourself over here."

�@✐✐

By the time Joe's third call to Kathryn on Monday went unanswered, even by her machine, he was livid. What'd she do, unplug the damn thing? Since Phyllis at Omni had been dodgy about giving up Kathryn's home number, he went straight to Zach Tolliver for the cell.

Ever the boss, Zach asked, "Something the matter?"

"Nope. Just touching base, must be a glitch on her land line."

"Okay, she has good cell coverage. That's how I get her."

Joe punched in the number Zach dictated and put his iPhone on speaker while he flossed his teeth. At least her cell rotated to voice mail. "Kathryn," he said, "call me. We need to talk."

Joe's buddy, Alex, roused earlier than the law of musicians allowed, lounged in the doorway. "Sorry about your call, man. Suze screens everything, and she can hear a phone a mile away."

"Yep." Joe shook the creases out of a laundry-folded shirt and whipped it on. "Really appreciate you guys giving me a place to crash."

College roommate Alex and his wife Suze were Joe's closest confidantes. They had witnessed his sham marriage to Phoenix, and they knew about Wrenn. Joe shoved his shirttail into his jeans and zippered in an annoyed motion as Kathryn's phone rolled to voice mail again. "Crap. She won't answer."

Sweeping a pack of cigarettes off the dresser, Alex

lipped one into place. "Special lady?" He searched around the room for a lighter.

Joe reflected on the Kathryn who had wowed him two days before. Sun-kissed and healthy, her glossy ponytail much more than an afterthought, and the rogue freckle he remembered beside her top lip taunting him. The sadness in the depths of her pretty brown eyes still tugged at him, and her approval of Kitty Quinn had taken on inexplicable importance. "Maybe," he answered.

Alex lit his cigarette. "If she's local, I can find out where she lives. My golf buddy's wife is big in real estate. Dee makes it her business to know just about everybody."

Joe sat on the bed and picked up one of his shoes. "Yep, do that. Kathryn Tribble. Grew up in Athens. Hold on," he whipped out his phone. "I have her maiden name."

"C'mon, man. She's not married is she?"

"Widow." Joe made a quick search of his contacts. "Morton. That's it, Kathryn Morton Tribble."

❡❡❡

A blur of blonde enthusiasm, Donna-Ray Lyndon orchestrated any hullabaloo into a concert of foods, friends, and drinks. Emphasis on drinks, since her Back Porch Punch contained enough peach schnapps to kill a horse. The caterer had brought in an army of Latino servers to make magic for her gardening friends.

A teen wearing the black-vested uniform of the catering company swooped an empty tray off the buffet and smiled shyly at Kathryn.

"*Hola*, Lydia," Kathryn said, having met the girl at Old Mill Village when Dee showed her the library.

The Mexican girl wore the beleaguered look of one

who worked too many hours for too little pay. She nodded and blended back into Dee's kitchen teeming with women in identical black vests.

Kathryn bumped into Lydia again as she came down the hall with a bowl of limes for the bar set up in Dee's Florida room. She fell in step with the girl. "I'm going to start teaching ESL, English as a Second Language, at the library. Would you like to come?"

"*Sí*—yes." Lydia rushed away, skirting the melee of aging Sorority Sue's and Fraternity Fred's reliving college days.

As Kathryn made her way toward Dee and Tommy, she caught a whiplash motion of Lydia's head. The bartender had grabbed the girl's arm and jerked her to him. Kathryn frowned and changed course for the bar. She arrived in time to hear Lydia's apologetic tone but not her actual words.

The short, thick-set man spewed a guttural stream of Spanish at his captive.

"Excuse me," Kathryn interrupted, "white wine, please."

Like a rabbit out of a snare, Lydia made a dash for the kitchen.

The bartender's vest, as black as his slick hair, matched the other servers and displayed a nameplate. "Eduardo," Kathryn read. "Are you related to Lydia? I hope to tutor her in English."

"*Soy su hermano*," he mumbled and poured a glass of Chablis.

Kathryn searched her paltry grasp of Spanish. "You're her brother? You must be proud of her. She works very hard."

Black eyes luminous and challenging, he clinked the wine glass down on the bar in front of Kathryn and turned dismissively to ice down a tub of beer.

She maintained her place and tasted the wine. "Would you put a little ice in this for me?"

His calloused brown hands contrasted sharply with the starched white cuffs of his catering shirt and the delicate silver tongs he wielded. Locking eyes with her, he splashed two cubes into the goblet. She felt a tendril of fear creep up her spine.

His warning for her to butt out was universal in any language.

A group of men jostled up to the bar and called Eduardo to tap a keg for them. One of the men was Kathryn's high school boyfriend, a former pro-linebacker, Steve Overby. He reached out and caught her around the waist. Marinated in Brut, he accosted her with a bear hug lasting a tad too long. "My God, Kay," he said, slurping foam from a mug, "you look wonderful. Now that I'm divorced, I'll be calling you."

"I heard you and Connee were separated," she said, stressing the last word and dodging his beer breath.

"Same difference."

Picturing his lovely wife and young sons, Kathryn frowned. "That's not the same at all, Steve, but since you think so, don't embarrass yourself by calling me."

He leered at a passing young woman and called out, "Hey there, hon, wait up."

Kathryn circulated and had used up her gardening small talk when Dee pulled her into a happy hug. "Let's go sit, gal pal. There are vacant seats over by the piano, and my dogs are barking. If I'm not mistaken, you're having a good time in spite of yourself. Come on, let me hear it."

Kathryn smiled. "Okay, you told me so. It's good to get out and see everyone."

Collapsing into a chair, Dee kicked off her shoes and wriggled her toes while her sharp eyes inventoried the guests. "I saw Steve make a move on you. Your old teddy bear has turned into a snake."

"What in the world has come over him?"

"Alcohol. Got bad after the pros cut him, worse since Connee left with the boys. She had to, though. He's a mean drunk. Real estate community wouldn't put up with him if his hip pocket wasn't full of properties." Dee scanned the rest of the crowd. "Sure do wish Alex Whitlow had come."

"You better not be trying to match me up with a rock star."

Dee put on her expression of doe-eyed innocence. "He's been married forever. Where Alex goes, his Suze goes. I was just wishing they'd come. We went to 40-Watt to hear his band Saturday night. Would've called, but knew you wouldn't go. Anyhoo, Alex has a buddy visiting from Los Angeles. Lordy, Kay, that man is so handsome he'd make you squint. And...drum roll...he's single."

Kathryn pretended to get up.

Dee waved her back down. "Okay, spoil sport, I'll hush." Subdued for only an instant, she added, "You know what, Matilda? We need us a film festival."

Kathryn caught the code for girl talk. Their film festivals dated back to sixth grade. They had gabbed about boys all night long, wolfed down Waffle House omelets, and swooned over back-to-back Brad Pitt and Tom Cruise movies. Watching Dee's husband aim his cheek at a couple of women making *mmuuah* noises at him, Kathryn said, "Does 'so handsome you'd have to squint' mean he's dark like Tom Cruise and Tommy Lyndon?"

"Um-hum." Dee massaged her tired feet. "That's why you and I never fought over boyfriends. You can have the blonds with big ole goofy grins."

Like Sam. The words came unbidden and dropped a

veil between Kathryn and the festivities. How could she sit here enjoying herself without him? Would she ever stop craving his easy smile and good-natured company?

For all Dee's seeming frivolity, she was astute at reading people. She gave Kathryn's hand a meaningful squeeze. "If you should meet Alex's friend, be nice. That's all I'm saying. Alex called earlier, asking where you live."

"Me? Why?"

"I dunno. The caterer showed up, and I didn't have time to ask."

"My, my." Tommy flopped into the chair beside his wife. "I'd like to be a fly on the wall over here."

"Gal-pal gab," Dee said. She rolled her eyes toward Kathryn, who had drifted far away again.

Joe Butler's voice rang in Kathryn's mind: *Movies and musicians make good bedfellows.* She knew exactly who was visiting Alex Whitlow.

Chapter 6

Armed with directions, Joe focused on finding Kathryn. As Alex's realtor friend, Dee, had said, he "couldn't miss" her sign at the estate she'd referred to as Charlie's Corner. Per Dee's instructions, he turned off Morton Road onto Morton Farm Lane. That took him down the side of the corner property where Dee had planted another of her in-your-face type signs. A sprinkling of mailboxes on The Lane hinted at houses out of sight. A pond on the right was the landmark for him to take the next driveway to the left. A half mile in, the gravel drive doglegged to the right and ended in front of a stone cottage. Tucked neatly into a stand of pines, the place was surrounded by a pretty, well-kept yard.

He remembered Kathryn saying, "The best place for a rewrite, back to the beginning." *Nice if you can get it.* Joe's life hadn't come with any do-overs.

He looked around for the Prius she had driven to Blue Willow Inn, but it was missing from the car shelter in the side yard. She wasn't home. He slammed his car door, and leaned against it. A Cujo-ish warning issued from under the porch as Joe wondered if she was purposely avoiding him. The message she'd left with Suze held a tone of finality. Maybe she did not intend on talking to him at all. He hadn't counted on that.

He approached the vintage fieldstone structure. The new-looking porch across its front seemed welcoming. "Good puppy," he coaxed, quieting the invisible pooch as he took all three front steps in a bound. With a perfunctory rap on the door, he added, "Like she wouldn't already know I was here, with your racket."

The porch was furnished with a rocking chair that looked about a hundred years old. A spindled bench backed up against a picture window made from individual panes of wavery, hand-blown glass. Bundles of drying lavender hung upside down from the ceiling. Gigantic I-bolts in a rafter held a sturdy oak swing that creaked under his weight as he sat down. Forty-eight hours ago he'd been rocking on a porch with her, yelling 'jinx' and laughing as if he didn't have a care in the world.

He sucked on a nicotine lozenge, glad he hadn't taken the pack of cigarettes Alex offered, and studied the surviving sections of a mossy rock wall. It undulated through her front yard like a sea serpent. What would life be like in a quaint, peaceful place like this? The quiet was broken by his cell phone ringing in his jeans pocket.

Joe frowned at the number. Colton's guard, Daniel, wouldn't be calling from Paris unless there was a problem. Joe gave his standard answer. "Yep."

"You coming over?"

"If I need to."

"Our man's costar is stirring up a stink. Fact is, he's been into her more than the movie."

Joe closed his eyes against a flash of anger. "I'll fly out of Atlanta tonight."

"Atlanta? You're not in LA?"

"Just glue your ass to Benny 'til I get there." Joe

pocketed his phone and slumped against the back of the swing. How much would this one cost him? He rose and stared without seeing over the porch rail. *Cursed, needy, grasping females.* With a half-grin, he amended his thought. *Except for Kathryn, who won't talk to me, and Wrenn who barely can.*

Striding to the car, he dug a business card out of his duffel and scrawled a note across the back. He returned to the porch and stuck it in a pot of pansies. Assailed by the fresh scent of lavender wafting past his nose and a final spate of barking from the dog, he growled, "If I had a place to hide, fella, I'd guard the hell out of it, too."

∽∾∽∾

The knot in Kathryn's stomach tightened when she listened to Joe's "we need to talk" message in her cell phone's voice mail. His voice had a gravelly timbre of controlled irritation. She didn't "need" anything except for him to leave her alone. She'd stayed deliberately late at Dee's reception and was relieved to find Goose the on-ly one at home to greet her. "You'll give him the devil if he shows up here, won't you, Goosey-boy."

By Tuesday morning she had relaxed. A man of Joe's stature wasn't apt to hang around, looking for her. She ran through her Pilates routine, bath, and breakfast before taking a glass of water to the porch pansies. She was startled to find the B&B Productions card of Joseph Enriqué Butler caught in the tangle of yellow and purple blooms. She narrowed her eyes and turned it over. Bold-ly, in sweeping script, he had written: *Without you ~ Kitty dies.*

"Well?" she queried Goose.

He cocked his head in reply.

Stupid man! In a fit of pique, she stormed into the

house and gathered up the manuscript he had so magnanimously hand-delivered. In the back yard, she flung all three hundred pages into the trash barrel and lit it on fire. Trash burning was one of Aunt Tildy's country practices that Kathryn embraced. Reducing waste to ashes had a cleansing effect that noisy, nasty garbage trucks couldn't achieve.

She spied the Bennett biography in the weeds where it had landed the day before when she threw it out the back door. She was about to add it to the blaze when a greedy flame licked at the cover and caused her to snatch it back. Shoving his "Kitty dies" note between the pages, she took it into the house and tossed it on a bookshelf.

ᏊᎣᏊᎣ

According to the movie hype "everyone loves Paris," but not Joe. He claimed one of the few first class seats available back to the US on Christmas Eve and considered himself lucky to make any flight. Nonstop to Atlanta, he held onto the peppery sensation of a nicotine lozenge in the back of his throat and scowled as he reflected on the four weeks it had taken him to pull Colton's butt out of a proverbial crack. Again.

His cousin hadn't banged the usual starlet looking to add the Bennett notch to her bedpost. Those were easy to buy off with paparazzi-filled club dates followed by a well-publicized break-up—industry standard for feeding the sharks and pumping up the box office. This time Colton had hit on his co-star, former sit-com darling Lila Manning.

And Lila had cried rape. Known now only for having been famous in the past, her history of revolving rehab had not diminished her international fan base. She posed a significant threat.

Joe had arrived to find French authorities riled, and Little Lila playing victim to the hilt.

Colton had rolled his eyes. "She's just a drama queen, Joey." After a moment, he added, "Y'know, she might be telling the truth."

"On Pet's grave, Benny, if you raped that woman, any woman, I'll let you rot in a French prison."

"Don't be all…" Colton let a shrug close the sentence. "She all but raped me. I'm just saying she'd had so much champagne, she might not remember."

Joe clamped his hands down on his cousin's arms like a vise. "Pig!" He dug his fingers into Colton's biceps and gave the star a teeth-rattling jolt. "Ever occur to you to leave her the hell alone?"

Colton winced and rubbed his arms. "It seemed okay at the time."

Joe must've run twenty miles that day, through parts of Paris no tourist guide recommended. He would've welcomed a mugger, an excuse to beat the crap out of somebody. As much as Colton profited from publicity, an international incident wasn't worth it. The likes of *TMZ* and *Entertainment Tonight* would have a field day over "The Cuz," as they dubbed Joe, coming to the rescue again.

A big dose of high-priced private sleuthing had finally uncovered the root issue. Little Lila was busy deflecting attention away from her latest oxycodone relapse. Joe held her contractual clean-and-sober clause over her head and offered her equal billing on the film if she retracted her accusation. He charged her agent with seeing to it Lila made good on the promise. He hadn't missed a single Christmas with Wrenn and he wasn't about to miss one now that she'd been taken to the hospital with another lung infection.

Joe gave Daniel, worth his considerable weight in

gold, orders to sit on his randy cousin for the rest of the shoot. Joe headed for Atlanta, fantasizing about bringing his little girl home for Christmas. Her present was engraved, wrapped, and in his carry-on bag—a silver horseshoe charm representing the pony Rusty had secretly stabled.

One thing the old cowboy and Joe had in common was horses. "She's a beaut," Rusty had bragged, sounding more excited than Joe had ever heard him. Joe's thoughts shifted back to figuring out a place to stash Colton until this latest debacle blew over. He hissed out a breath between clenched teeth. He must act quickly, before the next bimbo came along and jiggled her boobs at the star. Capitalizing on Phoenix's fear of flying, Joe had planted rumors about Colton staying in Europe after the movie wrapped, but the man couldn't be trusted that far out of reach.

Like a juggler with balls in the air, Joe checked his phone to make sure neither Daniel nor Anna was trying to reach him. On the periphery was also the hope that Kathryn Tribble might call. He frowned. He had devoted half a year of solid writing to capturing an intrinsic quality that woman possessed. How could his fictional embodiment of her as Kitty Quinn be so objectionable that she wouldn't even speak to him? He didn't understand it, and he couldn't think of a single way to make it right. His cheeks puffed out with the release of another frustrated breath. He couldn't fix things with her, any more than he could fix Wrenn.

He pressed the back of his skull into the headrest and closed his eyes. A woman without a price would be...what? Priceless. He imagined how light Kathryn would feel in his arms—the curve of her back, smooth as a calla lily. Readjusting his long legs, he crossed his ankles as far under the seat in front of him as he could. His thigh muscles tensed as he yearned for something more carnal than nicotine.

Somewhere over the Atlantic, Joe drifted into that magical state writers crave, a fictive dream where characters tell their own stories. A first-person narrator whispered the opening lines of a new book into Joe's psyche:

> *I make my home in the South, a rural estate*
> *at the corner of Morton Road and quaint little*
> *Morton Farm Lane. A finger of wood smoke ris-*
> *es in the distance as though beckoning me to*
> *her. If only she was there. If only.*

"Blanket, sir?" A well-intentioned flight attendant yanked Joe back into reality.

"Thanks." He pulled the cover across one shoulder, turned his back to the aisle, and gazed into the inky void beyond the fuselage window. The caged animal expression he so despised glared back at him.

Arriving in Atlanta, Joe felt the joy of Christmas as he anticipated seeing Wrenn. He stopped briefly at his condo to change clothes and collect his car. A black cattleman's shirt with red piping turned him into a cowpoke for Wrenn and dressed up his ostrich boots that were as broken in as his jeans.

By the time he reached the hospital, Wrenn was fretting to go home, but she lacked enough energy to mount a full-on campaign.

"The doctor said not 'til tomorrow," Anna cautioned. There was obvious worry in the look she gave Joe.

Wrenn slumped into her pillow. "In the morning?"

"Yep," Joe said. "I got a good report on you from your doctor and he'll be here first thing."

"He won't come," she sighed. "It'll be Christmas."

"Then he'd better release you early so he can get

home and see what Santa brought." Joe winked and presented his wrapped gift.

Anna snipped the ribbon with her crochet scissors and Wrenn picked up the silver chain. The horseshoe charm twirled and sparkled before her eyes. She immediately connected the engraving, *Miracle*, to the pony awaiting her. "That's her name," she said. "It's the only thing I want."

"Me, too," Joe said, blinking away the sting of tears. The fight was going out of his little bird. She really needed a miracle.

As promised, he engineered her early release on Christmas morning. Anna didn't object when Joe tucked apple slices in the blanket wrapped around Wrenn and carried her straight from the car to the four-stall stable behind the house.

Beaming, Rusty led Miracle, a riding pony he'd vetted through a trainer with a house full of girls, across the paddock. All the leggy little athlete needed to be a unicorn was a horn. She was petite, upright, and full of self-importance.

Wide-set eyes on the filly's exquisitely dished head showed her Arabian heritage and were full of youthful curiosity.

Hinting at her future palomino color, Miracle's straight, tippy ears flicked and homed in on Wrenn. She thrust her pink, velvety nose into the blanket and nuzzled for the apples. Wrenn giggled, her platinum hair intermingling with the pony's pale mane.

Miracle gently lipped her mistress on the cheek.

"She kissed me!" Wrenn caught her jingly red halter and kissed her back.

Rusty gave Joe a thumbs-up, and Anna laughed.

❧❦❧

Joe managed to keep business at bay until after the holiday but, in due course, his presence was required on the west coast. Bennetthurst was where he worked but he *lived*, in every nuance of that word, with Wrenn. He promised to be back for New Year's Eve, and made her repeat his cautions about the pony. Mischief in her eyes said she would try to ignore them, but he was confident Anna, Rusty, and her health would rule.

Reversing his airport routine, Joe drove back to the condo to leave the Lexus. They were the accoutrements of the normal life he indulged in imagining from time to time. In that life, he was married to an exceptional woman and his child had a certain future.

In the silent condo, he stripped off his cowboy duds and sat on the edge of the bed. Colton's way of dealing with his life was to go public with everything. Joe worked out his problems in private. This place gave him the freedom to panic, to pray, to cry, and to cuss as needed. It had come furnished, minimally, with less décor than a hotel suite. He wandered into the empty kitchen and stared at the only point of interest, glass fruit in a bowl on the counter, some decorator's idea of art. Beautiful in a garish way. Brittle. A bit like his life.

During the mechanics of showering, dressing, and packing, he conceived an idea that might help both Colton and him. He called Alex Whitlow.

"Only got a sec, man. I'm in New York. Playing a charity gig in Central Park on our layover from Berlin."

"Berlin?"

"Mixed the disc on our next studio album over there. Suze and I read about your fun and games in Paris. You ought to get off the radar and spend New Year's with us. We'll be back in Athens by then."

"Thinking that might be a good place to stash Benny."

"I dig it. Major out-of-sight time?"

"Yep. Put me in touch with your trusty realtor, will you? The one who gave me directions to Kathryn Tribble's place."

Alex exploded with a fit of coughing laced with laughter. "Right, Kathryn." Clearing the rasp out of his throat, he provided Dee Lyndon's name and number.

Joe walked out onto the condo's miniscule balcony while he connected with the realtor. By dropping Alex's name and feigning a music industry connection, he could handle the deal without putting Rusty in the know. "I'm interested in leasing a place I saw on the corner of Morton Road and Morton Farm Lane."

"Charlie's Corner," she said. "I have others in that price range you might like to see."

"Nope, that one."

"You sound certain."

"Yep. Can you get me a three-year lease?"

"Absolutely. I'll fax you the contract. Three years, you said?"

"With a five-year option, if that works."

"Great. I can negotiate a better deal if you go out that far."

"Won't say no to that." He chuckled in appreciation of her acumen. "I'll turn the papers around and set up the bank draft as soon as I get back to LA."

"And I won't say no to that." Dee laughed merrily. "Welcome to Athens, Joe."

He called Daniel in Paris to hash out the logistics.

"I got me a cousin in South Carolina," the big man said. "Marleen. I can get her to set up the house and stay on to see to things."

"Is she discreet?"

"Discreet! Be easier to slip dawn past a rooster than get something out of Marleen."

"Good. I chose the place for location, so I don't know exactly what it needs. According to the realtor there's basic furniture. See if your Marleen can have it ready by mid-January. Can she make it homey?"

"Done raised four children, cooks up a storm."

"Thanks, man. Keep Benny over there 'til she gives the nod. And get wardrobe to fix him up with a beard, sweats, and everyday clothes."

"I'm on it. Guessing you wanna tell him about it yourself."

"Where is he?"

"Sleeping off a late night."

"Alone?"

"Got that right. Ain't nobody slipped nothing by me, neither."

Grinning, Joe ended the call and speed-dialed Colton, ignoring his cousin's obvious hangover. "Don't know why I haven't thought of this before, Benny. I've leased the perfect get-away for us, an estate in Georgia—Athens where Alex Whitlow lives. That town is home to a boatload of bands. Nobody hassles Alex, and he says there's a good airport there. Realtor assumed I was in the music business. Daniel is seeing to the details. He'll know when it's ready."

"Sounds like a good chance to detox." Colton yawned. "I've been swimming in wine."

"No swimming at this place, unless you're cool with a cattle pond. The upside is it's secluded enough for jogging. All you have to do is use your Ben Thomas alias and blend in. With the University of Georgia there, football players and bulldogs are bigger celebs than you."

"Isn't Athens where Kim Basinger grew up?"

"Yep. And Kenny Rogers used to have a big spread near there. He's been married to a couple of Georgia girls."

"Juicy Georgia peaches."

"Keep it zipped, Cuz."

Colton laughed. "Don't worry, man. If I can't play the part of southern gentry, nobody can." He shifted to a sober tone. "Now that you mention it, I was thinking about Atlanta."

Joe's hackles rose. Atlanta was code for Wrenn.

"I was thinking. The sharks would drop this Lila Manning bull if they got wind of a better story. A rumor, say, about me having a kid."

Joe flinched at the word "kid" and bit off two words. "You—don't."

"Y'know, technically."

"Technically—you—don't." Joe held his phone in a death grip. "Listen up, Benny. I'm only saying this once."

"You don't have to get all—"

"Shut up! This is not about you, and it's not make-believe." Joe took a breath. He tried for an even pitch, but his voice was pure emotion. "This is about a real, flesh and blood little girl. *My* little girl. By a cruel fluke of genetics, she may not see another Christmas. Do you imagine I'd ever in a million years throw her to the sharks for you?"

"It was just an idea," Colton backpedaled. "I didn't say it was a good one."

Joe's head throbbed. "Go to Athens, Benny. Keep your nose clean. Can you handle that?"

"Okay."

"I'll send scripts for you to read and be there myself in a few weeks."

"Thanks, Joey. And hey, I didn't mean any harm. About Atlanta."

In the cab to the airport, Joe shoved two sticks of spearmint gum in his mouth and mulled over the conversation. Benny was weak, but with all his catting around, he was more duplicitous than malicious. First Pet, and now Joe, kept the man's life simple by design and by necessity. He existed in the alternate reality of movies. In real life, Joe had let him have every prize they ever fought over. But he couldn't have this one. Wrenn was Joe's little bird and he wouldn't let anyone hurt her.

Chapter 7

Teaching satisfied something deep inside Kathryn. To be a more effective tutor, she had signed up for an adult ESL methods class at the Georgia Center for Continuing Education. Taking a break from helping Dee dismantle the Christmas tree in the Old Mill Village library, she gazed out the window. The cotton mill, reborn into trendy lofts, preened in the distance. Its surviving array of village houses had been brought up to code and reinvigorated with an influx of Latino culture.

"I don't know why," she mused, "but I have a terrible feeling about Lydia Vasquez. I'm setting aside worksheets for her, but she's only been to a few sessions."

"No luck with the phone number and address I got from the catering company?"

"No. The one time someone answered, a man snarled at me in Spanish and then hung up. The address turned out to be a vacant lot. You'd think somebody out here would know her."

"I'm sure they do," Dee said. "I'll ask around some more. How many ESL students signed up for this session?"

"Six. I picked up three adults, parents bringing children for guitar lessons."

Dee pursed her lips in thought. "Do you think there's room under the windows for a couple of computers? That's my fundraising goal for the Board of Realtors Ball. You'll be there, of course."

Kathryn arched an eyebrow.

"I'm not pushing you," Dee assured her. "I just enjoy the hell-o out of having you at these things. We usually have it before Christmas, catch everyone at their most charitable, but there was too much going on this year. It'll be fun on New Year's Eve for a change, and I hope profitable."

"Sure, I'll go. Why not kick off the New Year in style? Are you using the same caterer as before?"

"You're worse off than I thought if all you can think about is the food."

"It might give me a chance to see Lydia."

"Okay, sure. I'll request her."

"While you're at it, can you get another bartender instead of her brother Eduardo?"

"Good gardenseed! Don't tell me he messed up, and I'm just now hearing about it."

"No, nothing like that. Never mind. I don't want to jeopardize his job or make him mad. Don't mention him, but do ask for Lydia."

"Whatever. Beats me how you know more about my kitchen help than I do."

∾∽∾

"Hey," Joe fussed, "can't do this with you wiggling your feet."

Wrenn fell back on the sofa in a fit of giggles. "I'm trying, but it tickles."

Anna shook her head at them and put down her crochet basket. "About time for Granna to go finish the *gorditas*."

The way Joe played with Wrenn reminded her of the big lay-about German shepherd she'd had as a child. She chuckled in remembrance of the patient dog letting her polish his toenails and tie ribbons in his fur.

"Nooooo." Joe's wail came predictably from the other room. "Not mine, too."

Anna laughed, washed her hands, and wondered how many times that handsome man had been caught with Wrenn's polish on his feet. She picked up a dish towel and opened the kitchen door, looking across the back yard at the pony in the corral. Attuned to Wrenn, the filly's head came up and she gave a hopeful snort. Anna went back to warm a pan of pretty little tortillas she hoped would tempt Wrenn. They'd come a long way since her tube-feeding days, but it was still a challenge to keep her nourished and strong enough to fight off the cycles of inflammation and infection. Anna prayed every day that Bapa would never have to let go of his little girl.

If the unspeakable happened, there would be no more answer for him than there had been for her when she'd lost her daughter Julie—or Phoenix as she had become. Always high-strung and difficult, Julie had grown up mired in the same mental illness that drove her father to murder two men. He had ended horribly, wasting away in an institution.

After his trial, Anna had fled Canada with her child, but she couldn't outrun insanity. Anna hadn't laid eyes on Julie since the day she, calling herself Phoenix, gave birth to Wrenn. Anna's overarching emotion regarding Phoenix was fear, fear for those she would harm. Anna crossed herself with a prayer to Saint Jude, the patron saint of desperate causes.

Wrenn quietly picked at her food, making an effort. Her hair pooled like corn silk on her shoulders.

Joe ate heartily and pushed aside his empty plate. "Decided on your project for the Home School Science Fair?"

"Rocks."

"Want some geodes? Petrified wood?"

She shook her head. "I'm gonna build a model to show what they have to drill through to get oil."

"Layers?"

"They're called strata," she informed him in the imperious tone of a student in possession of a new fact. "I want to show how old they are, how hard and soft. Things like that."

"Interest in 'things like that' makes you a smart cookie. My uncle's old books on drilling oughta be around here somewhere. You know me, I don't throw away books."

Her coy smile lifted the permanent little smudges beneath her eyes. "Where do you think I got the idea?"

Anna smiled, too. "I'll bet when Bapa was a boy he kept his nose stuck in a book, just like you do, Wrenn."

"Except when it was on a horse," Joe said, pushing back his chair. "Wanna go riding, Bird?"

"Only if you hold me."

He hoisted her onto his shoulder. "Haven't dropped you yet, have I?"

ひつひつ

Kathryn clasped on her mother's pearl choker and twirled around in front of her bedroom mirror. Unexpectedly giddy, she affixed a sparkly comb in her dark, upswept hair. Her green Chanel dress was not new or sequined, but its slender silhouette bespoke couture and never failed to impress. Glamming up her brown eyes with gold-flecked eye shadow, she applied tinted lip gloss before driving to the Botanical Gardens to welcome in the New Year. She traversed a lighted pathway from the parking lot to the conservatory with the second wave of guests and blew a kiss across the room to Dee.

Sheathed in a shimmery red gown, Dee resembled a holiday candle with her bouncing flame of golden hair. She juggled an armload of unlikely door prizes, garden shears festooned with party bows, and yelled out merrily to Kathryn, "The only way I'm giving you one of these is if it comes attached to a man." Two handsome junior realtors helping Dee pretended to chase after Kathryn with upraised pairs of shears. Dee's peals of laughter reverberated all the way to the bandstand.

Throughout the evening's mingling and munching, Kathryn eyed dark-vested women replenishing trays and whisking away discarded dishes. She was at first delighted and then dismayed when she recognized Lydia. The unsmiling girl was pallid, with an obvious baby bump. She didn't speak until Kathryn stepped directly in front of her and touched her arm. "*Hola* Lydia, I haven't seen you in a long time."

"*Sí*—yes," she whispered, eyes downcast.

"You're always welcome in my class."

Lydia glanced around at the crowd, a sense of desperation about her.

"Can I help you, somehow?" Kathryn asked. "Is there anything I can do?"

Lydia shook her head and fled.

Kathryn sought out Eduardo. Tending bar on the far side of the atrium, he didn't notice her approach. "White wine, please."

Garnishing a tray of martinis, he nodded a crisp acknowledgment. He poured wine into a crystal goblet and placed it on the bar in front of Kathryn. Raising a heavy brow in recognition, he dropped in two ice cubes.

"Thank you." Catching his eye before he looked away, she said, "Can you help me with Lydia? I'd like to tutor her if she can arrange it."

He leaned forward and, quite close to her face, growled, "Leave. Her. Alone."

Kathryn recoiled at the undercurrent of threat in his words, and further recoiled when Steve Overby, never far from a bar, hulked up and ordered a scotch.

Giving her a once-over, he said, "My God, Kay, you really are beautiful."

"We aren't going to replay this again, Steve, you're drunk," she said, catching a wave of his alcohol and Brut stench.

"No, I'm pretty sure you're beautiful. Wanna dance?"

She took a step away from him. "Not really."

He put a beefy hand on her arm. "Sure you do, come on."

Irritated by his air of entitlement, she decided to let him swing her around the dance floor rather than make a scene. Tommy Lyndon came to her rescue halfway through the tune and waltzed her over to where Dee was hugging a spare, shaggy-haired rocker type. Kathryn recognized him as Alex Whitlow from his album covers. He was dressed in skinny black jeans, tee shirt, and tuxedo jacket with sleeves pushed up to reveal an eclectic array of forearm tattoos.

Bursting with excitement, Dee fanned a check in Kathryn's face. "Looky-Look! Thanks to Alex, we'll have *three* computers, and just about anything else we want."

Kathryn's eyes popped when she saw the amount written on the check.

"Oh Yeah—Unh Hunh, Unh Hunh." Dee snapped her fingers in time with her little sing-song and ran off, saying, "I'm gonna put this bad boy in the till."

Tommy shook his head and laughed. "That's my wife. Money does that to her." He looked from Alex to Kathryn and back. "Do you know each other?"

"Not personally," Kathryn said, "but that big donation makes him my new best friend." Smiling, she shook his hand. "I'm Kathryn Tribble. Dee will put your money to good use. Thanks for being so generous."

"The band gives back when it can."

"I remember when your first album took off. That must have been incredible."

"Tubular." Alex's eyelids, inked with permanent liner, dipped by half as he cocked his head and studied her. "Are you Kathryn Morton Tribble?"

"Yes," she said, surprised. "I am. Why?"

"We have a mutual friend in LA."

Kathryn's mouth went dry. Alex was the one who had called Dee to get directions to her house for Joe Butler. "Right," she said.

"My old UCLA roomie. I've had some of my biggest hits scoring movies for him." Alex tilted a rapscallion's grin her way. "He's not a bad writer either."

Aiming to shut down conversation about Joe, she said, "Publishing was our connection, but we aren't working together now."

"Too bad. I have some crazy riffs for Kitty Quinn whenever he green lights that project."

Kathryn was struck dumb. She had not considered Joe turning the book he'd mined from her life into a movie. Before she could recover her voice, Dee started windmilling her arms from across the dance floor.

"Uh oh," Alex said, "she's got publicity written all over her. Splitsville." Before he left, he said, "Our friend didn't make it for New Year's, but he'll be here soon."

His parting remark, made with a thin-lipped, know-ing smile, put a pall on Kathryn's festivities. Strains of "Auld Lang Syne" wafted her onto the terrace, and she slipped away from the party. At the stairs leading to the parking lot, she paused with her hand on the banister and gazed into the starlit southern sky. She'd reveled in her five glorious New Year's Eves in Times Square, counting down the minutes in Sam's embrace, waiting for their midnight kiss. Even though she had been alone in her apartment last year, she'd had the promise of their baby. A wave of melancholy hit her. She descended the wide stone steps, just wanting to go home. She shouldn't have come.

"I was right." Steve stepped out of the shadows at the bottom of the stairs, a slur in his speech "You're beauti-ful."

She forced a laugh and tried to pass by him quickly.

He reached out and caught her arm.

"Come on, Steve." She glanced around the deserted lot. "Don't do this."

"Why the hell not, Kay?" He pulled her roughly to him. "You know you want to."

"What I want is for you to quit telling me what I want." Fed up and angry, Kathryn dodged his slobbery kiss and struggled against his barrel chest. "Let go!" she screamed. "You're hurting me!"

He ran his hands down her back and ground himself suggestively against her. "Remember how good it was?"

"Let me go!"

Steve snarled and gave Kathryn a look she could on-ly describe as vicious. Trapped in his vise-like grip, she was terrified.

A dark figure rounded the side of the conservatory. Short and scrappy, he leveraged Steve off Kathryn and threw him to the ground. Recovering her balance, she recognized Eduardo Vasquez.

The young Latino balled his hands into fists and took a menacing stance over the downed drunk. "*Vaya!*" he commanded Kathryn. "Go!"

Chapter 8

Toward the end of January, Goose had found himself a playmate, a high-energy boxer with a penchant for racing Kathryn's Prius down the Lane. Tan with a flash of white on her cropped tail, she resembled a white-tailed deer running through the woods. A jogger routinely called to the dog, and they would disappear into the back part of the estate on the corner. Whenever Goose was absent, Kathryn figured he was up at the big house visiting his girlfriend.

Charlie's Corner, named for Kathryn's universally loathed great-uncle, had been uninhabited for most of her life. She had financed her move to New York by selling it, along with most of her inherited Morton land, to a wine distributor. Sadly, the recession hit before the man's business got off the ground. Dee had been trying to sell the place for him ever since. Kathryn was pleased to know someone lived there again.

She spent the last Sunday of the month at Dee's watching a rare Georgia snowfall, as they made salmon chowder and worked on the tutoring schedule for the library.

"Steve was in my office this week," Dee said. "When he brought up your name, I pretended not to hear it."

"Good. One mauling from him is one too many."

"Thank God for that bartender. Wasn't he the one you didn't like?"

"Yes. Well, I like him now."

"I don't think I told you, but I saw Lydia this week," Dee rambled on. "She's working at The Taco Stand—the original one down from my office, don't care how many they open that'll always be the best. Looks like she only has a few months left before the baby arrives."

"A child having a child," Kathryn said. "How on Earth will she manage?"

"Now that we know where she is, we can at least keep an eye on her." Dee tapped the end of her pen on Kathryn's forearm. "You could use some tacos. Put a little more meat on those bones." She screwed up her face and studied the schedule. "Okay, we've got enough tutors lined up for next month. Let's go watch *Pride and Prejudice*."

Tommy groaned and rose from the recliner where he had been watching TV. "I'll catch the game in the bedroom. I can't stand you mooning over Colin Firth."

"But, Tommy, he makes me so ro-man-ti-cal."

Tommy thumped an imaginary cigar and waggled his bushy brows in a Groucho Marx leer. "Like I said, I'll be in the bedroom."

❧❧❧

Phoenix lingered at The Melting Point, listening to an evening jazz quartet and sipping scotch. She had been in Athens since New Year's, almost three weeks. Wrapped in the warmth and security of the cardigan Colton had given her before the wretched kid came along, she smirked. She'd gotten good at Joe's cat and mouse game and hadn't bought his media dodge about Colton staying in Europe. Not for a minute. Rusty'd tipped her off about Joe leasing a place in Chicago, but that was money wasted. A Whitlow Band roadie said Joe was hanging with Alex and his snarky wife in Athens. Something in her gut told her Colton would be there, too.

Phoenix played along. She went online and rented an apartment in Chicago with her debit card so Joe's people would see the charges. She'd even buy occasional tickets for Chicago concert venues to keep them thinking she was there. Meanwhile, her student flat and used van in Athens were charged to a credit card Joe Blow knew nothing about.

A scowl briefly replaced her smirk. She gnawed on a hangnail. She had to find their place here, and that would be tricky.

扰扰扰

Kathryn was irritated with herself for staying at Dee's far later than she'd intended. She inched her way home, watching for patches of black ice on the roads. She gave a sigh of relief when she pulled safely into her yard, until her headlights panned across the front of her cottage and she caught sight of Goose. Instead of snug in his nest of fresh pine straw under the porch, he lay prostrate on the steps. Kathryn's heart leapt into her throat. She slammed the Prius into park and sprinted across the snowy front yard. A whimper pronounced the dog alive, but she quickly discovered a rope around his neck had him tied to the porch railing. His thrashing on the icy steps had tightened the slipknot into a noose. She threw off her gloves and worked at loosening it. The cold instantly numbed her fingers.

She fetched her kitchen shears and raised blisters on her fingers before the nylon cord gave way and Goose took a raspy breath. "Poor baby." He dropped his head and Kathryn massaged his muscular neck. "I'm so, so sorry." She half-dragged, half-walked the disoriented dog into the house. "Come on, Goosey. We gotta get warm." Shivering, she fired up the gas logs and sat on the floor with him wrapped in a quilt with her. He leaned heavily against her side as she hugged her arm around him.

When Goose slumped down on the hearth rug, Kathryn fully expected him to sleep beside the fire. At bedtime, however, she found him hovering next to the front door in a silent plea for his outside realm. Kathryn obliged. She gave him a pat as he ambled out, and said, "Who would be mean enough to tie up my sweet boy?"

☙❧☙

Kathryn was in the midst of answering Phyllis's barrage of Monday emails when a movement in her front yard drew her eye. Through the wavery glass panes above her desk, she saw Goose's girlfriend bounding up the driveway. The boxer was accompanied by her jogger-owner. Goose loped alongside. Ears lowered submissively, he was tied to another length of the same butt-ugly yellow nylon cord she had found strangling him the night before. Kathryn flew out the front door. "Take that off him! Right—this—very—minute."

"Hello, I'm Ben—"

She sailed across the yard at the scruffy, red-bearded man. "I don't give a merry damn who you are. Get that rope off my dog!"

"He's been following my dog home. I don't want him to get run over."

Stooping down, Kathryn worked at loosening the

tether. "Right, so you'll choke him to death instead? Give me that!" She snatched the lead out of the man's hand and sat down on the ground to work the knot free.

"Yankee here chases cars."

"Well, Goose doesn't."

He tipped the brim of his sweaty ball cap back a bit. "Goose?"

Easing the rope over the dog's ears, Kathryn stood up and put her hands on her hips. "Yes," she flared her eyes at Red Beard. "His name is Goose."

"You don't have to be all… " He shrugged.

Kathryn waited for him to go on, to explain or apologize, but the dog no longer held the man's interest. Red Beard's eyes were assessing Kathryn in uncomfortable detail.

"Yankee is welcome here, Ben," she said sharply, "but you are not."

She turned and walked with Goose back to the house, unpleasantly aware of the man's blatant scrutiny.

e/ɔe/ɔ

Morton Farm Lane, with pastures on one side and woods on the other, continued a mile past Kathryn's driveway and dead-ended into a hayfield. Hers was the last residence, shielded from the road by its L-shaped tree line around a pasture that'd been carved out of the woods. Several days after her confrontation with Ben, she stopped her car at the mailbox on the way home and picked up her mail.

Shuffling through envelopes and ads, she eased along the driveway toward her cottage.

Without warning, the jogger's boxer shot out of the trees and assailed the car, snapping dangerously close to the tires. Kathryn stomped on the brakes. The Prius skidded in the gravel and hit the dog. The poor thing dropped like a rock.

"Omigod! Omigod!" Kathryn leapt out and ran to where Yankee lay motionless. Blood oozed from a gash in her head.

Grabbing an old blanket from her trunk, Kathryn tried to hold back her panic. "It'll be okay," she sobbed. "It's okay. I'll help you."

Jabbering in soothing tones, she eased the blanket beneath the limp dog and used it to hoist her off the cold ground and onto the back seat of the car.

"Hang on, baby. I'll get you to the vet. Here we go."

She turned the car around and fishtailed back down the driveway. Braking at the mailbox to make the turn onto The Lane, she glimpsed Ben jogging over the crest of the hill toward the dead end. She raced toward him, yelling out the car window, "Ben. Ben! Get in, your dog's hurt."

He stopped running and tugged iPod buds from his ears. "What?"

"Get in. I'm taking Yankee to the vet."

The skin visible above his beard and below his cap turned pale. "The vet?"

Kathryn leaned over and flung open the passenger door. "Get in the car!" As soon as he stumbled in, she executed a U-turn and screeched toward the main road.

"Stop at my house, I'll get—"

"No time." The estate flashed by as she whipped the car onto the highway. "Is she still breathing?"

He twisted around and knelt on the front seat to reach Yankee better. Feeling under the blanket, he said, "I can't tell. Wait, yes, barely." His voice reflected Kathryn's urgency. "You're right, no time. Where're we going?"

"My vet, unless you have one." She slowed, put on emergency flashers, and ran a red light.

"I don't."

"Don't what?"

"Have a vet here. What happened anyway?"

"Shut up and let me drive."

He recoiled like he'd been slapped, but Kathryn was far more worried about Yankee than his hurt feelings.

Pulling into the loading zone in front of the vet clinic, Kathryn threw the car into park. "Stay with her. I'll get help." Gone only a moment, she rushed back with a technician pushing a gurney, doing her best to answer the tech's rapid-fire questions. "Yes, she was hit by a car. No, not run over. Yes, a blow to the head. No, she hasn't tried to move."

In baggy running sweats and nondescript pullover, Yankee's master trailed behind as his dog was whisked away. He hesitated in the lobby, lingering beside the door while Kathryn approached the receptionist. "Hi, Billie, the patient is Yankee, my neighbor's dog," she said and gestured Ben forward.

"Your name, sir?" Billie asked.

He reached up and tugged at his ball cap.

The clerk repeated, "Your name, sir?"

"Uh, yes. Yes, it's Ben."

"Last name?"

"Oh, uh, my last name? Thomas. Ben Thomas."

"Okay, Mr. Thomas. Your address?"

"Y'know, I haven't been there long." He gave Kathryn a perplexed look. "Morton something."

"47 Morton Road," she supplied.

"Yeah, right."

Kathryn glanced at Ben. Despite his unkempt state, he possessed an air of refinement. Blond and buff, he was surprisingly handsome. His eyes were lavender and his eyelashes were the color of honey. The scraggly, reddish beard hid the lower part of his face, but she'd bet on straight teeth and a firm chin.

Billie looked up from her keyboard. "Since this is a new account, Mr. Thomas, I'll need a credit card on file."

"Oh, right. I don't—" He hesitated, scratching his beard.

Kathryn figured he wouldn't have a wallet because she had snatched him straight off the street. She also figured it was her responsibility to pay for the poor creature's injuries. "Use mine," she said, producing her credit card.

He passed it to the clerk and stepped aside, seeming disinterested.

Ben's air of entitlement canceled out any refinement and good looks Kathryn had previously credited to him. With an emphatic toss of her ponytail, she marched across the lobby and sat down.

He wandered over and took a seat beside her. "Yankee was running with me. What happened to her?"

"She darted out of the woods." Kathryn's voice trembled as she relived the moment. "It was so fast."

"*You* hit her? Weren't you paying attention?"

"It's not like I meant to. Anyway she wasn't with you. You were nowhere in sight." She clasped her hands. "I wouldn't have hurt her for the world."

"No," he said. "Of course, you wouldn't."

"And now," she gulped, "now—"

"Now, she's gonna be fine." He reached over and patted her hand, offering her a bright, eye-crinkling smile of reassurance.

Kathryn sat in silence. Sam had done that, patted her hand and grinned big when he wanted to jolly her into feeling better.

"Hey, you brought her to people you trust. She'll be okay," Ben continued in a kind voice.

"Lord, I hope so. It's surreal, like it didn't happen. But here we are."

"Yeah." He bent over and retied his running shoe while a young mother walked past juggling a toddler and a cat carrier. After a moment he sat up again and said, "So, you aren't still mad at me for tying up your dog?"

She shook her head. "You were right to be freaked out about Yankee chasing cars." She blinked back tears. "And then I went and hit her."

"Hey, don't you cry. It wasn't your fault. Anyway, you did something much worse than that?"

"What?"

"You told me to shut up."

Her lips curved as emotions tipped from misery to mirth. "Well, I must say you do take direction well."

He sobered instantly and bolted out of his chair. "You have no idea. Can I use your cell?"

Kathryn handed him her phone, but instead of placing a call he looked blank and shifted from foot to foot. "Something the matter?" she asked.

He wrinkled his nose and moved away, mumbling, "The only number I have memorized is the last one I want to call."

℃ↄℰↄ

When Joe's ring tone blasted out an Alex Whitlow hit, the quiet poolside ambience at Bennetthurst dissolved along with the sentence he was composing.

Kathryn Tribble's name displayed on his iPhone.

He shucked his custom-tinted readers and answered more calmly than he felt, "Glad you called." A nanosecond later, he flung his chair back and was on his feet yelling, "Benny? Talk to me!"

"Chill, Cuz," Colton said. "You don't have to be all—"

Joe could almost see the irritating shoulder roll that completed the phrase. "You're calling from Kathryn Tribble's phone?"

Joe listened to Colton's explanation of the situation that had landed him out in public without Daniel. "Hey, Joey, you're as big a fool over Yankee as I am," Colton said. "You'd have done the same thing."

"Not with your face. Get recognized by one person, just one, and Athens is history."

"I've got the drill—beard, sweats, cap. Y'know? I don't even know this chick's name; how come she's in your phone?"

Joe ground his molars. He had foreseen this conversation but not this soon. "She was my editor in New York on the Bennett biography. Her husband died, and she moved home to Athens. That's where I got the idea of Charlie's Corner." He took a breath and plowed on. It had to be said. "Between you and me, Cuz, she's Kitty Quinn."

"That's a real kick in the head."

"Between you and me," Joe emphasized, pacing across the pool deck. "She doesn't know I'm the one who leased the estate. And she certainly doesn't know you're there. Got the picture?"

"No prob."

"Listen up, Benny—" Joe stopped himself from warning his cousin away from Kathryn. Forbidden fruit was the sweetest to Colton. "Take down Daniel's number. He'll come get you."

"I don't need him. As soon as I get a report on Yankee, this Kitty chick can take me back."

"Use some sense, Benny! The woman's name is
Kathryn."

"Right."

"Now take down Daniel's number. Memorize it this
time."

"Lemme get a pen." Joe heard Colton call out 'Hey'
a couple of times and imagined Kathryn's reaction if his
cousin was dumb enough to snap his fingers at her. After
a series of fumbling sounds, Colton came back on the
phone. "Fire away."

Joe all but snarled the number and then tossed his
phone down on the table. He threw his cap so hard it
bounced off the towel hamper, then he sat back down and
laced his fingers behind his head. Pressing his neck
against the wrought iron rod along the top of his chair, he
glared into Pet's palms waving overhead. The preposter-
ous image of Colton Bennett sporting around Athens,
Georgia, in Kathryn Tribble's Prius bothered the hell out
of him.

Chapter 9

After Joe disconnected, Colton adopted his practiced stance of hip cocked languidly to one side and shot a covert look across the waiting room at Kathryn. This woman made a simple unadorned ponytail look classy. Sitting straight and a bit aloof, she was a study in neutral. Camel coat thrown across the lap of brown slacks, a tan hound's-tooth scarf draped twice around the neck of an ivory sweater. Poised, feminine, and perfectly normal unless you knew there was a Kitty Quinn lurking inside her.

He walked over and returned her phone. "How long do you think we'll have to wait?"

"As long as it takes."

"So what's your name?" He wanted to confirm that she was actually who Joe said she was.

"Sorry, I never introduced myself. I'm Kathryn Tribble."

He smiled, wholehearted and wide enough to cut a crease through his beard on either side. As co-owner of the Kitty Quinn movie rights, he would play the husband's role when Joe moved it into production. Joe regularly accused him of dumb luck and, damn, if he hadn't landed in the perfect spot to launch a character study of the actual husband.

Colton, in the guise of Ben, sat side-by-side with Kathryn, a bit like adversaries guarding the same post. After a time, the vet came forth with news that Yankee had suffered a concussion but only needed to stay overnight for observation and stitches.

Kathryn sighed in obvious relief.

As they got back in the car, she said, "I'm going to stop and pick up supper. You hungry?"

Colton shook his head. He was already one above his quota of unescorted jaunts in public. "I'll have dinner at home."

"Suit yourself. I'm just picking up Covered and Smothered."

"Covered and what?"

"Waffle House specialty, an omelet covered in melted cheese and smothered in sautéed onions. It's on the way home. Won't take me a minute."

"That can't be good for your figure," he blurted out. "Not that you need worry," he said, quickly covering his blunder. As far as he was concerned, she filled out her clothes exactly right.

She responded with good humor. "How do you think I got this figure in the first place?"

"Okay, then cover and smother me, too." She was stopping anyway and didn't have a clue about who he was.

Waiting in her shadowy car, Colton viewed the brightly lit diner as a movie set. He admired Kathryn's ease. Not bothering to put on her coat, she ran inside and called out what she wanted to the short-order cook. With her shapely derriere propped against the counter, she chatted with a waitress until a man, washed-up jock type, sidled up. Her bearing changed, subtle but apparent to Colton, to whom acting was as much body language as anything else.

In a statement of controlled emotion, she reached back and tightened her ponytail band. The hulky dude crowded in on her.

Old boyfriend, Colton assessed. The man seemed intent on walking her to the car, evidently apologizing for something. Whatever it was, her stiff carriage across the parking lot said he was unwelcome.

Colton tugged the bill of his cap down and slouched in the seat. As much as he would like to get rid of the guy, he couldn't risk recognition. Plus, this man was the size of a lumbering linebacker.

The genesis of Kitty Quinn deposited their take-out on the back seat, slammed the rear door, and squared off at the jerk. "You're a bully, Steve. I'm not interested in you or your excuses. I meant what I said, stay away from me."

She slipped behind the wheel, but the Steve guy reached out and caught her door before she could close it. "Well, now," he drawled, "I see you've got company."

Kathryn started the Prius and, without looking at either of them, said through clenched teeth, "Ben Thomas meet Steve Overby. Steve, meet Ben."

Steve stooped over for a look at her passenger. "You new to Athens?"

Kathryn put the car in gear.

"Hang on, Kay." Persistence personified, the man handed his business card past her nose. "What business you in, Ben?"

"I write," Colton lied.

"You got the right little lady for that," Steve said. He closed the door and stood aside while they drove away.

Colton noticed tension in Kathryn's jaw that could

rival Joe's. He cast around for a safe subject. Although he knew she wasn't, he asked, "So, you're a writer?"

"Editor," came her clipped response. She drove along a mile or so under the stars before she shook off her irritation. "What do you write?"

"Nothing."

"You aren't a writer? You said you were."

"Nah. My cousin writes. I borrowed that from him."

She frowned. "Why'd you say you were?"

He let out a cynical bark. "That guy's a prick. I'm not telling him what I do." As soon as he spoke, he wanted to take the words back. Now she would ask him what he really did.

A full minute passed. All she said was, "Fair enough."

They finished the trip in silence, making Colton wonder when curiosity would get the best of her. All the while her little white car was getting buzzed through the gate, negotiating the estate's dressed-to-impress entry, pulling past the limo, and stopping in front of the columned house, he was betting she wouldn't be able to resist prying. "Thanks for everything," he said, unfolding from the confines of her car.

"Don't forget your omelet."

"Right." He snagged one of the take-out boxes off the back seat.

Before she drove away, Kathryn lowered the passenger window and leaned over.

He gloated inwardly. *Here it comes.*

"You're right," she said. "Steve Overby is a prick."

Colton watched her gain the main road and negotiate the switch-back down The Lane side of the estate.

As her headlights disappeared, he muttered, "Damn! When Cuz finally decides to pick one, he sure knows how."

એઝિ

Kathryn next encountered Yankee a week later being walked down The Lane on leash by a spit-polished black man the size of a refrigerator. She got out of her car to pet the boxer. Yankee's stumpy tail wagged so hard her whole body swayed.

"Wonderful to see her well again," Kathryn commented to the dog's companion.

He gave the car, then Kathryn, an appraising look. "I'm Daniel," he rumbled, impressing her with the soft timbre of his voice and obvious affection for the dog. "Gotta keep our girl here leashed until she stops that car-chasing business. She's not use to so much freedom, and she sure misses your brown dog. What's his name, anyway?"

"Goose."

As Kathryn expected, the giant laughed, but it was a friendly chuckle. "Suits him, unusual name for an unusual dog."

"I think so. He's special."

"Yankee, too. Sit, girl." He flashed a gold tooth and produced a treat when the dog's rear end obediently hit the ground. "I understand you guaranteed the vet bill with your credit card. Let me know when you get the statement so Mr. Thomas can take care of it."

"That's not necessary. The accident was my fault."

"You probably saved her life by making us train her better. Anyway, they'll pay the bill whether you like it or not. Can't talk them out of it."

They? Them? Kathryn hadn't thought of Ben as part of a couple before. If so, she pitied his wife or girlfriend his wandering eyes.

એઝિ

On February tenth, Kathryn paid her bills online, including Yankee's sizeable vet bill. Within days, a reimbursement check showed up in her mail, drawn on a production company she'd never heard of. Mr. Ben-of-the-Big-House probably conned the amount out of Billie at the vet's office. It might be a pittance to him, but Kathryn was responsible for his dog's injuries. Right was right. Finding no return address on the envelope or the check, Kathryn stopped by Charlie's Corner to return it in person.

She came up against the wrought iron gate locked in un-neighborly fashion across the main entrance. Later when she came back on foot, cutting through the side yard shrubbery from The Lane, Goose trotted alongside. She rang the doorbell and knocked with gusto on the mahogany double doors. A peek through beveled sidelights revealed little.

Goose pricked up his ears at the sound of a rough-running motor approaching the back of the house via a service entrance off The Lane. Kathryn walked around the side and converged with a middle-aged black woman exiting from a banged-up blue Toyota.

"Everbody's gone 'round here but me," the woman announced. "I'm Marleen. I seen you before, going down yonder in your car."

"Hi, I'm Kathryn. I'm the last house down The Lane."

Goose loped over and offered his grisly head for the woman to pet.

"He's not usually quite so friendly," Kathryn said.

"Oh, I been romancing this fella." Marleen laughed. "You gets all my ham bones, don't you, mister."

"That'll do it every time." Kathryn smiled. "Marleen, do you know how I can reach Mr. Thomas?"

She shook her head. "Not me. His man Daniel—he's

my cousin—he'll call when they get ready to come back. I just keeps the house."

Mystified, Kathryn walked back to her cottage. She flipped open her phone and reached out to her most reliable source.

"Gal Pal, you'll never guess where I am," Dee trilled.

"Not at home, I gather."

"No, ma'am. I'm nekkid in a hot tub on the side of a mountain."

"What? Where?"

"Up in Blue Ridge. Tommy wanted to hide out in our cabin this week. What he calls marriage therapy."

"Pays to listen to the doctor, especially when he's your husband. Sorry I bothered you."

"Tell you the truth," Dee whispered, "I'm a tish bored. Whatcha got going on?"

"Looking for information on a guy named Ben Thomas. Did you handle the deal on Charlie's Corner?"

"Sure. I leased it to Alex Whitlow's buddy from California. Remember the one I told you was so handsome you'd have to squint. Some sort of music producer. I have his address back at the office."

Kathryn's mouth dropped open.

"Here's my Tommy." A clink of glasses pronounced Dee was no longer alone in her hot tub. "Gotta go." She giggled. "Oh, wait. That guy's name is Joe Butler, not Ben Thomas. Toodle-loooo."

The air whooshed out of Kathryn's lungs. She stared out the twelve-pane window overlooking her desk as if it had transformed into Alice's looking glass. Nothing made sense. And then, gradually, everything did. Joe Butler had come to her house last fall, shortly before Dee's for sale signs disappeared from Charlie's Corner.

By the first of the year, Ben-the-Jogger showed up

with his bedroom eyes, ever-present ball cap, and scraggly beard.

She picked up her phone and scrolled through the
call log. The number Yankee's owner had dialed from the
vet's office was the same one Joe Butler had given her to
call about his manuscript. Kathryn reached around and
slowly pulled the scrunchie out of her ponytail.

Ben Thomas had said, "My cousin's a writer. I borrowed that from him."

She combed her fingers through the length of her
hair and frowned at the check issued by B&B Productions. When Daniel spoke in plurals he meant Joe Butler
and Colton Bennett. "They" were a couple all right, a
couple who produced movies not music as Dee thought.
Leaping out of her chair, Kathryn twisted the band tightly
around her hair and shouted, "Hell's bells!"

Chapter 10

For the remainder of February and the entire month of March, Charlie's Corner remained as dormant as its sculpted Zoysia lawn. Kathryn passed the estate every time she came and went from home. It was a constant reminder that Colton Bennett, *the* Colton Bennett, was her scruffy neighbor. Random visions of him assailed her. *He was in my car. I hit his dog, for crying out loud! Oh, Lord, I made him eat Covered and Smothered.* Despite his disheveled look, now that she thought about it, he did have manicured nails and an air of culture, except for the tying-Goose-to-the-porch bit.

She pictured Dee swooning over his screen image, calling him a hunky monkey. Kathryn realized if she had been looking, really looking like a woman looks at a man, those eyes would've tipped her off.

Presumably Colton or Ben or whatever he called himself was in her neck of the woods at Cousin Joe's behest. She flashed on the Bennett biography. What was it Joe called the paparazzi? Sharks. Would she now be running into Joe, too?

There was no way she was going to keep their mon-

ey. Knowing Lyndon Real Estate's busy Five Points office would be closed for Good Friday, Kathryn wheeled
in to see Dee Thursday on the way to her ESL method's
class at The Georgia Center. Dee's receptionist waved
Kathryn down the hall where she barged in to find her
friend standing beside her desk in full scowl. One hand
had the phone pressed to her ear while the other perched
saucily on her hip. "You may well be within your rights;
I'm just saying it's not the right thing to do." Giving
Kathryn an eye-roll, she mouthed, "Steve."

Kathryn mimed gagging herself while Dee ended the
call.

"I swear, Kay, that man skates so close to the edge
he's gonna fall off one of these days. What brings you
here?"

Kathryn endorsed the check and handed it over. "Do
something for the library with this."

"Because?" Dee asked.

"I was going to send it back, but Mr. Butler can jolly
well make a donation instead." She kept quiet about his
Hollywood connection. As long as Dee thought Joe's
business was music, she wouldn't go star crazy. That
would've served Joe right, but privacy was a hot button
for Kathryn. She valued her own too much to intrude on
someone else's.

"Aren't you the stubborn little cuss."

"You don't call me Matilda for nothing. Gotta dash.
I'm tutoring a French woman before tonight's class. She
joined late, so I'm helping her catch up. What a character! Flaming red hair and calls herself Phoenix."

∽∾∽

Phoenix hunkered in a bathroom stall at The Georgia
Center and lit a second cigarette. Stupid concierge had

chased her away from the front entrance. Snotty town wouldn't let her smoke in bars either. She inhaled quickly, before some freaking bathroom police busted her. Pretending she wanted to buy a house, she had pestered realtors, ridden all over the place with them until she located the estate Joe leased. It was six miles from downtown on the eastern side of the county. That was where Colton would be.

She closed her eyes and leaned against the stall door. God, he was great in that last movie. Her lips puckered and played with the end of the cigarette. If there was ever a sequel, she *had* to be in it.

And she had to be near, ready when he was. Whatever he was waiting for must be about to happen. He'd signaled her just this week by wearing a blue shirt on Letterman. She hummed a little ditty, "Blue, blue, blue means he loves you."

Phoenix flushed the cigarette butt and went to the sink to swish out her mouth. Kathryn Tribble had agreed to tutor her before class. A quick web search of the county's tax records had identified the nearest neighbor to Joe's estate. Unlike the bitch housekeeper who hadn't given Phoenix the time of day, this neighbor-lady was the helpful type. Phoenix had brushed-up her grade school accent from Quebec and, *voila*, become *petit mademoiselle* struggling to master the well-grammared English. She reapplied dark maroon lipstick to her smirk. She was a much better actress than anyone gave her credit for. She'd only had to cross paths twice with this Kathryn person to have her bending over backward to help her.

Feathering her bangs into place, Phoenix exited the bathroom in time to see Kathryn leave the coffee shop. "*Mademoiselle*," Phoenix called out and hurried down the corridor toward her. "I am ready for being tutored."

"Oh, there you are," Kathryn said. "It's time for class

to start. I'll have to get together with you some other time."

"Why you not wait ten minute?"

"What do you mean? I waited half an hour. Now I'm going to class."

Phoenix clenched her fists. "Ten minute!" As the elevator closed between her and Kathryn, she yelled, "Why you not wait ten minute?"

ᘉᘉᘉ

"Beard the dragon," Joe muttered Easter Sunday when he opened his laptop and confronted his characters. Script revisions kept him from getting home for mass with Wrenn and Anna, but he'd marked the holiday by attending Pet's church. He'd hoped God would inspire him to write more than gloom and doom in his new novel. A purveyor of happily-ever-after in Colton's movie scripts, he was having trouble forcing what he didn't feel into his own work. "Cynicism," he grimaced. "My dirty little secret."

He took a sip of scalding coffee and walked over to the edge of the rock garden where Pool Kitty was stretched out in the sun. It would be easier if his new character wasn't in first person, but that was the only way the narrator spoke to Joe. With a hard set to his mouth, he went back to the computer and read the last words he had written:

> *I cannot be in love with her. Convention does not allow it. Cannot. Will not. Yet I am. She knows, and she hates me for it.*

Joe read over the passage a third time, then leapt up and stripped to his swim shorts. Taking a running start, he sprang into the air, grabbed both knees, and cannonballed into the heated pool. He swam along the bottom with long, languid strokes before bursting back to the surface, lungs begging for air. He broke into a freestyle crawl, fast and furious, and then switched to the butterfly, heaving his body through the water until he was spent.

Colton sauntered out of the house as Joe boosted himself onto the side of the pool. Yawning, Colton shed his terry robe and tossed it to Joe. "Hey, Cuz, remember what you told me last fall?"

Gulping in great, replenishing breaths, Joe said, "Gave you lots of advice." He wrapped up in the robe and went to flop onto a chaise longue. "Most you ignored."

"That thing you said about me needing a wife."

Joe squinted at Colton.

Flexing his arms, Colton strode to the edge of the pool. He jutted each lanky elbow overhead, in turn, and tugged on it with the alternate hand. "Got me a contender."

Joe sat up and straddled the chaise. "Benny? You crazy?"

Colton arced into the water, creating barely a ripple.

A sense of dread came over Joe. He stood and frowned down at the pool. His cousin was gliding across and back underwater. Might figure Colton's subdued attitude since returning from Paris would be about a new conquest in his sights, not being chastened over the Lila Manning debacle.

Colton surfaced and flashed an impish grin. "'Bout time I made another trip to The Peach State." Without waiting for Joe to respond, he launched into a series of breaststroke laps.

Joe pinched the bridge of his nose. According to his accountant, Kathryn Tribble had donated the vet repayment to some library. That could mean she had figured out Colton's identity. Perhaps she thought refusing Joe's money was another way of rejecting him. He shook his head, hoping he was wrong. It hadn't been necessary. Kitty Quinn was dead.

Joe hunkered down beside the water. If his suspicions were true, surely Kathryn was too savvy to fall for his cousin's movie-star routine. As Colton completed his reps and rolled onto his back, Joe shouted, "Did you forget? Post production for *Dog Tales*."

"Oh, right." Colton stroked to the side and hauled himself out of the water. Toweling off, he said, "Voice work is fun. Y'know, I wouldn't mind doing more animation."

"Bet on it, if this thing goes *Shrek* like they predict."

"How long will they need me?"

"Several weeks." Joe went back to the table and stared at his laptop. "Thinking I'll go back east 'til you're done."

Let Colton think Atlanta but Charlie's Corner seemed like the place for the fresh perspective he needed.

"I still don't understand why you're dicking around with new stuff. You could sell ten books about Kitty Quinn. Hell, man, she's 'Jane Bond.' Let's screen it." Colton's voice went up an octave as his enthusiasm grew. "We could have a rough cut in six months. You've got the script in shape. Get a commitment from Jennifer, and I'll nail the husband role."

Joe stowed his computer. "Not happening."

Colton shook water out of his blond mane. "Damned if I can see why not."

Joe's blistering glare sent his cousin running for the house, calling back over his shoulder, "I know, I know. Your book, your call."

∽✠∾

"No!"

The utterance came so sharp and quick in the dark that Kathryn wasn't sure she actually heard it. She was leaving the library late, having stayed to accommodate April fifteenth procrastinators photocopying income tax returns. She finished locking the door and held her breath, listening.

"Aiyyy," a woman's voice cried out.

Kathryn ran around the side of the building, triggering motion-activated lights mounted under the eaves. Lydia Vasquez was near Kathryn's Prius. One hand clutched under her distended belly, she was trying to pull the other free from Eduardo's grasp.

"Hey!" Kathryn shouted. "Leave her alone."

Eduardo let go of Lydia's hand and took an uncertain step backward.

"Aiyyy." Lydia doubled over the hood of the car.

"She's in labor." Kathryn ran to the girl.

"I have a place," Eduardo growled.

"A place?" Kathryn was incredulous. "She needs a hospital."

He side-stepped Kathryn and reached for Lydia. "No hospital."

Lydia grabbed Kathryn's hand. Her eyes were saturated with pain and fear.

Kathryn pressed the advantage. "I'm taking her to the hospital." She didn't look at Eduardo again, but she felt his scathing glare as she helped Lydia into the car and drove away. "You're going to be fine," Kathryn said, in what she hoped was a reassuring tone. "We'll be there in no time."

Lydia's teeth chattered. "I—no documents," she whimpered.

"Don't worry about that right now. I promised to help you, and I will."

Pressing her fist to her lips, the girl nodded and took rapid, shallow breaths.

"Is Eduardo really your brother?"

Lydia's head bobbed up and down.

"And not your baby's father?"

This time Lydia shook her head emphatically.

Kathryn put on her emergency flashers and concentrated on driving. Immediately upon reaching St. Mary's Hospital, an attendant took Lydia upstairs to Labor and Delivery. Kathryn called Dee.

"Aha," Dee said. "We thought she was illegal. That's why she's been so skittish. What'd you tell the hospital?"

"Nothing. It's pretty obvious she's having a baby."

"I meant admissions. Insurance."

"I signed a form."

"Kathryn! Don't you end up stuck with her bill the way you did when you hit that dog. This is not your responsibility. Is her brother illegal, too?"

"I don't know, but her family ought to be with her. I guess I'll have to go back to Old Mill Village and try to find them."

"You don't sound enthused about that."

"Well, I've already made her brother mad. I'm not keen on knocking on doors in the middle of the night, waking up people who can't understand what I'm saying. You don't know anyone conversational in Spanish who'd come interpret for me, do you?"

"A realtor in my office but she's at a concert in Atlanta. I'm down at The Globe having a beer with Tommy and his golf buddies. I'll ask around and call you back."

Finding Lydia comforted and monitored, Kathryn followed a nurse out of the room. "How long?"

The RN consulted her chart. "Hard to say. She really wants her mother. Is she coming?"

Kathryn's phone rang. "I'm about to find out. Tell her I'll be back as soon as I can."

"You're in luck, Gal Pal," Dee sang out. "A man in Tommy's foursome speaks Spanish. Um, Kay, he isn't from here, he's—"

"I don't care if he's from the moon," Kathryn shouted, running for the parking lot. "Does he know how to get to the Mill?"

"Says he does. He's leaving now."

"Wow, you work miracles."

"Matilda," Dee quipped, "sometimes they happen all by themselves."

თანთ

Back in Georgia since the first week of April, Joe had been splitting his time between Wrenn's Ranch and Charlie's Corner. The way Wrenn had bonded with the pony and was responding to her new treatment plan had surpassed all his expectations. His writing was back on track, and he'd started playing golf with Alex and Alex's friends, Tommy Lyndon and Steve Overby. Joe had taken special note of the Old Mill Village complex since finding out his money had gone there. He went so far as to drive to the library one afternoon but hadn't gone inside when he saw Kathryn's car in the parking lot. Warning her off Colton wasn't going to be easy, and he was not yet in the mood for another dose of her rejection.

She might very well refuse his help tonight as an interpreter. As a boy he had acquired a solid grasp of Spanish and an understanding of Latino culture from his summers in Texas. His uncle's Twisted B Ranch was within spitting distance of the border. Joe hadn't been keen on offering to translate, but then Tommy's wife, Dee, said it was her friend Kathryn and that she was desperate. Desperate was different. And so was Kathryn.

Joe sped past columned sorority and fraternity houses along historic Milledge Avenue. Athens was much to his taste, a meld of academics and artists, and an easy drive into Atlanta. Colton was still in LA polishing the animated film he had voiced.

He exceeded the speed limit as much as he dared and arrived at the Mill before Kathryn. For her to take a Latino girl to the hospital to have a baby was one thing, but to come back and confront a barrio of illegals was something else. Didn't she realize how Kitty Quinn that was?

Chapter 11

Kathryn felt completely out of her element. Since Dee was sending a golfer, she hoped he was fit enough to offer a little protection. If it came to that. Eduardo's anger seemed more like misdirected worry, but he had been really upset at her for taking his sister to the hospital.

She pulled up beside a high-end gray Lexus, obviously the golfer-turned-interpreter. Both she and the Lexus driver exited their vehicles at the same time. Recognition took away Kathryn's breath.

"*A su servicio, señora,*" Joe said, giving a mock-salute.

"You, you—"

Grinning, he supplied, "Golfed with Tommy, hung out at The Globe, here to back you up. Good job getting the little mama to the hospital."

Kathryn stared at him with her mouth open.

He gestured toward the hillside of slumbering homes. "Ready?"

She walked mutely up the hill to the first house. By the time the door was answered, she had found her voice.

"Ask if they know Lydia's brother, Eduardo, or her mother, Mrs. Vasquez. Say that Lydia is having her baby and needs them."

Joe fired off a round of words in the same brusque staccato as the men who hesitantly cracked their doors. One after another, the answer was negative, and the door abruptly shut.

"This is crazy," Kathryn muttered as they came to the end of a row of houses. "It's no use."

"Not their way to say anything outright."

"Then how do I find her blasted family?"

"Be patient. You'll see."

Kathryn sensed Joe was enjoying himself as they leapt on and off stoops and stumbled through dark yards. The easy way he soothed gruff dogs challenging their presence gave her confidence a much-needed boost.

Between two houses the timid voice of a woman wafted from the shadows. *"Mi Lydia está en el hospital."*

"Sí, señora," Joe replied in a reassuring tone. After several quiet exchanges, he told Kathryn, "Mrs. Vasquez speaks no English. I promised her we'd take her to her daughter." He held the woman's shawl-clad elbow and guided her down the rutted hillside. *"Cuidado, señora,* careful." Nearing the cars, he turned to Kathryn and asked, "Mine?"

"Okay. Everyone is used to seeing my Prius parked here." She buckled into the back seat while he settled Lydia's mother in front. Before pulling onto the road, he glanced around at Kathryn. "Want me to keep her talking, see what I can find out?"

"Yes, please, whatever she'll tell you. I really can't thank you enough for all this, Joe."

"No sweat. Nothing more exciting than a baby."

It was too dark to see if he winked, but Kathryn heard a grin in his voice. She thought he must have repeated his remark to Mrs. Vasquez because the woman covered her mouth and giggled.

Noticing two missed calls from Dee on her cell, Kathryn redialed.

"Where the hell-o are you, Gal Pal? If you don't get your Aunt Sass back here in a hurry, we're gonna have us a baby without you."

"You're at the hospital?"

"Of course. Me and Tommy. Lydia barely knows us from Adam's housecat, but she knows we're pulling for her—better change that to pushing."

"Joe found her mother. The way he's driving, we'll have her there soon."

Dee dropped her voice to a whisper. "Do we need to talk about Joe Hollywood?"

"No."

"Too bad."

ᕬᕔᕬᕔ

After healthy José Vasquez lustily cried his way into the world, Lydia's cheering section of Dee, Tommy, Kathryn, and Joe clustered jubilantly in the hall. Dee was bubbling over. "Have you ever in your life seen anything like that?"

"I did a rotation in obstetrics," Tommy said, "and it never fails to thrill me."

"Amazing." Kathryn shook her head in wonder. "Amazing."

Dee gasped and grabbed her arm. "Oh, Kay, I'm so sorry. I got carried away."

Kathryn saw a query flit across Joe's expression. "Don't be silly," she said, quickly hugging Dee. "I'm serious. There's nothing more amazing than childbirth."

She wondered for the millionth time where Joe had

gotten the idea to write a miscarriage into his Kitty story. Would Phyl have told him about hers?

A nurse, wheeling the bassinette with baby José out of the room, called to them, "Grandmother doesn't want to leave Mom. Anyone out here want to help give this little man his first bath?"

"Me." The word fairly leapt from Joe's mouth. At the group's collective look of surprise, he shrugged self-consciously. "Hey, I like babies."

After he rounded the corner with the bassinette, Dee grabbed Kathryn's arm. "Matilda, are you *positive* we don't need to talk about that man?"

Kathryn gave Tommy a look. He slung his arm around Dee. "Let's you and me go home and talk about a little miracle for ourselves."

Not wanting to intrude on Lydia and her mother, Kathryn wandered down to the nursery. Howls burst from beyond two swaddled infants napping in front of the viewing window. Off to one side, Joe, now wearing a sterile smock, held Lydia's son chest-down in one of his big, capable-looking hands. He seemed to be murmuring to the baby as he sponged his tiny back. Taking a towel from the nurse, Joe deftly rolled him over and cradled him close. He placed the little guy in the bassinette, blocking Kathryn's view with his broad shoulders. She felt as much on the outside looking in as she did in her dream where Sam turned away holding their baby—their baby who would have been almost exactly a year old now.

"Wouldn't have missed that," Joe said, when he came out of the nursery.

"You made him mad."

He chuckled. "Little critter wasn't too happy, was he? Want to go in and hold him?"

"No."

Joe frowned and glanced away at the sharpness of Kathryn's reply. It reminded him of Phoenix's refusal to hold Wrenn. Once Wrenn's tiny fist grabbed onto Joe's finger, he had never wanted her to let go. He'd taken her to the ranch and held her day and night until Anna moved in and took charge.

Taking another look at Kathryn, he wondered if she had been crying. He wasn't sure. Maybe she was tired. He wanted to talk to her about refusing to edit his book, and about Colton, but this wasn't the time or place. "Almost four a.m.," he said, "you're dead on your feet." He turned her around and guided her down the hall. "Glad you didn't leave with Tommy and Dee. I learned a couple of things from Mrs. Vasquez."

They peeked into Lydia's room to say good-bye. She was sleeping, and her mother spoke tearfully to Joe. Outside, away from the hustle-bustle of the hospital, Kathryn said, "I didn't expect you to be experienced with babies."

Pressing the key fob to unlock his car, Joe quelled an impulse to tell her about Wrenn.

Kathryn pulled open the passenger door and got in the car, seeming okay with his silence.

Exiting the parking garage, he said, "Mother and brother aren't illegal. Only Lydia."

"How did that happen?"

"Family fragmentation. Father had a government job in Mexico. Girl was young and stayed with him. Dad died suddenly, and Eduardo had to get her here any way he could."

"No wonder she's so frightened. If she's deported, she has no one to go back to. I'll bet her brother was trying to prevent exactly what happened, her getting pregnant. Was anything said about the baby's father?"

"Low-life druggie. Eduardo ran him off. Mrs. Vasquez has a nephew with a landscape business in Florida. She plans to move there with Lydia and the baby."

"That's great. With family support Lydia can make it. She's smart and thirsty to learn. Why was her mother crying?"

"Afraid I did that. Told her I'd get the girl a green card."

Kathryn gasped. "You can do that?"

"Hey, come on." He laughed. "It's not always bad being me. Celebrity has its advantages." While negotiating a series of turns in the narrow road, he considered how to warn her about Colton. "The Lyndon's don't know who I am," he began.

"I figured that was the case. Dee's so star-struck she would've told me."

"Look. Benny will be back here by May. Better if he doesn't realize that you know who he is."

"Better for whom?"

Joe frowned as they reached Old Mill Village and he pulled up beside her car. She had a way of making him answer the damnedest questions. "Mostly for you," he said.

Her face was flooded by the security light, but her expression was inscrutable. She clicked open her seatbelt. "If you knew me better, you'd know I'm a big proponent of truth. Thanks again for your help," she said, getting out of the car.

Watching her turn out of the library lot toward Charlie's Corner, Joe headed for Atlanta in the opposite direction. He frowned and wished he did know her better.

☙❧☙

Hank, the pilot of B&B's Gulfstream for over a decade, flew Colton into Athens on the last weekend in April. Joining him at Charlie's Corner, Joe put up with

Colton rehashing the Kitty Quinn production argument whenever they jogged past Kathryn's driveway.

Joe stood his ground. "Kitty's dead."

He no longer expected Kathryn to get over her adverse feelings toward the book. She'd had ample opportunity to rethink her position.

"Bring her back to life," Colton persisted.

"Nope."

They eventually boiled it down to three breathless words as they picked up their pace and huffed past her mailbox. "Still dead?"

"Yep."

Satisfied with the care of Wrenn's new doctors and bowing to business demands in California, Joe got Hank to fly him back to LA. Instead of working during the flight, Joe spent most of the time gazing into the clouds, puzzling over Colton's next move. Kathryn wasn't his cousin's type, per se, but she was female. The depths of her brown eyes drew Joe and that cute freckle on her lip tantalized him, but Colton lost his head over supple and shapely bodies.

Restless, Joe sat forward and picked up a stack of papers. Kathryn seemed perceptive, surely she would see through Colton. But he was an irresistible SOB when he was in the chase.

Actually, if his cousin was ever going to have a family, she wouldn't be a bad choice—good looking, smart, outside the industry yet worldly. Joe screwed up his face and tried to imagine her at Bennetthurst. Maybe.

He shook his head. He wouldn't wish his cousin on Kathryn. Like their grandfather, Colton would be as faithful as he could, but it went against his nature. Pet kept her marriage together, but the sharks had circled her relentlessly. Rubbed every one of her husband's indiscretions in her face. Kathryn didn't deserve that. Putting the pa-

pers down unread, Joe frowned and pictured the way
Kathryn had looked last June in New York. She might
not even survive it.

Chapter 12

Having finished her methods class, Kathryn signed up to teach ESL night classes in the Georgia Center's session slated to begin the sixth of May. Her separate tutoring commitments now included Lydia at the library, and the strangely demanding Frenchwoman, Phoenix, who was now taking Tai Chi classes at the Georgia Center. As Kathryn passed by the residence on the corner, she tried to erase Joe and Colton from her thoughts. She found herself plotting ways not to have to see them while simultaneously hoping she would.

Colton kept a low profile, though she saw him in the distance jogging, sometimes with his cousin. Joe was a part of Alex Whitlow's inner circle, which included Tommy and Dee. But he had lost favor with Dee by failing to show up for two of her special dinners. She complained to Kathryn, "Joe Hollywood must have a woman, the way he dashes off at the drop of a hat. Somebody in Atlanta says jump and he says how ding-dang high."

The second weekend in May, Kathryn was ready to put her tomato plants in the ground. She inspected the flat of seedlings sheltering on the porch. Phoenix had helped her pick them out. Kathryn constantly bumped into that weirdo—grocery store, post office, and, on the day she bought tomato plants, the garden center at Lowe's. Phoenix asked about the tomatoes every time she showed up for tutoring.

The kooky woman, waiflike in the shapeless cardigan she wore with its buttons misaligned, seemed to want friendship more than tutoring. But she was the kind of high-strung, needy person Kathryn usually avoided.

After itching for weeks to plant her tomatoes, Kathryn joyfully donned work gloves and located her trowel. Dee, with her battered Farmer's Almanac, had insisted Kathryn wait until mid-May. Kathryn picked up her flat of plants. "Come on, boys. BLT's here we come."

She circled the front yard, trowel held out like a divining rod. Purple Bearded Irises, delayed by a cold snap back in April, bloomed in the flower bed surrounding Aunt Tildy's stone birdbath. Dogwoods dotted the tree line and the Gingko had donned a frilly new dress. Beside the well-house, Kathryn knelt down and plunged the trowel into a loamy patch. Resting back on her heels, she chuckled over Dee's mockery of her gardening ability. "Look at your thumbs, Gal Pal, this one may have a tish of green, but that other one is jet black."

Without warning Yankee raced into the yard and bowled Kathryn over in exuberant greeting.

"Hello, you!" She tried to fend off the boxer and pet her at the same time, laughing and tumbling back onto the dirt.

"Don't do that, Yank." Colton ran up, scolding and pushing the dog aside. "Go find Goose. Get!" Quick and strong, he grabbed Kathryn and set her on her feet. "Sorry, I thought she had better manners."

"No harm done. It's good to see her so well." A noisy low-flying Cessna caused them both to glance up.

Shielding her eyes, Kathryn said idly, pretending he was a neighbor named Ben, "Have you ever flown a plane?"

"Heck no, but I might get a motorcycle."

"Yikes, a donor-cycle. I'd be hauling you off to the hospital instead of your dog."

"About that. You didn't keep the money."

She could well imagine that being outside the norm for him. "I told you it was my responsibility."

His sandy brows bunched together. "She's my damn dog."

"And it was my damn car." She knelt down again and stabbed a clump of dirt with the trowel.

He stood for a moment and then squatted down beside her. "What're you planting?"

"They look puny now, but you just wait. These are Better Boys."

"Better than…"

"Any tomato you can buy. I can't wait for the first BLT."

"My favorite sandwich. I'll bring the beer."

As though someone had snapped a photo of them, Kathryn pictured herself grubbing in the dirt, while Colton Bennett, nominated "Sexiest Man Alive," invited himself over for a sandwich and beer.

Dee would go crazy if she knew. His beard was shorter this time and the cap was Braves instead of Dodgers, but the eyes were the same. Those same dreamy eyes, that sent women all over the world swooning, were right this very minute crinkled in merriment at her.

❧❧❧

Colton had forced himself to wait until after Joe left for Los Angeles before making a move on Kathryn. Despite his cousin, maybe to spite him, Colton intended to

play Kitty Quinn's husband. He jogged daily, watching
for Kathryn, but until today she had eluded him. Relying
on what Joe deemed his "dumb luck," he'd taken off
Yankee's leash and chased after her to Goose's house
where they'd come upon Kathryn planting tomatoes in
the yard.

He'd come back every day the following week.
Bonded by their vet adventure, he found himself relaxed
in her company. She brewed iced tea and ragged him
about being a city boy when the mint he picked from her
yard turned out to be weeds. She was different from any
woman he had ever known. She wasn't nosey and sex
didn't drive her. She did her own thing, spoke her mind,
and didn't try to impress him. Oddly, before long he
wasn't trying to impress her, either.

Topics of conversation were sparse without his movie work to talk about, but the quietness about her calmed
him. On the flip side, she was like Joe when it came to
privacy, so Colton hadn't gleaned much insight for playing the part of Kitty's husband. One afternoon Colton
made a misstep. Helping carry their sandwich plates from
the porch to the kitchen, he'd spied Sam's picture on her
desk and blurted out, "Hey, is that your husband?"

She stopped dead in her tracks. "What makes you
think he's my husband?"

"Well, boyfriend then." He laughed, hoping he'd
covered well enough. At least he had discovered what the
dude looked like. Blue-eyed, blond Anglo. A golden boy
with a smile as big as all outdoors. *Helluva lot like me,*
gloated Colton.

The only subjects he managed to draw out of
Kathryn were Athens, travel, and teaching. He would be
glad to have her teach him a thing or two. Walking back
to the estate in the evenings, he imagined ripe breasts under her colorful tee shirts and the promise of a lithe body

beneath her jeans. She had a slim, kissable neck, and her lips were full and sexy. He couldn't wait to see them wet and—*whoa boy, not yet*, he admonished, tamping down his stirrings.

തൈൻ

A little more than a week after Ben started making his neighborly visits, Kathryn was on her porch checking bundles of drying lavender, listening to the whippoor-wills, and thinking about her unlikely and covert friend-ship with a movie star. He was much more fun-loving than she would have imagined. In constant pursuit of mirth, he could turn anything into a joke. The down side was that he didn't take much of anything seriously. Each time she tried to figure him out, she came up against the same question. What was this man's game? Was he co-zying up just to get in her pants? Because she was female and he was bored? Why else would a man with his pick of women be hanging around?

He certainly was a glib liar. She had already caught him claiming to be a writer, and he backpedaled mighty fast about recognizing Sam's picture. Joe had warned her not to tell Colton she knew his true identity, ostensibly for her own benefit. She wondered if Joe had given his cousin that same caution in reverse. Her trust in Joe wasn't particularly high, but she had a gut feeling he didn't prevaricate. He possessed a decisive quality that made her think he hit things head on, no matter how much it hurt.

At least Joe's eyes didn't undress her. Instead, his eyes held tenderness. She remembered Lydia's newborn in his big, capable hands. He didn't have to help that night at the mill. And he didn't have to continue helping Lydia. No telling how many favors the girl's green card cost him. But being less self-centered than Colton didn't mean Joe was any less selfish in the long run—his cousin, his family, his business—his, his, his. Maybe, as Dee suspected, his woman in Atlanta. Unexpectedly irritated, Kathryn buried her nose in her palms to inhale the essence of lavender. There was no equal footing for her with either of these celebrities. Even if she had any interest, they were out of her league.

Kathryn presumed Ben's abrupt announcement yesterday that he was leaving Charlie's Corner for a while had to do with his next movie. Joe was still in LA, so she would get a break from the conflicting emotions her neighbors created in her. With a feeling akin to relief, she started to go into the house but was stopped by the crunch of gravel that signaled a vehicle approaching. She walked out into the yard as Joe's Lexus rounded the curve in the driveway. She caught her breath.

Eduardo Vasquez stopped the car and walked across the lawn. Dressed in a blue security uniform like Daniel's, Eduardo extended a small gift-wrapped parcel. "*Mamá* send to you, picture of José."

"Oh, how lovely of her."

He shuffled his feet. "And I give to you my *apología*."

"You were only trying to help Lydia. Anyway, I owe you thanks for helping me at the New Year's Party. That makes us even."

Nodding, he withdrew a card from his shirt pocket and handed it to her. "Call me if ever you have troubles. This job is *official*. Soon I pay back the hospital money."

"For Lydia? I didn't pay her bill."

He scowled. "When I go to make a plan to pay, they say the money is paid already."

"Not by me." She cocked her head toward Joe's car. "I'll bet I can guess who."

The young man smiled. "*Mamá* say he is a saint."

Watching Eduardo leave, Kathryn murmured, "*Mamá* may be right."

❧❧❧

Phoenix drove past Charlie's Corner at least four times a day and was rewarded with occasional glimpses of the limo, a sign of Colton's comings and goings. That was all she needed right now.

She dared not run into Joe. He was hard to pin down since he mostly drove himself, but she hadn't seen him around lately. The old manse didn't have much of a staff, only a live-in housekeeper and a Latino security goon. She'd checked that out several weeks back. After following the limo to the airport and watching the Gulfstream until it was out of sight, she'd returned to the house. The goon left in Joe's car, so she had seized that chance to chummy up to the housekeeper. Phoenix drove her van through the service entrance and boldly up to the rear of the house, but the nasty woman had walked down the back steps and confronted her before she'd had a chance to switch off the engine.

"What you want?" the troll had demanded, an inscrutable expression on her black face.

Quickly realizing she would be about as easy to move as a locomotive, Phoenix used her most innocent voice. "Is this where the Browns live?"

"No it ain't, and you ain't got no business coming up in here."

Joe had obviously picked this battle-ax, Phoenix thought. She put on as engaging a smile as she could muster. "Can you please tell me where the Brown's house is?"

The woman had crossed her arms and with the

warmth of a glacier said, "Ain't no Browns live 'round here. Now you git."

∽∾∽

Colton had zipped in and out of time zones all his life. He relied on fast and furious jogging to remedy jet lag. After a London shoot dragged on for three weeks, he arrived back at Charlie's Corner in the wee hours of June tenth in need of such a run. Joe would flip out to know Colton was outside without his disguise, but what Joe didn't know wouldn't hurt him. Daniel was cool. Colton left a note on the coffee pot for the sleeping giant and escaped out the kitchen door. He didn't bother with Yankee's leash. Tasting freedom, man and dog sprinted through the side yard and onto The Lane.

Early morning light streamed through distant pines as they ran past disinterested cows grazing behind fences. A tractor trundled past pulling some sort of contraption, headed to a field down The Lane. The driver acknowledged Colton with the indigenous two-finger steering wheel salute. Thinking it looked like a peace sign Colton returned the gesture and found himself wondering if Mr. Farmer had a Mrs. Farmer at home. Colton laughed out loud. "Proving you right, Joey, my man. Always thinking with my little head."

At Kathryn's mailbox, he imagined jogging up the drive and jumping into bed with her. He could also imagine Goose chewing his leg off. Kathryn was a walker, not a runner. During his last stay at the Corner, he had become pretty good at timing his cool-downs to coincide with her morning treks. Angling across the pasture to intersect with her at the pond was a pleasant start to any day.

By the time he had run The Lane a couple of times

this morning and hit the five mile mark, the sun still wasn't high enough for her to be out.

He loped down to the pond anyway. His approach silenced a cricket chorus and sent a frog or two splashing back into the water. He ambled across the dam and picked up the remnants of an old pulpwood road he had seen Kathryn follow. A series of bends took him deeper into the woods than he had gone before. Soon abandoned by Yankee, he grew uncertain as the road narrowed to a footpath. Briars snagged at his pants legs, and he was about to turn back when he broke into a clearing. In the middle stood an enormous tree, tall and regal, as if it had been there since the beginning of time. Lesser trees rimmed the meadow, subjects of the king.

His iPhone registered a text from Daniel, awake and checking on him. Colton sat down on a tree root and replied, *1 hr.* He rested back against the trunk and wondered if this tree figured into Kathryn's walks. It might be a good place to meditate if she was into that sort of thing. Yawning, he shifted to a comfortable patch of moss on the ground. A fresh fragrance on the morning breeze proved soporific. He drowsed almost immediately.

Chapter 13

Kathryn stood beside the pond and stared at a spindly bug using surface tension to skate across the water. Colton Bennett skimmed the surface of her life much the same way. One day he was tending her tomato patch with childlike anticipation, and twenty-four hours later she'd seen media coverage of him at some distant red carpet event. Next day he was back, sprawled on her porch with the dogs. Three weeks ago, he disappeared to London. She had planned to enjoy his absence but, as much as she didn't want to, she missed his quirky visits.

"Lydia is bringing the baby to see us this afternoon, Goosey Goose. Aren't you excited?" She imagined a shrug from the dog as he swaggered past.

His subsequent woof had nothing to do with news of little José but was all about spying Yankee, chest deep amongst the cattails on the far side of the pond.

"What are you doing out here, happy girl?" Kathryn called to her. "Is one of your daddies back?" She glanced around for Colton since he was the most apt to leave her off leash.

The boxer frolicked over to Goose, and they chased each other across the pasture.

"Stay out of the road!" Kathryn yelled, as though the pair could understand or would heed the warning if they did. She turned and strolled into the woods. Birds sang and small creatures scampered unseen out of her way. Snakes also moved around on warm June mornings, so she kept an eye out for them.

She was surprised to find Colton sleeping under Sam's oak. His fair hair seemed aglow as his head lolled against the trunk. With a quick intake of breath, Kathryn stepped back into the shadows. Mere feet from where she had scattered Sam's ashes, this Adonis was snuggled in the embrace of a gnarled root. From a distance and without his beard, he could have been Sam. A yearning came over her, a desire to slip into his arms and let the tree hold her, too. She immediately felt ridiculous. Sam was gone. She crossed the meadow, shuffling leaves and stomping loud enough to wake Colton.

"Hi there," he yawned. Rising slowly, he stretched. "Jet lag. Just got in from London. Something the matter?"

"No."

"You don't look glad to see me."

"Sorry." She gazed across the meadow. "As you've discovered, it's restful here."

He stretched again, yawned loudly, and craned his neck to stare up into the canopy. "This is one big-ass bipolar tree."

An impulse Kathryn recognized as irrational compelled her to get this shallow, conceited, pin-up boy away from Sam's oak. He didn't know what the tree represented to her, but she could not bear to hear it mocked. Moving away, she beckoned him to follow. "Would you like to see something pretty?"

"I'm looking at her," he flirted.

Near the far edge of the meadow, she stepped behind him. "Turn and look at me."

"Gladly," he leered.

"Will you stop? I want you to get the full effect."

Her lips pursed in thought as she put her hands on his shoulders and lightly positioned him to face her. "Now, take ten steps straight back," she said. Holding his shoulders square, she walked him backward and counted, "One, two, three—" Stepping aside as Colton reached out for her, she said, "—eight, nine, ten. Okay. About face."

He turned to find himself on the brink of a down-slope carpeted with blooming lavender. Inhaling deeply, he said, "So that's what I smelled."

"Aunt Tildy's Provence Lavender planted half a century ago. It really puts on a show this time of year." She waded into the field, tilted her face to the sun, extended her arms, and twirled like a ballerina.

Colton gave chase.

She managed to pirouette halfway down the hill before falling.

He took up where she left off and spun off toward the bottom. She followed him this time. They landed on the flat, wrapped in the pungent aroma, gazing dizzily back up the bluff.

"Told you it was pretty."

"You are given to understatement."

"My friend, Dee, is a gardening guru but it never does as well in her yard. She says that's because lavender doesn't like to get its feet wet. It loves the slope of this hill and the sun hits at the perfect angle." Kathryn tucked a spire behind her ear and said, more to herself than to him, "Sam surprised me with bundles and bundles of this when we moved to New York."

"The guy in the picture? Was he a romantic?"

A soft smile played on her lips. "He was an adventurer, but he had his romantic side." The smile faded when she realized Colton had referred to Sam in past tense. She hadn't said Sam died. Joe must have told him. This actor wasn't very good at pretending when he went off-script.

Her voice strengthened. "I sold this parcel along with Daddy's land, but it's too steep to farm and too land-locked to develop. I think Aunt Tildy's secret garden is safe."

"But you told Dee about it."

"I tell Dee everything."

"I'm glad you shared it with me."

An odd weariness came over Kathryn. Her intent had not been to share but to get him away from Sam's oak. She was weary of playing Joe's petty identity game. She raised her eyes and locked onto Colton's. "You keep my secret, Colton Bennett, and I'll keep yours." She was amazed at how fast his come-hither expression vanished.

The cocoon of make-believe dissolved. Colton's hand flew to his naked chin, and his hypnotic eyes narrowed. "How long have you known?" The tenor of his voice was one of demand, void of its usual lilt.

"For a while."

"At the vet?"

She shook her head. "I found out when I tried to return the check for the vet bill. Your cousin shouldn't have been pig-headed. He should've let me pay it."

"That doesn't give you the right—"

"You have nothing to do with my rights, mister, neither you nor Joe."

Colton looked confused. "What's Joey got to do with it?"

"I worked on the Bennett biography with him at Omni. We've had what you might call creative differences over his subsequent work." She yanked a piece of foliage out of the earth and twined it through her fingers. "We've agreed to disagree."

Colton's eyes widened into an incredulous expression. "Don't tell me you can hold your own with my cousin?"

She huffed out a breath. "Both of you must realize by now I'm not going to infringe on your privacy. I know who you are. Big deal. It doesn't change anything."

Colton fell spread-eagle into the lavender. "*Au contraire, mon chérie.* This changes every little-ole thing." He reached up, pulled her down on top of him, and planted a kiss directly on her mouth.

"Hey!" She pushed off him and scrambled to her feet. "What do you think you're doing?"

"What I've wanted to do ever since you bawled me out for tying up your dog. Now I don't have to worry about you discovering who I am, I can be myself."

"If you think 'being yourself' means you can manhandle me, you'd better think again, buddy."

"Seriously?"

She jabbed her forefinger into his chest like a loaded pistol. "Behave yourself. And get your butt out of my flowers." Technically, they were his flowers since the hill was part of the estate property, but she was too irked to care. Ponytail swishing, she climbed back to the top of the hill and trudged across the meadow before he caught up and stopped her.

"Hold on, Kay. I get it. If you aren't going to treat me different, I can't treat you different either."

One of her eyebrows darted up.

He pulled a sprig of lavender out of his hair and looked thoroughly perplexed. "I've had a lot of women in my life but not a single one of them ever wanted to be my friend."

Kathryn recognized the sad truth in what he said. He

could probably count his friends, those not out to gain from him, on one hand. She took the lavender spire from him and passed it under his chin. "Aunt Tildy said if you tell a lie your neck will turn purple."

A boisterous laugh burst out of him. "Last one back to the pond is a rotten egg!"

かめか

The country cemetery almost directly across Morton Road from Charlie's Corner was the eternal resting place of the Morton family. Hiding behind a monolithic gravestone weathered to about the same color as her dirty van, Phoenix kept tabs on when Colton's limo or Joe's car showed up.

One Saturday afternoon in late June, she was at her vantage point listening to her iPod when Kathryn's car popped out of The Lane and headed toward town. That woman lived way too close, and she drove past all the time looking for Colton.

Bitch! Phoenix pulled in behind and tailed her to a boutique in Five Points. *What's she getting gussied up for?*

Following her nemesis inside, Phoenix shoved hangers around on a rack in front of the dressing room Kathryn had disappeared into.

"Oh, hi, Phoenix," Kathryn said when she exited. "This sale on blouses is great, isn't it?" She held out a blouse she had tried on. "This jewel-tone green would look great with your red hair."

Phoenix took the blouse and sulked into an adjacent dressing room. She pulled the garment off the hanger and glared at the mirror on the wall. Unconsciously twisting, viciously wringing the blouse, she jumped at the sound of her name.

"Hey, Phoenix." The door of Kathryn's dressing room opened and closed. "Do you like it?"

"*Non,*" Phoenix uttered hoarsely.

"Okay. I've decided on blue. See you soon."

Phoenix's head pounded. *Blue? That's Colton's signal. To me.* Steadying herself against the wall, she dropped the green blouse on the floor. After Kathryn completed her purchase, Phoenix trampled the blouse in her haste to lurk beside the shop door. Her eyes narrowed into slits as Kathryn drove away. *I've got a lesson for you, teacher.*

こうこう

Kathryn had not yet broken the news about Colton to Dee when Dee showed up unexpectedly for lunch. Munching a BLT, Dee kicked off her shoes under the kitchen table and rested her feet on the empty seat beside her. "Is your man as yummy as your tomatoes?"

Sitting across from her, Kathryn frowned. "What man?"

Dee cocked her head toward the back door. "The one who belongs to that baseball cap and those big ole sandals."

"Ah," Kathryn swallowed the bite of sandwich in her mouth and took a sip of tea. "I want to tell you about that."

"I'm all ears, Matilda."

"It's not what you think." Kathryn reached back and tightened the band on her ponytail. "Promise you won't go all crazy on me."

"Me?" Dee pressed a hand to her chest and pretended offense. Fully engaging her southern drawl, she said, "What Prince Charming has done gone and discovered my little ole Snow White way off down here in these piney woods?" When Kathryn hesitated, Dee slapped her hand on the table. "Come on, Gal Pal, spill it!"

Like ripping off a bandage in one fell swoop, Kathryn blurted out, "Colton Bennett."

Dee didn't move. She grinned quizzically as though she had missed the punch line of a joke. Kathryn waited as question marks erupted in Dee's head.

"Not? I mean? You don't mean? The—no—not *the* Colton Bennett?"

Kathryn nodded. "Remember, I told you about working on the Bennett bio before I left New York."

For the first time in Kathryn's memory, Dee was at a loss for words.

"Joe Butler wrote it. Alex's friend, the one you call Joe Hollywood. He's Colton's cousin. B&B produces movies, not music. Butler and Bennett." Seeing words still failed Dee, Kathryn rushed on. "Joe saw Charlie's Corner for lease when he came to my house. It's a perfect get-away from the press. After Colton started coming here and jogging in The Lane, our dogs introduced us."

Dee gaped at Kathryn like she had grown an extra head. "How can you make all that sound normal?" She leapt to her feet. "Do you mean to tell me—*Colton Bennett sat in this chair?*"

Kathryn couldn't suppress a giggle. "I think he even ate off that plate."

Dee wind-milled her arms and shrieked. She ran screaming out of the kitchen, twice around the sofa in the day room and back.

Outside under the porch, Goose added his ruckus to Dee's.

When both friend and dog finally settled down, Kathryn said, "Emphasis on 'get-away.' This is where he comes to get out of the public eye, away from cameras. He calls himself Ben Thomas when he's here." She reached over and squeezed Dee's hand. "You can't tell anyone, Dee, not a single soul except Tommy. Joe was planning to tell y'all at some point."

"J—Joe Butler," Dee sputtered, "of course. The Bennett orphans. Here. Right here." Standing up, she plucked the ball cap off the wall hook and clutched it to her breast. "Col-Ton-Ben-Nett," she intoned and then dropped dramatically back into the chair. "What's he like? In person?"

"About as crazy as you are. Impish, kid brother-ish. He crashed my ESL class last time he was in town, made-up to impersonate a bawdy Irishman. Everyone totally bought the act, even me until he let me in on it by mentioning a dog named Goose."

"Nobody recognized him?"

Kathryn shook her head. "Nobody. He's that good an actor."

"Have you—" Dee arched her brows and widened her vivid blue eyes. "—you know?"

"No, we have not. I told you, we're just friends."

With exaggerated care, Dee placed the ball cap dead center on the table. "Think what you want, Matilda, but hunky monkey has marked his territory."

Chapter 14

Joe broke away from Wrenn whenever commitments called him to LA. For most of the summer, Colton traveled heavily and tension grew between them whenever their schedules coincided at Bennetthurst. The bangs of doors ricocheted across the rotunda. Colton usually started the arguments, and Joe finished them, slamming into his suite in the north wing of the house. Next time their paths crossed, Joe started them up again, and Colton finished them by slamming into his suite in the south wing.

Daniel, on guard for the next round, kept the staff out of the line of fire.

In mid-September Joe jogged up from the beach through Pet's rock garden as Colton climbed out of the pool. They sat down together and slugged back breakfast smoothies that Daniel had strategically placed on adjoining patio tables. Joe paged through *The Hollywood Reporter,* and Colton gazed out over the ocean.

At length, Colton said, "Y'know, Joey, I just don't get it."

"Can't make it any clearer. Told you a hundred times. Kitty is dead. Period. The end."

"Why? That's what I want to know. B&B bought the movie rights. She's my property, same as yours."

"Name your price. I'll buy your share."

"That's not what I want."

"All you can have. Get off my back!" Joe stalked into the house and rattled the hinges slamming his heavy mahogany door.

Colton did likewise to his.

Shaking his head, Daniel cleared the glasses from the tables.

Joe slouched into the leather chair behind the desk in his library and glowered at the *Daylight to Darkness* manuscript sandwiched between his first edition Mark Twains. He was so angry he felt like his head would explode. Whatever possessed him to leave that note? *Without you—Kitty dies.* He never expected Kathryn to let that happen. He'd never expected her to matter so much.

He rubbed his eyes with the heels of his hands. Would he ever get anything right in this life? He couldn't have a woman worth having as long as he was stuck with Phoenix; he couldn't get rid of Phoenix without blowback on Wrenn.

⌒⌒⌒

At the opposite pole of the house, Colton lay spread-eagle on his bed. What a diabolical twist. Joe as the problem instead of the problem solver. A maddening hour passed without Colton coming up with a single idea for getting around him. When his cousin was entrenched, there was no moving him. Colton rose and went to the mirror. He cocked his head and finger-combed his wavy forelock. A wicked grin replaced his frown. "Y'know," he said to his reflection. "I don't have to play Kitty's husband. I can just *be* him."

After the men ate separate lunches, Colton tapped on Joe's door and received an unwelcoming, "What?"

"I'm going to Athens."

Joe took his feet off his desk and removed his reading glasses. Frowning at Colton, he said, more calmly than he felt, "Hardly worth it if I pull this publicity tour together. Anyway, you're the one who promised to be a presenter at that awards show in London"

Colton licked his lips. "Still time for me to take a peach break."

"Come on, Benny. If you mean Kathryn Tribble, don't go trifling with her life. She's been through enough."

"Don't be all—" Colton shrugged, letting Joe fill in the expletive. "I've read about Kitty Quinn."

"That's fiction, dammit. Use some real sense."

"You can keep your fictional Kitty. I'm going after the real one."

"Crazy talk."

"Hey, you're the one who sent me to Athens. Hiding out with her is a helluva lot better than hiding out alone, y'know?"

"No," Joe fumed. "I do *not* know. Pray enlighten me."

"You have no idea how great she is."

Biting back his own feelings, Joe said, "Tell me, then."

"I dunno. She's just neat. Sews pretty quilts, grows tomatoes, makes lavender sachets." A childlike grin split Colton's face. "She perks coffee and makes sandwiches exactly the way Pet used to. Even small things are important when Kitty does them."

Joe caught the misnomer. "Blast, Benny. Have you no idea what's real and what's not?"

"You want real, Cuz, try sleeping on sun-dried linens."

Joe flinched at the idea of Colton between Kathryn's sheets. Would she fall for his act? Had she already? "You can't have Kathryn," he snapped.

His voice deep and husky, Colton said, "We'll see."

၄၁၁၁

As much as Kathryn resented Colton's knee-jerk reaction to half-maul her, his kiss had turned a page. Whether she was ready or not, he had spiced up her summer considerably. His was a far-removed world of sheer fantasy, so she kept her signals of friendship clear.

When he sent her Lavender from Provence, she knew this man of make-believe had some sort of place in her real life.

She was less certain about whether or not he would still be around when it bloomed again next spring. Although she couldn't imagine anyone giving a hoot about her mail, he sent tokens of his travels to her via Charlie's Corner.

They came addressed to Yankee Morton, a name which made Kathryn imagine set her Rebel ancestors spinning in their graves. She looked forward to Marleen knocking on her door with his outlandish gifts.

Marleen was as steady as Stone Mountain. "Daniel needs somebody he can trust," she told Kathryn, "and that'd be me." Her loyalty and affection soon extended to Kathryn. "That man do take the cake," she would say, laughing over Colton's escapades. "I hollered from here to Sunday when he hid in the pantry with that bird mask on his head. You know what else that rascal do? He put a rubber snake out by the back steps. I took hold of a hoe and chopped that thing in 'bout twenty pieces 'fore I got a good look at it."

Kathryn shivered. "I'd have probably had a heart attack."

Marleen laughed. "I gets wise when he goes to buttering me up with that Domestic Goddess foolishness." Her toothy grin faded. "That other one, though…"

"Joe?"

"I don't understand him much a'tall. He's right lively with Mr. Colt and Daniel around, but he gets broody on his own. Seem like something dark turning over in his head 'bout all the time."

In early September, Marleen delivered a fresh orchid lei Colton sent from Hawaii. Kathryn immediately phoned Dee. "I have to give this to you. You're the orchid queen. They're all white except for four enormous purples. Marleen took the tuberoses lining the box. They were sickeningly sweet."

"Orchids are packed that way because they don't have much scent on their own. I can't wait to see them. And your timing couldn't be better. I was about to call you to come over for dinner. I won't cut flowers for the table. We'll use the lei."

�/Ე/Ი

On the Lyndon's deck, digesting Dee's latest dinner creation, Kathryn told Tommy she had finally stopped thinking about the abyss. "Feels weird, sort of Rip Van Winkle, like I've lost time."

He nodded. "Grief isn't on the clock, Kay. Don't overthink it. Relax and enjoy your new friend. See where it goes."

Dee sashayed up behind them, arranging the lei

across her bosom. "Your old friend loves the hell-o out of your new friend."

"I must say you've been the soul of restraint," Kathryn said.

"What'd you expect me to do, swoon at the mere sight of him?"

Kathryn snickered. "Something like that."

"Well, it's different to know him, isn't it? Not the same as seeing him on screen."

Tommy squeezed his wife's hand. "He eats, he sleeps, like a real live boy."

Dee made a pouty face. "Anyway, Tommy bribed me."

"Whoa," Kathryn said, "with what?"

"Whatcha think?" Tommy laughed suggestively. "I'm a real live boy, too."

"Soon to be a real live dad," Dee announced.

"What?" Kathryn yelped. "When?"

Tommy's eyebrow went up. "Notice she didn't ask how."

"Shush," Dee said. "Oh, Kay, we had to tell you first. We're having an Easter baby."

Kathryn hugged and kissed them both. "I knew this was a celebration dinner. I thought you'd scored a big real estate deal. I can't wait to tell Mr. New Friend what great timing he had with the lei."

⚬⚬⚬

Kathryn heeded Tommy's advice to relax and enjoy Colton's friendship. Impressing it on Colton, a man who related to women by bedding them, was an entirely different matter. She redirected his romantic overtures by poking sisterly fun at him. Silliness prevailed. He contented himself with giving her bone-crushing bear hugs and noisy smooches on her cheeks. He was prone to swoop her up in the air and twirl around with her, but she landed squarely back on her feet, unmolested. Thus far.

She was one-hundred percent unprepared for him to turn up at her door the fifteenth day of September proposing marriage. She stared into his beautiful eyes and said, "What?"

"Y'know, bride and groom, happily ever after."

"Are you drunk?"

"Nah, I just want to get married. What's wrong with that?"

"Nothing—with the right person—at the right time."

"How 'bout with you, next week?" He took her hand and led her toward the couch. "I've been thinking about this."

"Well, I haven't," she said, pulling her hand away. "Let's have some coffee and sober you up."

"Only thing I'm drunk on is love, love, love."

She poured two mugs of hot coffee. "Ben Thomas-Colton Bennett, you are not in love with me."

"I must be. I miss you like crazy." He sat down at the table. "Come on, babe, marry me, travel with me."

She sat across from him. "Why would I start jetting all over the world? I have a job, remember, and I'm a teacher. Well, sort of a teacher."

Pitching his voice low and sexy, he said, "You can teach me anything you want." When that got no response, he lightened. "Hey, you could coach me with my lines. Grandfather knew this old Brit whose wife built a tree house in the garden where he hung out and practiced his lines."

"Sounds like she was trying to get him out of the house."

"Where's your romance. When she died, he didn't live a month."

"Oh, that's sad. I can't see you being that dependent on anyone except your cousin."

He laughed. "Yeah, my shrink called Joey the over-functioning side of our relationship. C'mon, babe, you could teach online like you do your editing stuff."

She tut-tutted at his self-absorption. "You have no idea what a marriage is."

"Yes, I do. Compatibility. We're only incompatible in lifestyle." He raised an eyebrow. "Say, you aren't worried about the physical stuff, are you?"

"No, not really." In truth, she couldn't quite picture herself sleeping with anyone except Sam. "It'd be a leap, though."

"I'll catch you. You can trust me."

Without knowing it, he had put his finger on the crux of the matter. She didn't trust him. He lied at the drop of a hat. And a celebrity "showmance" was of no interest to her. Before she could form a serious reply, he bonked himself on the head with the heel of his hand. "How stupid of me! I didn't bring a ring. I'll have the Hope Diamond here by morning."

"Stop it, you goofball! See, that's just it—"

"A ring? For real?"

"Don't you dare get me a ring," she fairly yelled at him. "You aren't anywhere near ready to get married. Not to me anyway."

Over the next few days they replayed variations of the proposal/refusal scene until Kathryn thought it pretty well defused. She became so good at anticipating him that she would shake her head as soon as he opened his mouth about it.

"You remind me of Joe," he grumbled.

She had read the Bennett biography manuscript backward and forward but had not completely grasped the enormous role the cousins played in each other's lives until she found herself privy to their tug-of-war phone conversations. One in particular came on the last hot day of September. Colton was hiding from the heat and the world. Lounging beside Kathryn's desk, enjoying the cool feel of the wide-plank oak floor, he was studying a new script spread out on Aunt Tildy's braided rug. He whipped his iPhone out of his khaki shorts at the first note of his ABBA ring tone, and shouted, "Told you, Joey, I'm not going!" He paused briefly for what was no doubt a clipped response from Joe. "Too bad. We should've talked about Shanghai before you finalized the dates."

Joe couldn't be aware of Colton's marriage scheme. He would never sanction that. She had not spoken with Joe in the five months since Lydia's baby was born, but Kathryn had no trouble imagining his fury at being defied. Although Colton was blond and dazzling like Sam, the dark and serious Joe more often came to her mind. Lanky and angular, an inch taller than Colton, Joe's loping stride was distinct from his cousin's more fluid gait. And, as Phyl would say, he had "those shoulders."

Kathryn eyed Colton sitting cross-legged at her feet. His muscles were less defined and he was softer in physique and manner. He switched to listening mode, absentmindedly stacking inside his size twelve surf sandals the small flip flops she had kicked off. At length he retorted, "Plenty of reasons." Pausing, he flashed a smile at Kathryn. "Not just that. Howard gave me three months to put on thirty pounds for his new gig. Thing is, I just don't want to leave."

Tensed for an angry explosion from one or both, Kathryn was surprised by them coming to an instant agreement.

"Okay, that'll work." Colton ended the call with his favorite verbal backslap, intoning in his Shakespearian best Captain Picard's catchphrase to his first officer in *Star Trek: The Next Generation*, "Make it so, Number One."

Kathryn laid her reading glasses on the desk. "You two might as well be brothers."

He stretched his arms out in front, hands together like a diver, working kinks out of his back. "Always been us against the world. Like you and cutie patootie, Dee."

Kathryn laughed. "I like that. Serves her right for calling you hunky monkey."

Colton gathered up his script and clambered to his feet. "She knows her way around a kitchen. Tell me again what she called that veal stuff last night."

"Grillades and Grits, her new signature dish."

"She can sign my name on another one of those. She's the dish, though."

"Don't be fooled by all those curves and platinum curls. Dee's an MBA, CCIM, and everything else it takes to broker a real estate firm. If a man underestimates her, she'll sell the ground right out from under his feet."

"Since Joey didn't tell her about me, I'm glad you did."

"Remember, Dee and I don't keep secrets from one another, especially not a secret as big as you."

His left eyebrow quirked upward, an unconscious gesture that sent his fans over the moon. "According to this," he riffled the pages of his script, "not big enough."

"Yikes, do you really have to put on thirty pounds?"

"Joey didn't sign off on it when he negotiated the deal, but Howard thinks it'll give me an edge." He glanced around the room, "Could have its perks, y'know? Any of those chocolates left?"

"Not a sole survivor." Kathryn was not about to admit she and Marleen had gobbled up an entire box of Belgian delights the very afternoon they arrived. Marleen had earned her share the previous week by disposing of a rotten wheel of cheese he'd sent from London. However, both women were smitten the instant they laid eyes on his gift from Germany, a 1903 Steiff bear. Kathryn had christened him Benny and installed him beside her fireplace in a child's rocking chair Marleen picked up at a yard sale.

Rummaging in the freezer, Colton called out, "Hey, what about ice cream?"

Kathryn called back, "Don't they have fat suits you can wear?"

He peered through the arch from the kitchen. "Not if I'm serious about getting into character. I get to play the bad guy for a change. Y'know, maybe Tommy can hook Joey up with somebody like Dee."

"Are you in the habit of finding your cousin's women?"

"Hardly." He lounged against the door frame and put a glint in his eye. "Pun intended. I'm just saying, it'll take an extraordinary woman for him."

Kathryn gave a derisive little sniff.

"What exactly have you got against Joey?"

"Ask him."

"Special kind of hell," he muttered, "when a man's best friends don't get along."

"If you must know, he's a thief."

"A thief! Joey? Not in this life."

"That's exactly what he stole—my life. Think about it. Where did Kitty Quinn come from?"

"He invented her."

"Wrong." Kathryn got out of her chair and paced into the kitchen. "What's her profession?"

He frowned. "Literary editor."

"Where?"

"New York."

"And she became a spy because…"

"Insurgents blew up her husband."

"What was her husband's profession?"

"Okay, I see where you're going—he was a photo-journalist. But you're wrong."

Kathryn took a box of crackers out of the cupboard and handed it to him. "I am not. It's exactly like Sam. *My* husband. They killed him, too."

Colton popped two crackers in his mouth and mumbled, "All this time, you thought Joey took your story?"

"He most certainly did. I was sick with grief and just about cried on his shoulder at Omni. He was a wonderful listener—or so I thought. *Daylight to Darkness* is me, me and Sam." Her voice trailed away and then came back with a hard edge. "Only I haven't done a damn thing to avenge my husband's death."

He shook his head slowly back and forth. "You inspired him, babe, that's all. Your story drove the plot, but Joey was writing about his mother."

Kathryn executed an about-face from the counter where she was arranging a plate of cheeses. "His mother?"

"I doubt he even realized it, but he's hell-bent on creating what our mothers might've been. Y'know—brave, feisty, successful, independent, victorious—stuff we dreamed for them. It's all there."

A pang of empathy hit Kathryn. "I forget you never knew your mothers."

"Yeah. Betty and Peggy." He looked off to one side, "The sharks call them Beggy and Petty."

"That's mean."

His moment of gloom dissipated. "Y'know," he said, spreading goat cheese on a cracker, "they're fair game. Kardashians of their day."

"So where did Joe come up with Kitty's miscarriage?"

"From his mother again. Joey was her second pregnancy. Grandmother Pet told us."

Kathryn's eyes misted. "Maybe so." More to herself than to him, she added, "I didn't remember saying—"

"Oh, God." Colton pulled her to his chest. "That was you, too." He pressed his lips on top of her head.

She stayed there momentarily before stepping away, clearing her throat. "Okay. I'm done crying on shoulders."

"I'm sorry that happened. Joey will be, too."

"For goodness sake, don't say anything to him about that. The story hit me so close to home I couldn't see past it." She handed him a bottle of water from the refrigerator and unscrewed the cap of one for herself. "You really think he's writing about his mother without realizing it?"

"Absolutely." He took a swig of cold water. "We used to make up lives for them all the time when we were kids. His had to be a fighter like *Wonder Woman* or *Xena: Warrior Princess*."

"And yours?"

He waved her off. "It's silly. You'll laugh."

"Probably." She crooked her index finger in a "come on" gesture and sipped from her bottle.

"Okay—Barbara Walters."

She coughed to keep from inhaling water. "Why Barbara Walters?"

"Feminine but mentally tough. Y'know, like Dee."

"Maybe I shouldn't encourage you and Dee to be friends. I might land in that special hell you mentioned where best friends don't get along."

"Serve you right, being mad at Joey all this time."

"Guess I'd better get over myself. There's more at play here than me."

"The happiest I've ever seen Cuz was when he was writing Kitty. He's stupid to let her go. Get them back together, will you? He'll be here while I'm on this Asian blitz he cooked up."

Chapter 15

Colton couldn't originate an international flight from Athens' Ben Epps Field. However, Atlanta's Hartsfield-Jackson, the world's busiest airport, was surprisingly hassle-free. Media targets like him cleared security privately and were escorted directly onto flights. The morning he was to leave, Joe drove in from the ranch and met Colton as he was waiting to board. The agenda had him in Tokyo the first week, Beijing and Shanghai the next, and then on to Hong Kong, Taipei, and Jakarta. Casting their differences aside, the cousins greeted one another with lattes and back slaps.

"Hey, man," Colton said, striking a pose, "great minds think alike and great bodies dress alike." His attire differed from Joe's only in the shade of yellow Polo shirt they each wore with their jeans.

"Pathetic." Joe laughed. "Together wa-a-ay too long."

They found a table and Joe took a few minutes updating Colton's itinerary. Returning the iPhone, Joe cocked his head and studied Colton.

His cousin caught the look. "What?"

"You're mighty relaxed."

"Good old southern hospitality." Colton grinned. "Don't tell my fans, but my partying days may be over."

A furrow cut across Joe's brow.

"Not that I'm actually engaged or stuff."

With an edge of triumph, Joe said, "What? Fair maiden didn't succumb to your charms?"

Daniel appeared at the door. Colton rose and chucked Joe on the shoulder. "Go to Athens. Resurrect Kitty. I wouldn't be going halfway around the world if you hadn't promised."

"Said I'd *think* about it." Joe narrowed his eyes in a mock glare. "Blackmailers go to jail, Cuz."

"And workaholics die." Colton ducked under Daniel's arm and headed out the door. "I'll be out of your hair for a few weeks," he shouted back. "Get your head out of the smog and find yourself a southern belle."

℘℘℘

Kathryn had shared Colton's *bon voyage* dinner, made heavy on carbs at his request. Laughing about him wanting to gain weight, Marleen baked her unrivaled biscuits, deep dish chicken pot pie, and buttermilk pound cake. Kathryn was still on overload the next day when Dee called.

"Puh-leese go to Evelyn's tonight without me, Kay."

"I only agreed to go to keep you company," Kathryn sputtered. "Book groups aren't my thing and you know it. Why does either of us have to be there?"

"I put her off all summer but I promised we'd be there in October. You've already read the book. I didn't know this baby-making would eat up so much of my energy. After I leave the office, all I can do is go home and crawl in my bed."

"It would've been fun with you, but I'm not inclined to go by myself."

"You won't be by yourself. You'll have Evelyn. You might even meet somebody."

"If this is some kind of set-up—"

"No way. I don't have enough energy to set a table. I'd—I'd go if I could."

Kathryn responded to the catch in Dee's voice. "Okay, don't get all hormonal."

Dee sniffled. "You know how it is."

Kathryn sighed. "Get some rest. I'll go."

She tossed her cell phone into her purse and stared out the window. What a dreary day. Fall seemed to have come overnight. Dee was the second person that day hounding her about something she didn't want to do. Phyllis had bombarded her again that morning about editing Joe Butler's book. Kathryn survived the volley, but just barely.

"So who pushed him into fiction in the first place?" Phyl had demanded.

"Well—me."

"Why was that?"

"He had talent."

"So now he doesn't?"

"No, of course, he does, Phyl. I'm just not comfortable with his storyline."

"And your comfort trumps his success?"

"I didn't say that."

"Didn't you?"

A high-pitched tone emitted by Kathryn's fax machine receiving a document jarred her back to the present. Out came a page bearing Omni letterhead with the word *urgent* scrawled across the top, and boldly underlined three times.

Phyl was nothing if not persistent. Kathryn folded

the paper crosswise, stuck it in the book club tome, and slammed out the front door.

She trundled over to the neighboring county, begrudging every mile. Evelyn O'Hara had assembled a congenial group of three men and five women in a comfy conversation area off the main foyer at Blue Willow Inn. Kathryn poured a cup of hot cider and joined them. The book under discussion was the first offering from a famous mystery writer's son. After his father's death, he had done an exemplary job of picking up the reins. Some of the group embraced him and his story whole cloth, while others picked apart both. All agreed on one point: they were waiting with bated breath for a sequel. The son had his father's ability to capture imaginations and suspend disbelief. The editor in Kathryn knew that was exactly what would happen when Joe's *Daylight to Darkness* hit the shelves. The kind of lightning every author, editor, and publisher on the planet dreams will strike.

She savored the feel of the book club's selection in her hands. Light on plot, it was substantial in size. Noting cover graphics in the father's style, Kathryn hoped the son fully appreciated his leg up in the publishing world. Bored by a man blathering about premise, she paged through the front matter and came upon the Omni fax. Phyl had sent the dedication page of Joe's manuscript. Words swam up and floored Kathryn. *To Kathryn, whose courage to change her life changed mine.*

True, she had challenged Joe to write fiction. And it probably did change his life. Novelists said writing changed everything, but his life of privilege hardly needed changing. What could he have interpreted as courageous in her flight of sheer desperation from New York? She reached out and ran an index finger lightly over the single line of type centered on the page. As pithy as the man who wrote it. Joe's intensity was off-putting and

made him impossible to predict, but he was magnetic
when he let his guard down. She flashed on him holding
newborn José. Shaking the image out of her head, she
looked around to find she was the only person still seated.
The meeting had concluded without her noticing. She
donned her parka and was about to leave when Evelyn
sidled up. "So, Kay, tell me about your beau."

"Beau?" She tried to come up with a quick dodge
about Colton. Evelyn had fed him at least twice disguised
as Ben.

"Last fall." Evelyn laughed boisterously and drew a
crocheted shawl around her ample bosom. "Tall, dark,
and oh-so Hollywood handsome."

"Oh, you mean Joe." Kathryn was simultaneously relieved Colton hadn't been recognized and amazed Evelyn
pegged Joe so perfectly. "I told you that was business."

"Business, my foot," Evelyn scoffed. "That man was
drinking you up like sassafras tea."

Waving good-bye, Kathryn ran to her car through a
cold drizzle guaranteed to last all night. She figured her
friend was being fanciful, but the memory of Joe's husky
voice on the phone sent a shiver up her spine. Had Colton
been stretching the truth again or was Joe really happiest
when he wrote about his fictional woman? Envy shot
through Kathryn at Kitty Quinn's singular ability to make
Joe happy.

Driving home, Kathryn didn't notice the vehicle behind her until its headlights loomed too close for comfort.
It seemed to spring from nowhere as she crossed the rail-
road tracks at County Line Mill. She slowed to let it pass
before they reached the bridge over the mill trace. Oddly
it switched to high beams and crowded her rear bumper.
From the height and size of the glare, she gauged it to be
an SUV or a van.

Five dark miles from home, she flipped her mirror to

night view and strained to see the two-lane road. Few cars were traveling that wet, curvy stretch, but the vehicle on her tail didn't take advantage of any opportunity to pass. It was still breathing down her neck after she executed two of her turns toward home. Panic rose. Leading the tailgater to her isolated cottage was unthinkable. Deliberately passing the Morton Road turn, she went another mile and whipped into the Olde Lexington Gardens subdivision. As she gunned away from its well-lighted entrance, she caught a glimpse of the vehicle, a light-colored mid-size van.

The gap between them was closing rapidly. Kathryn took her right hand off the wheel long enough to scramble for the cell phone in her purse. Coming up with it, she thumbed 911 and wedged the phone between her ear and shoulder, gripping the wheel with both hands again. An alert dispatcher answered her call on the second ring.

With the van bearing down, Kathryn yelled, "I need help—in Olde Lexington Gardens—someone's trying to run me off the road."

"Can you make it to the fire station on Whit Davis Road, ma'am?"

"I'll try."

"Give me your name and vehicle descript—"

The van bashed into the Prius bumper. Kathryn screamed. The phone dislodged and fell to the floor. Clutching the wheel, she accelerated through the quiet neighborhood. Cutting back out onto the main road in a death-defying move in front of an oncoming car, she forced the van to wait for it to pass. The risky maneuver cushioned her mile run for the fire station.

The instant she pulled into its bright-as-day parking lot, four firemen exited an engine bay and took positions at each corner of her car.

The van, a tan Odyssey like a zillion others on the

road, flashed by too fast for them to see the driver or get a complete tag number. Kathryn's adrenalin was still sky high when a police cruiser rolled up. The officer requested her license and took down details of the chase.

"There's no reason for anyone to do that to me," she insisted.

"Never know about road rage, ma'am. Smallest thing sets off some folks. Might've even thought you were somebody else they had a beef with. Let me see your registration and proof of insurance."

She took the documents out of the glove box and handed them over.

"Wait here, please," he instructed and returned to his car.

Kathryn thought that was just peachy. Some idiot tried to kill her, and she got the license check. Why couldn't she have had a Kitty Quinn moment, shot out that van's headlights, and cuffed the driver all by herself.

The officer returned her papers. "You're good to go. More'n likely a random occurrence, but I'll follow you home to be sure."

Feeling like a wimp all the way home, she parked in her detached carport, Aunt Tildy's old pottery workshop, and hurried across the yard into her house. Goose barked furiously the whole time the police car was making a slow U-turn, floodlights piercing the shadows as it went.

She locked the front door and went straightaway to heat a cup of tea in the microwave. Her shaking hands sloshed as much as she drank and she felt exposed by the dark windows above the wainscoting in the kitchen. With miles of dense woodland behind the house, she had left them uncurtained to invite nature into her home. And any prying eye so inclined. She verified the back door was locked. Flipping on the outside light, she returned to the front door and rechecked it. She left the porch light on

and went room to room checking window locks and closing curtains. In her bedroom, she took Aunt Tildy's shotgun from the closet. With a knot in her stomach, she
dropped in two shells and closed the breach. That robust
metallic snap was the most satisfying sound she had
heard all day.

Kathryn lay in bed reading her Kindle into the wee
hours before she fell asleep. At Goose's bark, she came
wide awake and snatched up the gun. Without turning on
a light, she padded down the hall and peered out the bathroom window into the front yard. Past the halo of porch
light, the dog was a moonlit silhouette snarling and barking toward the curve in the driveway. The rain had
stopped, but the pine thicket beyond cast the driveway in
impenetrable shadow. Long minutes passed. She grew
weary from tension. The barrel of the shotgun sapped
warmth from her body. Nothing moved, but Goose didn't
let up. Something or someone was out there.

A pinpoint of light materialized. Kathryn squinted at
it. The trace of light arced. The fiery tip of a cigarette.
Who was it? Had the van followed her home after all?
She shifted the shotgun and dialed Charlie's Corner. Daniel was closer than the police.

"What the hell time is it?" Joe growled.

"Oh, sorry," she whispered. "I was calling Daniel."

"Kathryn? Thought you were Benny. Why Daniel?"

"I—well—" Something inside her rose up and refused to let her admit she was scared.

"Kathryn? Tell me."

"Never mind," she said, but her voice wavered. "I
forgot he left today. I'm a bit rattled. Somebody followed
my car earlier tonight."

"Followed you?"

"Yes, tried to run me off the road."

"Are they at your house now?"

"I think so. Goose is throwing a fit, and I saw a lit cigarette out there." Her phone went abruptly silent. "Joe? Joe!" She felt bereft to lose the strength of his voice but was immediately comforted when a flare in the direction of the estate indicated headlights heading her way.

The cigarette moved side to side—a red line slicing the darkness—the smoker obviously drawn to Joe's lights. Goose took a couple of steps forward and tamped down his racket. Kathryn detected the telltale crackle of gravel, a vehicle retreating. A sense of relief washed over her as she awaited Joe.

When he drove up, she flung open the front door and ventured as far as the porch railing.

He leapt from the car and ran toward her. "Nothing but pitch black out here."

"I heard it back down the driveway as soon as I saw your lights. If you didn't see anything, it must've gone down The Lane until you turned in."

"What's this all about, Kathryn?"

She scanned the darkness and shivered. "I honestly don't know."

He glanced around the yard. "Want me to stay? See if they come back?"

"It'll be light soon. I'm okay." Kathryn realized she had spoken the truth. In the course of five minutes, her emotions had shifted from fright to a sense of security she hadn't felt in a very long time—not since Sam's presence left her. "Anyway." She gave him a sheepish grin and pulled the shotgun from behind her back. "I have Matilda."

"Whoa!" Joe held up both hands. "I believe you know how to use that thing."

His awkward gait as he picked his way back across the yard, pointed out that he was shoeless as well as shirtless. A pair of baggy sweatpants slung low on his hips was all he had taken time to put on. She cleared her throat. "Thanks for coming so quickly. It—it means a lot."

He looked back at her. "Anytime."

Chapter 16

Having promised he'd write at Charlie's Corner while Colton was gone, Joe moped around for four days in search of his muse. Marleen suggested the old estate office built onto the far side of the house, but he wasn't one to write at a desk. The cushioned bamboo chairs and table gave the sun room adjoining the kitchen a semblance of poolside atmosphere. To Marleen's obvious dismay, he settled there and struggled to create new characters, trying not to mourn Kitty.

Even without Colton there to prompt him, Kathryn's driveway taunted Joe when he and Yankee jogged The Lane. He hadn't crossed paths with her since the night she'd called. What a vision she had been standing on that porch, dark hair spilling over her shoulders, shotgun at the ready. He had been tempted to call her Kitty. He chuckled at the thought. That would've brought on the buckshot for sure. As far as he knew, she hadn't had any more nighttime visitors, but he had Eduardo keeping an eye on her place, just in case.

After his runs, Joe found himself resting longer and longer at the pond. It was on his side of The Lane, about midway between his house and hers. The air down there had a pungent, earthy smell of the ages. And there was peace, real peace, the kind he could sink down into. Taking along pen and paper, he scribbled snatches of dialogue and fleshed out scenes that had previously eluded him. As he brooded over a passage, a fish breached and slapped the surface of the water only a few feet from him. He laughed out loud. How long since he had done that? He tracked the ripples until they smoothed out in the rushes.

Joe wandered into the woods on what seemed to be an old road. It narrowed into a path and eventually led him to a clearing that surrounded a big oak tree, a grandfather of the forest type. Fairies might've danced there. Druids might've worshipped there. He walked over and put his hand on the tree, glancing back over his shoulder with a feeling he should've asked permission first. Near his hand two hearts had been carved in the bark, one more weathered than the other. Why two hearts? Two couples? Two loves? Two lifetimes? He propped against the tree and wrote:

> *I have dreamt of this place for so long it doesn't seem real. I could never have imagined the real thing would be so much better, so full of surprises. I stop and kiss her every other step. I want to remember each of her small, tender touches. I am safe and I am at home.*

∽∾∽

At the beginning of Joe's second week in residence at the estate, in the middle of October, he returned from a joyful weekend of pony training with Wrenn and Miracle. Marleen flounced into the sun room and announced,

"UPS left off something for Ms. Kathryn down yonder. You mind taking it to her while I finish fixing supper?"

"What?" Joe shifted his glare from laptop to housekeeper. "Why'd they leave it here?"

"Mr. Colt always send her gifts here, addressed to the dog."

Joe shucked his reading glasses and knitted his dark brows. "Oh?"

"Oh, is mighty right." Marleen giggled and deposited the package on a chair.

Joe squinted at the last page he had written, decided it was trash, and deleted the whole thing. "Damn!" He grabbed the box and tore it open. Two seconds later he slammed out the back door, totally forgetting Yankee's leash.

Yankee's restrictions had put a crimp in Goose's playtime, so Kathryn was happy when she stepped out of the shower and heard them romping on the porch. She zipped on a chenille robe and blotted water out of her hair as she walked through the house to fling open the front door. "Oh!" she gasped, finding Joe's fist poised to knock.

He thrust a delivery box at her. "How long has this been going on?"

Twisting the towel into a turban, she became the cryptic one for a change. "Meaning?"

"This came from Benny."

"So?" She took the box, turning away from the door and from him.

He followed her inside. "It's a kimono."

A cat whose tail he had trod upon wouldn't have whirled around any faster. "How dare you open my mail!"

He shrugged. "Benny doesn't have secrets from me."

"Apparently, he does."

"Listen, Kathryn." Impatience was clear in his tone. "You're in over your head. You don't know what you're doing."

"No, you don't know what you're doing. Opening my mail is a federal offense." She brandished the box at him.

He thumped the label. "See your name on it? Explain why he's sending you a bridal kimono."

"I don't have to explain anything to you," she retorted before his actual words sank in. "Did you say bridal?" She pulled the garment from the box. Fine handmade silk, it was as red as red could be and lavishly embroidered with swans. "Wow. This is a lot better than some of the things he sends." Amused by Joe's stricken expression, she said, "Relax, it doesn't mean anything. He asks me to marry him a couple of times a week."

"What the hell?"

"Lighten up," she scoffed. "I'm not out to hook me a movie star, yours or anybody else's. Anyway, I'm hardly the glamour puss he's used to, I'm just ordinary."

Joe shook his head. "Glitz and glam are his ordinary, not a real woman like you."

"That's as backhanded a compliment as I've ever heard. I've come too far to get carried away with a crush." She shot him a look. "You ought to know. You saw me at my worst."

His purple eyes captured her gaze and made her keenly aware of being naked beneath her robe. She held up the kimono like a shield. "I—I—" she stammered, "I can't quite see it—myself, I mean—in this, can you?"

The hint of a smile softened his features.

Kathryn thought this was a good chance to explain her overreaction to Kitty Quinn. "Now that you're here, can we talk? I just need a minute to get dressed."

He cleared his throat. "Sure, no problem."

"There's coffee in the kitchen. I'll be right back."

Joe watched her hurry barefoot down the hall and heard a door close. For the first time, he realized she must have come to the door straight out of the shower. He shook his head, his thoughts returning to her kimono question. He had no trouble at all seeing her in the garment. Or out of it, as his unexpected arousal attested. The way her Natalie Wood freckle at the corner of her top lip rose and fell with the curve of her smile really got to him.

He strode through her front room into the adjoining kitchen. Running the length of the house, it was bright and cheerful with an abundance of windows. On the dining end, tubular aluminum chairs sporting red gingham seats surrounded a white enamel table. A matching hutch displayed an array of Fiestaware dishes and added to the retro ambiance of the room. Seeing she had set out a yellow mug for herself, he chose a green one and poured coffee in both from a percolator reminiscent of his grandmother's.

"Thanks," she said, coming in quietly, still barefoot. Wet hair pulled into a low ponytail, she had dressed in denim capris and a turquoise tee-shirt.

As Joe crossed the room with their mugs, Colton's surf sandals caught his eye. Unmistakably orange, looking very much at home, they remained in a basket by the back door after she took out her flip-flops. Grimacing, he sat down at the table. Why had he expected more? She had caught him off guard. He would give her that. The respite from his cousin's bimbos since Paris didn't mean Joe had forgotten how to get rid of one. "So, how much do you want to keep your mouth shut about sleeping with Benny?"

Kathryn's brown eyes widened and then narrowed. The way her knuckles turned white as she held the yellow mug, Joe figured she was quelling an impulse to dash hot

Jamaican brew in his face. She would not be the first to do that either.

She forced down a sip before looking directly at him. "You're an idiot."

He snorted. "I know all the tricks."

She rose and threw open the back door. "Get out of my house." Her tone was low and even, but he saw fire in her eyes.

He kept his seat. "I'm willing to negotiate."

She whipped her cell phone out of her pocket and punched in a nine and a one. With her finger hovering over the number one, she said, "Negotiate yourself off my property unless you have some insane desire to spend the night in a Georgia jail."

Okay, that's a first. He got up and walked to the threshold.

"Now!" she barked, barely waiting until he was clear before slamming the door.

Kathryn could not remember a time when she had been so angry. She waited for the loathsome man to get home before driving past his place on her way to class. Edgy about a string of midnight hang-up calls she had received since he ran off the cigarette smoker in her yard, she felt a sudden emptiness no shotgun could fill. That somehow made her angrier.

Returning home after class, she prepared for bed and hoped for uninterrupted sleep. That included Colton. He had not been in the habit of calling her until this Asian trip. The time difference made his days her nights. At first, she had enjoyed snuggling into her quilts and following him around his suite based on background noises. Lively music, microwave ding, crunch of popcorn, muffled voice of shirt pulled over head, zip of trousers, but the flush of a toilet had brought her bolt upright in bed.

"Hey, did you just pee?"

"One does."

"Not in this one's ear, one doesn't."

That had launched him into a series of Jimmy Fallon jokes that left her in stitches.

Tonight, though, she was in no mood to talk to Colton. Joe's crass remarks were too fresh. Dumping on Colton so he could crucify Joe would feel great in the moment, but she wouldn't foster a feud between them. They were family, what precious little they had left.

Kathryn dozed but her eyes snapped open as soon as her cell phone rang. She sat up and stared at the dresser where it was charging, then turned her back and let the call go to voice mail. She was still awake an hour later when the phone rang again. Although she didn't answer, she decided to listen to her messages.

The first was Colton's flip, "Catch you in an hour, babe." The second held a playful tinge of concern, "Hey, babe, if you don't answer my next call, I'll have Joey on your doorstep."

The third time the phone rang, Kathryn said, "Hello."

"There you are," Colton said. "Did I interrupt your beauty sleep?"

"That's okay."

"Something the matter?"

"Not really, I'm just tired."

"You sound sort of depressed."

"Definitely not good company. Good night."

"Hey, hold on a minute, Kay. What's happened?"

"Nothing," she whispered, hoping tears wouldn't betray her. "It's just not a good time." She hurried to hang up before he got it out of her. "I have to go."

"Wait! There's something you aren't saying."

Kathryn didn't trust her voice to answer.

"For heaven's sake, babe, don't shut me out."

His concern made her even sadder. She had never

known him to worry about anything. "Please," she choked.

A long, deathly silence ensued. "Okay," he said, gruff, edgy. "Get some sleep."

e/se/s

By daybreak, Kathryn was sleep-deprived and prowling the house. She threw on jeans and a lightweight hoodie and summoned Goose for a loop around the pond. "Get your old self moving," she grumbled.

His heavy paws, like socks of sand, plodded reluctantly behind her until they reached the half-mile mark, the mailbox. There his head lifted, along with his spirits. He tested the air, woofed, and loped into the woods.

Kathryn tramped through the pasture toward the pond. At least she'd had the satisfaction of throwing Joe out of her house. Pretty much like she had thrown out his book. Good reminder not to delude herself. Colton was not some regular guy with an out-of-town job. She thought about their marathon games of Monopoly, poker with Dee and Tommy, country drives in the sexy Porsche convertible he'd bought, dining out with him in disguise. All myth.

She stepped onto a granite shelf that jutted out over the pond. The conflict with Joe was too upsetting. Did he hate women in general or just her specifically? One thing for certain, Joe was an integral part of Colton. And they played on the world stage. A vapor cloud hovered above the green water. A terrapin ventured onto the knot of a submerged tree branch and turned its face to the sun. *That's me. Head poking out of my Matilda shell to soak up Colton's warmth. I'm a perfect idiot.*

Goose arrived in a tussle with Yankee and sent the little turtle plopping back into the depths. Brimming with canine zeal, the dogs trounced onto the flat rock with Kathryn.

"Hey!" she shouted, pushing them away. "You knock me in, you're in big trouble."

They didn't wait to find out if she was scolding or teasing. Goose splashed into the pond drinking noisily, and Yankee rolled on the grassy bank.

Kathryn went to pet Yankee, and then let out a shriek when Goose bolted over and slopped cold water on her. She sank down in the grass and hugged an arm around each dog.

Uphill, Joe leaned against the trunk of a large catawba tree. The ground was littered with its autumn bean pods. Kathryn had passed twenty feet away but hadn't noticed him. He watched her administer a tummy rub to Yankee, stretched out long and lean on one side, and an ear massage to the muscular mutt hunkered down on the other side of her.

He knew the dogs would give him away as soon as she stopped petting them. He also knew he had to talk to her. Benny had made that crystal clear in his 2 a.m. phone call.

"What the hell have you done to Kay?" he'd demanded.

"A *bridal* kimono?" Joe growled back.

"If I like. You wouldn't understand."

"Damn right. Found you a place to get out of the limelight, and you screw it up."

"I did not," Benny yelled. "More to the point, I'm not screwing Kay either."

"What'd she tell you?"

"Nothing, she won't talk to me. Whatever you've done, Joey, you'd better fix it."

"Did what I usually do about these messes."

"This mess is all yours. If I don't hear a smile back

in her voice by tomorrow, I'm getting on the next flight home. Take that to the bank."

Joe had rarely heard his cousin so adamant, and never about a woman. Kudos to this one for not sniveling about her hurt feelings, but if she continued to refuse Colton's calls, the film promo was dead. Joe figured the best he could do was approach her on neutral ground and try to reason with her. He had chosen the pond, but now he wasn't so sure. No surprise; he wasn't sure of anything when it came to Kathryn Tribble. With an inward groan, he walked reluctantly out of the shadows and toward her.

When the dogs alerted Kathryn clambered to her feet. Her spine stiffened when she saw Joe. Did his expression soften when the dogs romped up to him, or was that only a shift of light? He appeared larger than life and madder than hell as he steamed downhill at her. Backed up to the water, she gripped the cell phone in the kangaroo pocket of her jacket.

"Talked to Benny," he said, stopping barely a foot away.

She fixed her eyes to his left, intent on escaping around him toward the road.

He cleared his throat, like a guttural admonishment. "I owe you an apology."

She darted past him, hurrying toward The Lane.

"Dammit!" he shouted. "We need to talk."

Out of breath by the time she reached the fence, she opened the gate and reconnected the chain before looking to see how close he was following. "Go away," she yelled.

"Nothing would suit me better," he yelled back, "but Benny's gonna ditch this whole Asian tour if we don't play nice." His jaw jutted out, and he skewered her with his eyes.

Separated from him by the fence, Kathryn crossed

her arms and glared back. She clenched her teeth and said nothing.

"I jumped to conclusions," he said. "From experience—well, in the past, protecting him."

"Buying off his women, you mean."

"You read the papers."

With an unwilling nod, she said, "You were right about one thing. I'm in over my head." She turned and trudged along The Lane toward the dot that was her mailbox.

Vaulting over the fence, Joe came alongside her. Neither spoke.

Oblivious to any discord, the dogs threaded happily in and out between them.

At her driveway, Kathryn stopped and looked at Joe. She pulled in sufficient breath to add weight to her words. "Please. Leave me alone."

Joe opened his mouth and then closed it without uttering a sound.

"I want Colton to leave me alone, too. But I'll wait until after his trip to tell him. I'm not an actress, but I can keep up a front for that long. I won't interfere with him or with you. Kindly afford me the same courtesy."

Goose peeled off to walk his mistress home.

Joe watched them disappear around the curve. Neither looked back.

Chapter 17

For two sleepless nights, her eyes—bleak and brown as the catawba leaves—haunted Joe. There was a disconcerting finality about her. She was the kind of person who only cried wolf when it was time to load the gun. The third morning, he stood on the sun porch, staring off in the direction of her cottage, and wished for a cigarette. He had accomplished what he set out to do. Or had he? He raked his teeth across his bottom lip. Her declaration of not being an actress brought to mind the legion of sycophants he knew who shamelessly promoted themselves as such.

Joe's stomach roiled and he lost his yen for tobacco. *This isn't about Benny. And it isn't about me. This is about her, the embodiment of Kitty Quinn. She faces down the demons in her life. She is done with Benny, and with me.*

c/sc/s

Phoenix's interest had flitted away from Charlie's Corner and Kathryn Tribble. She was consumed with the

Far East. She devoured every morsel she could find on Colton's trip. Where he went. Who with. How he dressed. What he said. She also kept up with what he didn't say. He never spoke her name, but she knew the code. He pretended to call everyone "babe" but that was his special name for her. Whenever he said it, he was sending her a message. She was giddy about the newest tabloid buzz saying he was in love. He was, with her. She surfed the Internet, playing and replaying his interviews on YouTube, zoomed in with Google Earth on clubs and hotels where he had been sighted. She inserted herself into every place she knew he had gone, imagining what he had seen, smelled, tasted, thought. She felt as connected as if she had actually been with him. It was only a matter of time before she would be.

☙☙

True to her word, as Joe expected she would be, Kathryn put Colton back on his course of charming the far side of the globe. His lack of womanizing drew more attention than if he had been sporting Lady Gaga on his arm. Pundits grilled his co-stars about him on the talk show circuit. Lila Manning set off a firestorm by insinuating he was in love, her sly way of garnering millions in free publicity for the film in which she'd co-starred.

Joe kept his promise to Colton and remained mostly in Athens. He'd managed to delegate work in LA to his production staff, but he let Rusty think he was going back and forth to Bennetthurst, throwing in mythical trips to Chicago for the old coot to feed to Phoenix. In actuality, when he wasn't at Wrenn's Ranch, he played golf with Tommy, Alex, and their friend Steve, wrote incessantly at Charlie's Corner, and stewed over the deal he and Kathryn had struck. Things concerning her had a habit of turning around and biting him. He jogged in the afternoons so as not to interfere with her morning walks, but she was never far from his mind.

Colton, on the other hand, was absolutely predictable. If Kathryn followed through on rejecting him after he returned to the states, the star would pull out of post-production on every project in the pipeline. He would proceed to whore around as publicly and shamefully as possible, and no director in his right mind would risk casting him. Joe came to the same conclusion every time he mulled it over—no way could he honor Kathryn's directive to leave her alone. Not even if he'd wanted to.

Damage control was his bailiwick, but the end of October was near before he devised an actual strategy. Again, he chose the pond as neutral ground and moved there to write.

Marleen was obviously delighted to get him out from under her feet. She packed him off with hot coffee, sandwiches, and a motherly admonition to keep an eye on the weather. "It's s'posed to come up a cloud."

"As in cloudburst?"

"Sooner or later one gonna bust all over you and that computer."

"There's not a cloud in the sky."

"Go on ahead then. I'll leave you some towels by the back door."

Watchful lest Joe reappear under the big catawba overlooking the pond, Kathryn froze the first morning she found him sprawled there, plugging away on his laptop, Yankee at his side. Before she could alter her course, Goose and Yankee sprinted to one another. Joe glanced up, nodded, and went back to his work, seeming resigned to let her pass in silence if she chose.

She chose exactly that, and the dogs followed her across the dam. Aware of being in Joe's line of sight, she turned abruptly up the pulpwood trail and walked all the way to the meadow, past Sam's oak, and halfway down the slope of resting lavender. She sat down and hugged her knees to her pounding chest. These walks were meant to be relaxing, not a boatload of anxiety at the prospect of dealing with Joe Butler. She closed her eyes, breathing in the calming aroma of lavender mixed with pine sap and moist earth. An image of Colton emerged, one of him laughing and twirling with her on this hill last spring.

A fall breeze played with wisps of her hair that had escaped from her ponytail. The sunshine warmed her face. She touched her lips and remembered Colton's kiss. What would it be like to make love to him? He had promised to catch her, but both he and life were liars.

She ran her tongue over her lips and imagined kissing Joe. Would he be as protective in love as he was in life?

A flutter deep within brought her abruptly to her feet. She circled home through the woods, avoiding the pond and the disturbing man who lingered there.

After the weekend, Kathryn purposely put off her Monday walk until almost dusk to avoid seeing Joe again. But when she left The Lane and crossed the pasture, there he was, stowing his laptop in a backpack. He slung it over his left shoulder and approached her.

"I'm not stalking you," he said. He hooked a thumb toward the pond. "Seem to write better around water."

She zipped up her parka and nodded. "It's good that you're writing."

"I guess." He hitched the backpack higher. "'Bout ready to throw it in the lake. Like dancing, it moves around a lot but doesn't really go anywhere."

"Dee likes to say 'dance like you know what you're doing 'til you get it right.' That also applies to writing."

Frowning slightly, he put the backpack down and settled his eyes on her face.

A prick of conscience prompted her to say, "I wanted to talk to you about Kitty Quinn."

"Oh?"

His intensity made her heart skip. She flushed. "I was wrong."

He raised a skeptical brow.

"Wrong about everything except you being an inspired writer. *Daylight to Darkness* isn't my story, but I felt like it was."

He nodded and seemed to expect her to go on.

She fidgeted with the band on her ponytail. "You have to admit the parallels."

"I wanted to explain, but you insisted on reading it first. By then—" Grimacing, he threw up his hands.

"I know. I know." She shook her head. "But imagine how exposed and exploited I felt when the worst part of my life jumped off the page at me."

"That's the last thing I meant to do." He shoved his hands deep in his jeans pockets. "I'm sticking to my word. Kitty's dead."

"To be totally honest—" Kathryn looked at the ground, feeling her face redden. "—I'm jealous of her."

Glancing up and finding a query in his eyes, she hesitated, wanting to make him understand. "Instead of crawling home like I did, your Kitty Quinn goes out and does something about her husband's death."

"Kathryn..." Joe reached out as if to steady her, barely grazing her shoulders with his palms. "This is fiction. Benny gets it mixed up with real life. Don't you fall into that trap."

She nodded, a half-hearted smile on her lips. "It's really good fiction, Joe. That's what I'm trying to say. I'm sorry it took me so long. You can't let Kitty die. She's a winner."

"Ha," he barked. "I don't even know where she is anymore."

Kathryn didn't believe that for a moment. A writer's words came from deep within. Hard fought and rarely discarded. "Well—" She crossed her arms and gave a Jack Benny eye-roll. "If you should happen to run across her, I'll edit for you."

Joe's expression changed to something akin to a smile. "Always said you don't pull any punches." He shifted his weight to the other foot and hesitated as if he was unsure of himself. "Do you love my cousin?" he finally asked.

Kathryn crossed her arms and reflected a moment on the difference Colton made in her life. The genuine delight she felt from his friendship, his unabashed silliness. "Yes, I think he's become my cousin, too."

"Then you can't give him up." He took a step away but stopped, his gaze coming back and washing over her. For a moment he stood there as though deciding what else he wanted to say. "Just remember, Colton Bennett is a leading man. He isn't interested in supporting roles."

A fat drop of rain hit Kathryn on the head. She held out her hand and felt a couple of smaller ones. "You're about to get your laptop wet."

Joe looked at the sky. "Oh no! Marleen was right. 'It's coming up a cloud.'"

They both laughed at his falsetto impression of the housekeeper, and he loped off toward home.

Kathryn called after him, "You said you liked to write around water."

"Around," he yelled back. "Not in!"

☙❧

Tuesday morning Kathryn awoke to the comforting sound of rain pattering down on her tin roof. She fired up the gas logs and stood in front of the hearth, warming her backside and sipping her first cup of coffee. Her thoughts drifted to the two men who threatened to take up more room in her life than mere neighbors. Could she get along with them both? Apparently, Joe now accepted her friendship with Colton, though he clearly had misgivings. Maybe he was right. She moved to her desk and looked at the front yard through the curtain of water plunging over the porch eaves. The deluge had started stripping the gingko of its leaves. Envisioning the tree as a wood nymph with a golden gown pooled around her feet, Kathryn was startled by the phone.

"That *Gone With The Wind* restaurant?" Joe asked on the other end of the line.

His lack of preamble made conversation easy. "Blue Willow Inn," she said. "Do you need directions?"

"Hoping you'd go with me."

"Oh?"

"Can I pick you up at seven?"

"Okay." As Kathryn put down her phone, she said, "Humph!" A smile played across her face at the prospect of dinner with Joe.

Chapter 18

Dressed in black slacks and a white silk blouse, she brushed her hair onto her shoulders in loose brunette waves. With her left hand poignantly unadorned, she graced the middle finger of her right hand with an onyx ring to complement sterling drop earrings. Five minutes before seven, she ran back into the bedroom to exchange the clingy blouse for a classic oxford shirt and to smooth her hair back into a ponytail.

Joe's gray Lexus wrapped her in a light scent of the same Ralph Lauren cologne Colton wore. The hint of it that Joe used was far more masculine than Colton's heavier application. No jewelry, per usual, Joe wore a long-sleeved blue shirt with the collar open and khaki slacks. Kathryn placed her red sweater on the back seat next to his navy blazer.

Joe ducked his head boyishly and stashed a pack of Nicorette lozenges in the console. "A reminder," he said. "You navigate. I'm terrible with directions."

"This is where I gloat about you giving me permission to tell you where to go."

He rumbled a low sound of amusement. "A Georgia jail, last I recall."

"You deserved that."

"Indeed I did. Forgive me?"

"I wouldn't be here otherwise."

He nodded. "Okay, lead me to that caramel cake I've been dreaming about all year."

She noticed his light touch on the steering wheel. Tanned, tapered fingers with a dusting of dark hair. "I take it you don't like Colton's convertible any better than I do."

"I call it a skateboard," he snorted. "Ridiculous."

"You have me to thank for talking him out of a motorcycle, and for getting the roller skate in red and black. He blends nicely with UGA's Fortune 500 alumni."

Maneuvering up an S-curve from the Oconee River, Joe coughed back a laugh. "Hard to picture Benny blending. Driving is a treat for him, though. Both of us, especially out in the country like this." He slowed and relaxed back into his seat. "Green really pops after a rain."

"God's neutral," she said.

"Wasn't it Cummings who wrote about 'leaping greenly spirits'?"

"Yes, and 'blue true dream of sky.'"

They drove along, silently appreciating the fertile Piedmont landscape. Stately houses with mobile homes in side yards bespoke family, and Holsteins ambled across pastures toward dairies in the distance. As they passed by an orchard, Kathryn said, "Dormant peach trees remind me of witch's hands, fingers reaching up out of the ground."

Joe tapped the brakes for a look at the gnarled, twisted limbs. "Fitting image with Halloween coming up. Never had trick-o'-treaters. Don't suppose we'll have any out our way."

Kathryn shook her head. "No, we're too far from town. Too far from peach season, too. I'm as crazy about Dee's peach cobbler as you are Evelyn's caramel cake."

"Impossible."

"My mouth waters just thinking about it. I can't make it, though. When the crop comes in I eat my peaches over cereal."

"Why can't you make cobbler?"

"To be a good cook, I'd have to like to cook."

"Whether they like to or not, most women pretend they do."

Kathryn shook her head. "I don't like pretending any more than I like cooking."

Joe glanced over at her and smiled. "Bet you pour a mean bowl of cereal."

She laughed. "Anyway, Dee loves to make me beg for cobbler."

"She said she wanted to live at your house when you two were growing up. Was she talking about the cottage?"

"No, she loved the old Morton homeplace. It was at the far end of The Lane where the hay field is now. Over the hill—literally and figuratively. A falling down old monstrosity by the time it came into my possession. I sold it with the land."

"Selling your family property must've been tough."

"Not really, Daddy intended for me to sell it. The cottage was a different matter. I spent most of my time there with Aunt Tildy while my parents worked in town. I couldn't let it go."

"So if I were to exercise my lease option and buy the Corner would I own land you sold?"

"You would. For some reason Charlie's property went to Aunt Tildy. Then it all went to Daddy and I ended up with it. Are you thinking about buying it?"

"Hadn't planned to until I found this spectacular oak back in the woods past the pond. A once in a lifetime kind of tree." He paused and then added, "More like once in two lifetimes."

"Why two?"

"Many more, I'm sure, but there are two hearts carved on it. Bet you know the one I mean. Stands in the middle of a clearing. Sort of...I don't want to sound too 'out there' but it was like I could feel a presence around it."

She smiled. "Yes, I know that tree. I get the same feeling."

"If you hadn't kept your Aunt Tildy's cottage, where would you be now?"

She looked out the window and sighed. "I really don't know."

Joe glanced over at her. "Sounds like you're as attached to your place as I am to Bennetthurst." Approaching a junction, he said, "Highway 11, I know the way from here. Who was the Charlie of my house? He a Morton?"

"Yes, a first cousin of Tildy, who was actually my great aunt, Grandpa Morton's sister. Grandpa always said I looked like her. I loved her dearly but I count myself lucky not to have known Crazy Charlie. He was a drunk and mean as a snake. The whole county hated him. Grandpa didn't even want to bury him in the family cemetery, but he relented. It's kind of sad. Charlie was the end of his line. Never married and dropped dead in his fifties with a bad heart."

"As Dolly said in *Steel Magnolias*, 'There's a sto-ree there.'"

"By the time I came along, except for his house and grave, it's like he'd never existed. Nobody so much as spoke his name around Grandpa or Aunt Tildy. She was a remarkable woman, a mystery in her own way. Never married, either. Stayed in France after serving in the WACs during World War Two. She moved back about the time Charlie died. My memories are from when she was in her seventies, content in her cottage with her art. Her quilts were priceless, and her pottery flew off the shelves in Daddy's store."

"Did she make the blue churn by your front door?"

Kathryn nodded, surprised he had noticed.

He turned in at the restaurant but was forced to drive past the full parking lot to a secondary one behind the building.

"I didn't make a reservation," Kathryn said. "Did you?"

"Don't mind waiting. How 'bout you?"

She appreciated his good-natured reaction. Colton would have fled the scene. Stars of his caliber were not accustomed to waiting and he wouldn't have risked being recognized.

Getting out, Joe opened the back door, shrugged on his jacket, and met her at the front of the car with her sweater. His dark blazer and tailored slacks emphasized his lean build. His hair bespoke style, as opposed to mere haircut. Even his shoes were elegant, she noticed as he matched his stride to hers.

Evelyn O'Hara was personally in command of her ship. Joe and Kathryn were barely in the door before Evelyn waved them forward. As Kathryn made her way across the crowded foyer, a boisterous woman brandishing an empty wine glass knocked into her. Kathryn pitched toward the floor, but Joe caught her around the waist.

"Easy," he breathed, his lips against her ear.

Aligned behind her, he reached his arms around and shielded her as they inched over to Evelyn. Once there, he propped both hands on the reservation lectern, one on either side of Kathryn.

Effectively pinned, Kathryn's head reeled. He had become as powerful and protective as his cologne was light and seductive.

Evelyn adjusted her bifocals. "Unh hunh." She nodded approvingly. "Mister 'Just Business,' I got a table upstairs for you." One of her young hostesses in antebellum dress led them up the central staircase and into a small dining room away from the hubbub.

Kathryn found her voice as Joe seated her. "You sure you didn't make a reservation?"

He nodded. "What was that 'Just Business' about?"

"Her way of saying she likes you." Kathryn leaned forward slightly so as not to be overheard. "Unlike the *gauche* Mr. Ben Thomas I brought here."

Joe cocked his head. "Do tell."

"Evelyn does not take kindly to one dining in a baseball cap."

He emitted an amused rumble. "Surprised she didn't throw him out."

"She told me to teach him manners before I brought him again. He didn't want to come back anyway." Kathryn smothered her laughter with her napkin. "He said she glared at him the whole time."

Joe grinned, flashing teeth that were not quite as cosmetically perfect as Colton's. An off-kilter canine added character to his tan face. Evelyn wasn't the only one who responded differently to the Hollywood cousins. Whenever Colton whispered in Kathryn's ear, it tickled and made her giggle. But Joe's single utterance sent a ripple all the way to her toes, touching places along the way that weren't accustomed to being touched.

He made a raw, throat-clearing sound and extracted a memory stick from the inner pocket of his jacket. "Peace offering." Reaching across the table, he placed the stick in her palm and closed her fingers around it. "Don't worry," he said, his hand warm on hers, "I did some rewriting. You won't see quite so much of yourself in Kitty this time."

Reclaiming her hand, Kathryn stammered, "I'm—uh—I'm over that. I'm almost used to her name."

A crease appeared in his forehead. "What's wrong with her name?"

"How did you come up with it? The Kitty part I mean?"

"Pool Kitty at Bennetthurst. Soft and sweet but scrappy when she needs to be. Like my protagonist. Able to take care of herself. Why?"

"That's what Sam called me." She couldn't begin to explain how much she had loved the sound of her pet name on her husband's lips. "As much as I might like to be, I can't be a Kitty Quinn."

"Kathryn's a beautiful name." He captured her gaze. "Exactly who you are."

Feeling in danger of him reading her confused emotions, she said, "Well, who I am right now is hungry."

"We can fix that." He rose and held the back of her chair while she stood.

Evelyn's upstairs buffet was not as elaborate as the one on the main floor, but they preferred it to the din downstairs. Kathryn added skewers of grilled okra to her usual delights. "Oh, look," she said at the dessert table, "Evelyn is already making fresh coconut cake. That puts me in the mood for the holidays. Want some?"

Joe answered with a wink and slid a second slice of caramel cake onto his dish.

They ate companionably, conversation reduced to exclamations of gustatory delight.

Finishing his fried chicken, Joe licked an index finger and blotted the corner of his mouth with his napkin. "When do you think you'll read it?"

"As soon as I can, but I have a couple of Omni assignments to get out of the way first."

He nodded. "In the interest of full disclosure, you're right. Kitty is fiction, Kathryn, but your courage that day in New York inspired the hell out of me."

She waited until a server pouring their coffee moved away, and then said, "Is that what you call a panic attack? Courage."

His eyes grew serious. "It's what I call a conscious leap of faith, acting on the heart. You know the origin of the word?"

"Courage? French probably."

"Latin *cor*, to French *cuer*, heart."

"Hmm. That helps me understand the book dedication, but I don't really deserve it."

"Courage isn't for the moment a person is struck down. You made the long climb back uphill. Last thing I intended was to impede you." He frowned, hesitated, and then added, "I never would've pushed Lydia's baby at you that night at the hospital if I'd known about your loss. You have to believe me."

"Oh," escaped her lips.

Joe flinched. "You don't have to believe me, of course, but I hope you will."

"I believe you." She stirred cream into her coffee. "It's just, I asked you-know-who not to tell you about it, that's all."

Joe forked a bite of caramel cake. "Cuz isn't on the same wavelength with everyone else. You ought to know by now, he lies like a rug."

Kathryn smiled and nodded, realizing Joe's candor reflected a new level of acceptance of her. He expected her to understand what would otherwise seem disloyal.

"Yes. I get that. Do you know about his Freudian take on Kitty Quinn being an idealized version of your mother?"

Joe pursed his lips and looked down, toying with the hem of his napkin, clearly mulling over what she had said. She glimpsed vulnerability in him and wondered who protected the protector. She didn't want him to be hurt by a remark from her. "Forgive me, Joe. You've had a lifetime of being second-guessed. You don't need it from me."

He looked up, a slow smile turning his eyes from black to plum. "Poor thing didn't get much of a shot at real life. A fictional one couldn't hurt."

Chapter 19

After the dinner with Joe, Kathryn no longer felt discomfited whenever she came across him at the pond. Their evening had ended without so much as a handshake, so she put aside any misguided attraction to him. But it was nice to know she was still capable of such a response.

It was enough for her to be back on friendly terms, and he seemed to feel the same. They chatted briefly when she passed by him near the pond and went on her way, leaving him to write. So far, he hadn't shared his new story with her, saying he wanted to finish the first draft before revealing the plot. Having worked with authors who talked so much energy out of their stories they never got around to writing them, Kathryn felt his instincts were right.

Colton was back in Los Angeles and Joe was to join him at Bennetthurst on November seventh. The morning before Joe planned to leave, Kathryn found him sitting on the granite shelf dangling his feet in the pond. "It's unseasonably warm this week but isn't the water a bit nippy?"

"Let's call it refreshing, but I wouldn't take a swim."

"You look Huck Finn-ish with your jeans rolled up like that."

"Feeling a little like Huck."

"All you need is a fishing pole."

He looked abashed and chuckled.

"You don't know how to fish, do you?"

"Like you do?"

"Of course I do. Aunt Tildy and I caught our supper down here lots of times. Catfish." She leaned down and opened her palm. "Ever eat scuppernongs?"

He shook his head and took one of the orbs between thumb and forefinger. "Pretty," he said, holding it up to the sun.

"Native grape. The skin is tough, so bite a hole in it first."

Following her lead, he bit off a plug and spit it into the reeds.

"Okay, now squeeze the pulp into your mouth."

With his mouth full, Joe said something that sounded vaguely like, "Delicious." Chewing, he said, "Yuck, bitter."

"Don't bite the seeds, spit them out. If you swallow one, a scuppernong vine will grow out your nose."

"Will not."

"Will too." Laughing, she gave him the last few scuppernongs and stepped down on the bank to rinse her hands in the water.

"You ever swim in here?"

"Not since I put my hand on a water moccasin. I was about fourteen, practicing handstands in the shallows."

"Good lord!" Joe yanked his feet out of the water with a big splash.

She laughed. "Don't worry, wrong time of year for snakes. Aunt Tildy was fearless. She swam across this pond and back every day, winter and summer, 'til the day she died."

"How old?"

"Eighty-six. One morning she just didn't wake up."

"Did you find her?"

"No. I would have, but Daddy stopped by for some reason that morning."

"I found Pet, my grandmother."

Kathryn heard a faraway tone in his voice. "Did she die that way, in her sleep?"

"Yep. A stroke. I sat beside her for the longest time before I told anyone. Just me and Pet." He blew out a long breath. "I don't know what's harder, losing someone suddenly like that or slowly through illness."

"There's no good way."

He gazed out across the water. "Nope."

e/ɔe/ɔ

Joe joined Colton at Bennetthurst satisfied that he had mended fences with Kathryn. He was well-pleased with the success of Colton's publicity tour and made sure there was post-production work in LA to keep the star busy until early in December when he would go on location in Canada. Relieved to discover Kathryn was not falling for Colton's flights of fancy, Joe looked forward to her notes on Kitty Quinn. When his thoughts strayed past that point, which they had the unsettling habit of doing, he stopped himself cold. As long as Wrenn remained young and fragile, he was stuck with Phoenix. Damned if he would involve Kathryn with that lunatic.

e/ɔe/ɔ

Colton showed up unannounced at Kathryn's door on

December fifteenth. The face she made when she saw how much he had already blimped up in preparation for his new role, gave him a laugh. "Think of it as more to love, babe."

"You're so different." She marveled at the changes in him. He had grown a stubbly beard, cultivated to add menace to his demeanor. She wrinkled her nose. "Not sure I like it."

He sailed his ball cap across the room and sprawled onto the sofa. Eye level with the antique bear he had sent her from Germany, he said, "Hello there, Benny Bear. Why are you still out here? Shouldn't you be in the lady's bed by now?"

Kathryn was aware that Colton, typically, was referring to himself. "He knows his place."

"Cold." He laughed and stuck out his tongue at her. "Look what I brought you for Christmas."

She pulled a ticket out of the envelope he handed her. "Oh, Colton, I've never been to a premiere. I can't go to a red carpet affair."

"Yes you can. I need you to help launch my new movie. Hank'll pick you up."

"You'd send the jet for me? Can you do that?"

"Just say the word, the word being yes."

"Oh my, I'll have to think about it. I've never imagined myself at something like that." Going into the kitchen, she said, "Of course, I've never imagined you with a bad boy buzz cut, either." She switched on the burner under the coffeepot and looked back at him through the square lintel arch. "I hope being this heavy won't wreck your health."

"My sweet little polite peach, I'm not heavy. I'm fat. Don't worry. I'm not gonna kick off at fifty like Grandfather did. Daniel has turned into a nutritionist. Biggest diff is no jogging."

She frowned. "Joe can carry that weight. You can't."

"He only has me by a coupla inches. Not my fault his father was a tall ole Texan."

"So, does he have family other than you?"

Colton leaned over and picked up his cap. "None to speak of."

Kathryn recognized her parents' we-don't-speak-of-Charlie-Morton tone from childhood. She respected boundaries. She had her own. Coming back from the kitchen, she said, "It's good to know you keep Joe's secrets. I asked you not to tell him about my miscarriage."

He sat up on the sofa and made a grab for her which she sidestepped. "C'mon, babe, don't be all… "

She sat down in the chair opposite him. "I'm not all anything except wishing you'd be honest."

"I didn't promise not to tell him."

"You led me to believe you wouldn't." She gestured to Sam's picture on her desk. "You also pretended not to know Sam was my husband."

"If it doesn't make a diff, what's it matter?"

Seeing that Joe had been right, the truth wasn't in Colton, she changed the subject. "You mentioned Joe's father. Do you ever wonder about yours?"

"Nah. I knew who my mom was and lotta good that did me. Grandfather and Pet were our parents." He raised his shirt a few inches and pinched his new layer of flab. "Can you believe this?" Distracted, he asked, "Did Joey behave?"

"Mostly." She went to check on the coffee pot. "For your information, we're resurrecting Kitty Quinn."

He sprang to his feet, dazzling her with a smile, his dreamy eyes dancing. "That's exactly what I was hoping would happen. You're editing?"

"Who else? I'm calling him on Monday with my first set of notes."

"Don't tell him you've seen me. He's in Atlanta and he'll blow a gasket about me sneaking off set."

"If he's that close, he might just show up and catch you."

"Nah, he never mixes his business in Atlanta with anything."

The specter of a woman in Joe's life flitted through Kathryn's mind. "I'm not worried if you aren't. His Kitty Quinn has best-seller written all over it."

Colton swooped her up and twirled around.

"Watch the weight-lifting," she laughed. "I have a gift for you, too."

"A 'yes' to the premiere?"

"A challenge. I'll accept your gift if you accept mine."

"Uh oh, what is it?"

"A ticket to the Realtor's Christmas Ball."

"When?"

"Three hours from now."

Chapter 20

Joe snatched up his phone on the first ring. He had been so preoccupied with Wrenn's sudden lung infection, he'd failed to switch his cell to silent when he reached the hospital. Organizing his thoughts to deal with a call from Colton or Daniel, he was unprepared to hear Kathryn.

"Hi there. You said to call when I had notes."

He closed his eyes and held on to the lilting sound of her sweet voice like a drowning man thrown a life preserver.

"Sorry," she said into his silence. "I must have caught you at a bad time."

A respiratory therapist exited pediatric ICU and signaled Joe to go back inside. "Can I call you later?"

"Sure."

Kathryn hung up, figuring she had interrupted him in a meeting. She had spent every spare moment since the Christmas Ball working on his manuscript. Not initially drawn to the title *Daylight to Darkness*, she kept an open mind and made three passes through the manuscript: once for the story line, once for plot points, and once to see Joe through Colton's eyes. The suffering man behind the creative mind was there. Something within fueled his writing, not money and certainly not fame.

The phone had emphasized the husky edge in his voice and was reminiscent of his whisper at Blue Willow Inn. She found herself checking the charge on her phone, wondering why he was taking so long to call back, convincing herself that she was just anxious to continue work on the book. But there was no mistaking the thrill she felt when his return call actually came.

Saying that he was in a restaurant, he kept the conversation so focused on the book that Kathryn wondered if he was dining with whomever it was that drew him to Atlanta. She detected background conversation, clinking silverware, and a muted intercom. Even if he hadn't been in public, she couldn't imagine him moving around attending to personal tasks as Colton did while on the phone with her. Joe probably wouldn't, in a thousand years, flush a toilet in her ear. His voice echoed intermittently as if he was in a well, evidence of her being put on speakerphone while he made notes.

She ticked off the last suggestion on her list. "That's all I have for now."

A long moment passed before he said, "You can't imagine how this helps me, Kathryn."

She frowned. There was gravity in his words she hadn't expected. "It's mainly a global edit. Keep an eye on your opening and the end of the third chapter. Go through it again, and I'll clean it up with a final line-by-line edit. You've got a bestseller going here, Joe."

"If you say so."

He seemed distracted. Kathryn sensed he wanted to say something else, something that had nothing to do with the manuscript. Like Evelyn said, it didn't always have to be about work.

"I'll get on this as soon as I get back to LA," he said and abruptly ended the call.

Kathryn blinked. When might that be? So he was in Atlanta. It shouldn't matter, but she wished she knew what, or who, had such a hold on him.

Before she put her phone away, Kathryn called Dee. "Are you stuck at the office?"

"No, ma'am. I got my hair done, and now I'm about to go get myself a pedicure."

"Make me an appointment, too. I'll join you."

Arriving at the nail salon, Kathryn studied the kaleidoscopic array of polishes, found the one she wanted, and claimed the spa chair beside Dee. "Let the pampering begin."

She dunked her feet in the hot water and flexed her toes. Removing the scrunchie from her hair, she slipped it on her wrist like a bracelet and relaxed into the massage chair.

Dee scowled critically at her. "If that ponytail ever becomes a bun, you're in trouble."

"Don't start picking on my hair because you just gave yours the works. How are you going to manage high-maintenance hair after—what are we calling her—Fancy Nancy arrives?"

Dee smoothed a hand across her belly. "Her daddy can stay home, or he can put a car seat in his golf cart. Mama's gotta have her spa day. What polish did you choose? I'm trying a new one called Argenteeny Pinkini."

"You just liked its name, didn't you? I'm sticking with Sunrise."

Dee rolled her eyes. "Boring." After a moment, she leaned over conspiratorially, "Bet you can't guess what man we know wears toenail polish."

"Nobody. You-know-who gets manicures and pedicures but his nails are buffed, not polished."

"Ole hunky was a trip at the Ball. Not a solitary soul but us knew that paunchy man in the ill-fitting tux was him." Dee flourished her neon pink bottle in the air. "I mean po-lished. Who is it?"

"Nobody I can think of."

"I don't call him Joe Hollywood for nothing."

"No!" The word burst from Kathryn with such force, the Vietnamese technician clipping her nails jerked his hand away. "Oh, no, not you," Kathryn hurriedly reassured him.

Peals of laughter poured out of Dee.

"You devil," Kathryn scolded and snickered all at once. "Why would you say a thing like that?"

"It's the truth. Honest. Tommy saw his toenails when they were changing out of their golf shoes. He said Joe took off his socks and his toenails were as red as my roses." Dee ran the tip of her tongue over her lips. "Mmm, how kinky is that?"

Kathryn gaped. "I'd never believe you if it hadn't come from Tommy. That's a whole different side of Joe Butler, for sure." Kathryn started giggling. "I'm buying green fabric on the way home to stitch his profile onto Lydia's baby quilt." Laughing harder, she had to take a deep breath to get out the rest of her thought. "Maybe I should get Argenteeny Pinkini instead."

❧❧❧

Two aisles away from Kathryn's car, Phoenix sat in her van, ripping open a new pack of cigarettes and fuming with renewed anger. *Looks like you could keep your butt at home on Saturday. You run around all week.* Phoenix had been looking forward to hanging out at the cemetery, watching the estate. She and Colton were so connected, he didn't have to actually be there for her to feel close to him. *But, no! I have to tail you and watch you priss your ponytail around Beechwood Shopping Center with a million other Christmas shoppers.*

Narrowing her eyes, Phoenix filled her lungs with nicotine. Colton definitely had been at the estate over the weekend because the limo was there. She could only watch the front since she didn't dare go down The Lane anymore. No telling how many henchmen Joe had there now. They damned near caught her one night in smarty-pants' driveway, but she'd had to risk that. She had to put that woman on notice. As a reminder, Phoenix called her every few nights to deliver the same message telepathically. *Keep your grubby paws off my man. I can do a lot more than ram your stupid little car.*

Wrapped in her beige cardigan, she took a protracted drag off her cigarette and threw it down on the ground as she climbed out of the van. Ponytail had angled across the parking lot to a nail salon, so Phoenix went down the breezeway and sidled past the door. Her foe was laughing like a hyena with some bleached blonde. A wave of bitterness engulfed Phoenix. She had given up her time with Colton because this piece of trash wanted a pedicure. She glared into the salon. *You'll freaking pay for this!*

⋖⋗⋖⋗

Throwing a crocheted afghan over her legs and prettily polished toenails, Kathryn lounged in her big wing chair and tried to sketch a likeness of Joe's face in profile to transfer onto Lydia's quilt. Dee's tale brought to mind the time he jerked his bare feet out of the pond at the mere mention of snakes. He'd made an adorable Huck Finn with a golfer's tan, legs brown only as far down as ankle socks. Kathryn would not have missed polished toenails. No way. Likewise, Tommy wouldn't have mistaken such an oddity. Some woman must have hog-tied Joe or gotten him drunk. Why didn't he remove it, then? She raised an eyebrow. Maybe he did have a kinky side.

Phooey, she couldn't quite draw his nose right. Concentrating on not being attracted to him had kept her from paying attention to his individual features. She anchored her pencil in her ponytail and went to the computer. When in doubt, Google. She spent an hour, scrolling through images and following links to his production credits. Impressive for anyone in the tough movie industry, let alone a man in his thirties. She printed out a picture of his profile. It was actually the brow she had wrong, not the nose. His nose was straight and patrician. The brow was decisive.

അ**∂**അ

With Colton safely on location in Canada, Joe had planned on going to Athens, but Wrenn's health kept him in Atlanta. She had come home from the hospital, but she hadn't bounced back this time. He spent most of the two weeks before Christmas within eyesight of her while incorporating Kathryn's notes into his manuscript.

Despite his best efforts, Kathryn played on his mind. He realized she had grown much more important in his life than he should have allowed. He had even told her about sitting with Pet after her death. No one knew about that, not even Colton. Oh, how he ached to tell her about Wrenn. But that would dredge up Phoenix. Maybe he should mail his revisions to Kathryn and be done with it.

Anna had quashed his plan to give Wrenn a hand-tooled saddle for Christmas. His little bird wasn't fit enough to ride again, not yet. He delighted her with a new generation iPod instead and they passed a subdued but happy holiday, downloading music.

The evening of December twenty-seventh found Joe rambling around his condo, preparing to join the hubbub of post-holiday departures from Hartsfield-Jackson to LAX. He usually enjoyed the prospect of working at Bennetthurst, but he couldn't shake a hollow feeling. Not about Wrenn—she had slipped a notch but she seemed stable.

He yanked open the condo's refrigerator. Empty. He walked out onto the patio and watched the never-ending queue of incoming flights. His gaze eventually wandered past the lights, east in the direction of Athens. Turning abruptly, he whipped out his phone and cancelled his reservation.

Eduardo let Joe in the back door of Charlie's Corner at midnight. Another big empty house like Bennetthurst but he slept better than he had in weeks. He awoke to the aroma of biscuits fresh from the oven.

"I know you's the cereal type." Marleen said as he entered the kitchen, "but I gonna be mighty 'fended if you don't try my catheads."

"Catheads?"

"Biscuits big as a cat's head. Been a while since I could scare up somebody to feed 'round here. I gone fix it, and you tell me it ain't the best thing you ever tasted." As she talked, she pulled open one of her golden delicacies and steam rose from its flaky innards. Arranging it open-faced on a plate, she drizzled it liberally with syrup that was almost black. "This here's pure sorghum I bought side of the road up in the Blue Ridge."

Joe reached for the plate, but she brandished her knife at him. "Gotta have hoop cheese. And it gotta be the right temp'ature." She microwaved a thick slice of orange cheddar a few seconds and then nestled it beside the biscuit. Arms crossed, she gave a satisfied nod. "Now."

Joe took the plate to his laptop in the Florida room off the kitchen. While his computer booted up, he forked a bite of sorghum-laced biscuit and a cube of warm cheese into his mouth. He walked to the door and shouted into the kitchen, "Marleen! Make me about a hundred more of these, please."

She chuckled. "Uh huh."

Joe gobbled three biscuits while cleaning up his email. He arranged to Skype into the Los Angeles meetings he had ditched and then set his mind on Kathryn. Where could they get together to go over his rewrite? Her house, too intimate; a restaurant, too public. Maybe the conference room at Dee's real estate office or a classroom at the Georgia Center.

Marleen popped in to refill his coffee and collect his empty plate. Studying him, she said, "'Scuse me, but my biscuits ain't s'posed to make a fella look like a thundercloud."

"Sorry. Best thing I ever put in my mouth. I'm trying to figure out where I can hold a business meeting."

"What's wrong with your office out yonder?"

"Office? I'd forgotten this place even had an office."

"I clean it but don't nobody never use it. Probably 'cause you got to go way round the side of the house. You want me to get the key?"

"Yep. Let's take a look."

Marleen walked him to an unobtrusive door under a shed roof offset from the rest of the house. "I b'lieve this used to be a porch," she said, handing him the key. "I leave you to it. It ain't a very friendly sort of place."

Wood paneled and dominated by an antique roll-top desk, the room was otherwise furnished in ox-blood leather. A fresh scent of lemon polish hung in the air from Marleen's last cleaning. Pulling out his phone, Joe sat down behind what had likely been Charlie Morton's desk.

Slivers of light filtered through oak blinds and did little to soften the atmosphere of the room or Joe's mood. He dialed Kathryn.

"Hi there, Joe." Her voice held its usual lilt as it vied with acoustic guitars playing a merengue in the background. The music receded as she evidently distanced herself.

"Bad timing?" he asked.

"Guitar lesson in competition with you, that's all. I'm outside now. I've been wondering about you. That is, how you were getting along with Kitty."

"Rewritten and ready for your magic touch. Got time to stop by the Corner?"

"I promised to stay and lock up the Old Mill Village's library at six. I'll be finished tutoring by three, though. Why don't you come over here?"

Joe's eyes settled on a group of staid oils on the far wall of the office. They told the grisly story of an English hunt. "Sounds like a plan," he said. "See you at three."

Chapter 21

Even though writing wasn't Joe's first priority, Kathryn had expected to hear from him before Christmas. Especially after Colton made Dee's star-struck dream come true by going to the Realtors' Ball. Only Kathryn, Dee, Tommy, and the Whitlows knew the true identity of Ben Thomas, the plump, bearded man in the wrinkled tux. They had danced until their feet hurt and then adjourned to the Waffle House. All six crowded into a single booth to gobble pre-dawn omelets before Colton's Gulfstream whisked him back to Quebec.

Kathryn wondered how different that evening would have been with Joe. She said good-bye to her last student and went about shelving and straightening books, waiting for him to arrive. Stopping in front of the mirror to run cinnamon balm over her lips, she reflected on the genuine pleasure she had detected in his voice. He sounded as enthusiastic as she about working on the manuscript. Frowning at stubborn wisps escaping from her ponytail, she removed the band and pulled her fingers through her hair. It flowed prettily across her shoulders, and she considered leaving it that way.

She glanced at the window as cheers rang out from the parking lot. "*Tres puntos*! Three points!"

"*Suerte*, luck." Deep laughter signaled Joe had scored in the boys' perpetual game of basketball.

Kathryn hurriedly swept up her hair and secured the band before he opened the library door.

Joe thought her angelic, backlit by sunny windows. Instead of her ubiquitous tee and jeans, she wore a winter-white sweater set with a flowing skirt. A becoming shade of teal, the skirt appeared to be suede-cloth and, in his opinion, had just the right amount of cling. Halting strains of beginner guitar music wafted from a huddle in the far corner of the oblong room. A quilted wall-hanging harmonized with rainbows of books and art. How could he ever have imagined her in Charlie's depressing office? Joe felt like an abashed schoolboy, as he proffered his manuscript to her.

"Super," she said. "Let's sit here."

She pulled out a chair at a low table in the middle of the room. The rungs, backs, legs, and seats of the chairs were painted brightly in primary colors, and inscribed with words of encouragement and humorous sayings.

"Bit like Gulliver," Joe said, folding himself into one of the youth-sized chairs. He gave the table a thump. "My money buy this?"

"Absolutely not. You filled those." She made a sweeping gesture at the shelves. "Dee painted the furniture, Alex gave the computers, and I made the quilt."

"That was in your office in New York."

Kathryn nodded, surprised he remembered. "I made it for Sam. I would've buried him in it if I'd had the chance, but it looks nice here."

"Work of art."

"Thanks. I stitch stories like you write them. You're in the one I'm making for Lydia."

"A quilt? Me?"

"I'll show it to you when it's finished." She opened the envelope. "I can't wait to see what you've done with me this time."

"Less and less." He winked. "Kitty has become her own person."

Kathryn wasn't sure if his occasional winks were contrived or not, but she went a bit weak in the knees when he aimed one at her. She situated her reading glasses and opened the reincarnated Kitty Quinn.

He snapped his fingers. "Glasses!"

"Try these." She handed hers to him. "From the drugstore, but they work."

He perched them on his nose, tried reading, and nodded. "Thanks. And you?"

Already fishing in her purse hung neatly on the back of the chair, she said, "If we're lucky, I have a spare." Momentarily she held up a second pair, sparkly turquoise decorated with gaudy pink flamingos.

"Dude!" he said, taken aback.

"Dee gave them to me. Wanna swap?"

He shook his head, laughing.

They delved into the manuscript, dissecting text and rearranging scenes. After several chapters, Kathryn said, "You're throwing me off, grinning like that."

With pretended innocence, he said, "Like what?"

"Like a mule eating briars."

"Grandfather used to say that same thing. I'm just finding it hard to take you seriously in those glasses."

She plucked the plain brown frames off his face and handed him the flamingos.

He groaned but put them on, pushing up the sleeves of his pullover and buckling down to business again.

After the guitar teacher departed with his students, Kathryn became aware of being alone with Joe. Dark hair on his forearms brushed against her hands as they traded pages, jotting ideas and making corrections.

He shifted his lanky frame in the cramped chair and popped a mint into his mouth, making a sour face. "Nicotine lozenge."

"They helped you stop smoking?"

"*Mas o menos.*" He waggled his hand in the air. "More or less." Coughing back a short laugh, he said, "Addicted to these dumb things now."

"We've done enough for one sitting, anyway. Dee would get a kick out of you in her silly glasses."

He took them off and wrinkled his nose at the flamingos. "Confirm her view of me as Joe Hollywood, wouldn't it?"

"That's high praise. She only nicknames people she likes." Kathryn suppressed an image of his polished toenails and buried her laughter in busyness, gathering up the manuscript while he corralled their notes.

"I hadn't forgotten how good an editor you are, Kathryn."

"I'm glad you think so. I only see what you put on the page. Authors tend to leave a lot in their heads."

"Somehow you critique the hell out of my stuff without getting judgmental." He laced his fingers behind his neck and stretched out his legs under the table.

Kathryn liked this relaxed version of Joe. "That comes from my earthy upbringing. Daddy used to say everybody puts on his drawers one leg at a time."

"Good equalizer. Probably accounts for you accepting me and Benny as normal."

She reached over and lightly pinched his wrist. "Sure feels normal. One time I asked if the drawers rule applied to Uncle Charlie and Daddy said he doubted that old fool wore any."

Joe chuckled. "Poor maligned Charlie Morton."

"How can you possibly sympathize with him? He was so vile nobody would've spit on him if he'd caught on fire."

"Characters get stuck in a writer's brain, and he was definitely a character. Went round and round with him until I spent time in his office today. Figured out his story."

"What, pray tell, might that be?"

"Simple. Not being able to have Matilda drove him nuts."

She widened her eyes. "They were cousins, for heaven's sake."

"Therein lies the problem. That was a deal breaker in their day."

"Good lord, you're dark." She frowned out the window. "Only you could turn Crazy Charlie into a Heathcliff."

Joe chuckled. "Miss Bronte has no competition from me."

"Don't be so sure. Your Kitty Quinn will have quite a following. You were teasing earlier about her being less like me, but I sure do wish I was more like her."

He shifted the lozenge in his mouth and gave her a serious look. She waited, but he didn't verbalize whatever he was thinking. Strangely enough, the actor cousin was an open book and the writer cousin an enigma.

She brushed off his non-response with a sideways grin. "You just can't please some folks, huh?" She fastened the envelope containing his manuscript. "Kitty is about ready for the publisher. You ready to let go of her?"

Joe looked down at the table and rubbed the side of his nose. That same indication of emotion she had noticed before. "Nope," he said. "Not yet."

Kathryn went around the room, turning off the library computers.

"Don't suppose you'd be interested in a movie," Joe asked.

She looked at him in amazement. "You make movies, and you go to them, too?"

"Have to keep up with what the competition cranks out. Gotta get in a couple this week."

"I really would like to, but I'm meeting Dee and Tommy downtown."

"No problem, I screen plenty by myself."

Kathryn slipped on her overcoat and picked up a gift bag along with her purse. "Come with me to Dee's birthday dinner, and we can go to a movie afterward."

"Wouldn't want to crash a party."

"No party, just us. You know Dee will be thrilled. My car has a parking sticker for the historic district, so we ought to drop yours off at home on the way into town."

"Okay." He put on his parka. "Gives me a chance to trade this for a dinner jacket."

☙❧☙

Kathryn parked in the small lot beside The Last Resort, Dee's all-time favorite restaurant. Joe didn't make it two steps from the car. He was mesmerized by the psychedelic mural covering the entire side wall of the building. Joining him, Kathryn said, "I take it you haven't been here before."

"Helluva vintage piece of art."

"Classic '60s, beloved by all." They rounded the corner of the restaurant and found an overflow of patrons on the sidewalk waiting to be seated.

"Lots of those beloveds here tonight."

"Never fear, Dee'll have a table." She ducked inside when Joe opened the door.

A glass case featuring desserts caught Joe's eye. "Hey, isn't that—"

Kathryn shouted through the din, "You're not the first to appreciate Evelyn's cakes." Rather than yell, she reached back and grasped a couple of his fingers to steer him past the packed bar, up a step into the original dining room, and through an arch cut in a brick wall. Dee and Tommy sat amidst a throng of diners on the enclosed patio.

"Kathryn!" Dee leapt out of her chair, gaping like her best friend had developed a third eyeball. "You brought Joe Hollywood!"

Kathryn placed her hand playfully in the crook of Joe's arm. "So I did."

Catching on, Joe covered Kathryn's hand with his and aimed one of his winks at Dee. "Happy birthday."

Dee sat down with a whump. "Well bust my bloomers and call me Clyde."

Dinner was pecan encrusted trout and beef medallions. Dee made a face at her glass of water when Joe ordered a good bottle of Merlot. She patted her middle and said, "Okay, Fancy Nancy, that's another one you owe me."

Joe's brow shot up. "A girl? Hadn't heard. Tommy, buy this woman a vineyard."

"Par-dahn me." Dee held up her wrist, sketching curlicues in mid-air to show off her new diamond bracelet. "He did very well, thank you."

Kathryn handed over the gift bag she had brought. "No diamonds in here."

Dee tunneled through the tissue paper and pulled out a baby quilt. Clutching it to her breast, she burst into tears.

Tommy leaned over and embraced his wife, kissing her cheek.

Kathryn grinned happily.

Taking a sip of Merlot, Joe looked from one to the other.

Kathryn smiled toward him. "I think she likes it."

"Like it?" Dee blubbered. "*Hopes and Dreams*. Oh, Kay, you gave me *Hopes and Dreams*! Look, Tommy." She held it up. "I stitched these squares with rainbows when I was ten. Kay made the ones with clouds. Old Aunt Tildy wanted to teach us how to embroider flowers, but we were stuck on rainbows and clouds. She called them our hopes and dreams."

Joe rested his hand on the back of Kathryn's chair and pulled it out when she went to hug Dee. Reseating her, he leaned close and whispered, "Outstanding."

After dinner when they were back in her car, Kathryn said, "You didn't know I had that up my sleeve, did you?"

"You set the bar high with your part of the evening. Pitt's movie better not let me down."

"Pitt? As in Brad Pitt?"

"Yep. His Plan B Entertainment group produced this one. Sony distributed."

Keeping her eyes deliberately on the road, Kathryn said, "Alex says you're planning to make your Kitty Quinn book into a movie."

"He ought to know better than to listen to Benny."

"Meaning?"

"It's not happening. I just haven't been able to convince my cuz."

"He can be very persuasive."

"Yes he can. I watch his back, my dear. It's you who'd better watch his front."

Biting her lip, she said, "Point taken."

At the multiplex Joe flashed his industry ID and guided Kathryn past the ticket windows. When he stopped to buy a large bucket of popcorn, Kathryn gasped. "Oh no! We're too full for popcorn."

He laughed. "Part of the movie mystique. You'll find room. Nosebleed section okay? I get a better read up there."

"I'm with you." She followed him to the topmost row of the crowded theater. Pulling down her seat and settling in, she said, "What do you look for?"

"Everything. Casting to set design."

"Special effects?"

"Not so much. Colton's niche is romance, not action."

"Which is why Kitty Quinn isn't for him."

"Exactly."

As the lights dimmed she glanced toward the projection booth. "Guess it's all computerized now, but I miss the old blue beam of swirling dust. I used to imagine a whole world in it, sort of like *Horton Hears a Who*."

Joe cocked his head and looked at her. "Would you believe that's my earliest memory? The projection beam in the screening room at Bennetthurst." Plunging his hand into the bucket of popcorn, he laughed at finding hers already there. "Told you so."

"I hate it when you're right," she teased.

The main feature began, pulling Joe intently forward, elbows propped on knees, chin resting on a double fist of interlaced fingers. Kathryn settled in and gave herself over to the story. She rode the waves of emotion, flinching and sighing and even sniffling.

On the way home, he said, "Really touched, weren't you?"

"I love happy endings. Were you too focused on the process to enjoy the story?"

"Research doesn't ruin the art. It's magic when all the variables come together."

"A bit like me being aware of editing in a book but still loving to read."

They traveled along in comfortably good humor. Nearing his house, Kathryn asked, "How long are you staying this time?"

"A few days. Never know for sure."

"Your schedule is dizzying. My life must seem dull to you."

"Nope. You said it best: there's beauty in being. You did right coming back here, Kathryn."

"New York seems like a dream now." She turned toward him as the Prius idled silently beside his front steps. "I did the things expected of me, but life got too heavy. I couldn't carry it around anymore."

"You were instinctively drawn home to heal."

"All I did was sleep." They soaked in the quiet for a moment. "It was weird, fatigue from doing nothing."

"How'd you get better?"

"Time, I guess. I hibernated at Dee's until my place was ready. Once I moved into the cottage, little by little, I seemed to wake up. Goose was a great therapist."

"Good as they get."

"Learn from me, Joe, and don't ever let your life get too heavy."

With a rueful laugh he opened the car door. "I *am* the heavy. Hasn't Benny told you that?"

Kathryn took a tinfoil packet out of her purse and handed it across the passenger seat. "A little heavier won't hurt, then. This'll beat the heck out of your nicotine mints."

Going inside, he peeled back a corner of the foil and groaned over the rich aroma of Evelyn's caramelized sugar on a thick slab of buttery cake.

Chapter 22

Kathryn subbed for Dee in the church choir on Sunday so the Lyndon's could have an extra day at their mountain cabin over New Year's.

Monday morning was filled with Phyllis's barrage of calls and emails, so it was well into the afternoon before Kathryn rounded up Goose for a walk. She was pleased to find Joe at the pond. Instead of writing, he stood beside the water, slouched to one side, hands shoved deep into pockets of jeans as washed and worn as her own. He wasn't handsome in the classic sense, but he had rugged good looks. The unkempt way his hair curled at the nape of his neck was especially appealing. She did exactly as Dee had long ago predicted. She squinted.

Joe seemed lost in thought and didn't notice her until Goose romped up to him. He turned and waved, but his eyes weren't smiling.

"Sorry to interrupt your train of thought."

"Thinking about Dee. How emotional she got the other night."

"Yes, I should have given her the quilt at home. I forgot what a number pregnancy does on hormones."

He squared off at Kathryn with an intensity that caught her by surprise. The expression on his face was almost angry. "That quilt was yours, Kathryn. You can't give up your hopes and dreams, not even symbolically."

She averted her gaze out across the pasture. His conclusion was correct. As a young girl she had planned the *Hopes and Dreams* quilt to use one day with her own baby.

She cleared away the knot that had formed in her throat. "My hopes and dreams are safe with Dee. She'll give them back should I ever need them." The dogs sailed off into the woods, barking uproariously at the white tail-flip of a deer. Watching them go, Kathryn asked, "Who owns Yankee? You or Colton?"

"She belongs to both of us. What's his is mine."

"She seems more bonded to you."

"Benny is wishy-washy. Dogs need boundaries."

"How'd she get her name?"

"Baseball."

Kathryn laughed. "I should have known. Those old Y chromosomes."

He drew back in mock surprise. "Ridicule from one who calls her dog Goose?"

"Not my choice," she protested. Kicking at a loose stone, she picked it up and skipped it into the pond. "That was already his name. I kept guessing until he answered to it."

"Uh-huh."

She was aware of Joe watching her as she flung another stone. When she dropped her shoulder, he reached out and touched her arm.

"That's your story?"

A light breeze crossed the pond and cooled the sweat breaking out on Kathryn's neck. "And as they say, I'm sticking to it," she said, her voice growing small.

"You do that." He smoothed his palm down her windbreaker sleeve and interlaced his fingers with hers.

Kathryn caught her breath, but she didn't pull her hand away.

He leaned in and gently touched his forehead to hers.

Her hand came up almost involuntarily and cupped the side of his jaw as she met his gaze. What she read in his eyes sent slow, melting warmth down her spine.

A deep ache Kathryn hadn't felt in a long time coursed through her. Joe pulled her into a kiss. Closing her eyes, she floated with him on the current that connected them.

She felt like she might faint. Or explode. She matched him kiss for kiss and moan for moan, but when he staggered, pinning her roughly between him and a tree, she became aware of his ferocity. He seemed to realize it, too, and reined himself in letting his lips play gently on hers. Wrapping her in his arms, he buried his face in her neck. She felt his pulse gradually slow from full gallop.

At length he raised his head and gazed into her eyes. "You were saying," he whispered. "About the dogs?"

"I don't even know any dogs," she murmured.

Watching a languid grin ease his lines of habitual gloom, Kathryn relished his rough, staccato laugh.

He placed a gentle kiss on the side of her smile and tugged at the band falling out of her disheveled ponytail. Recoiling slightly, she reached back and pushed his hand away. Finger-combing her hair, she stepped to the side and twisted the band back into place. "What are we thinking?"

He cleared his throat, a hesitant look on his face.

Kathryn's core values were in conflict. The boundary of honesty and fidelity had never been so indistinct. Colton was talking marriage, and here she was falling for the

most important person in his life. Reaching up, she traced
Joe's dark eyebrows and read the intensity of his desire in
his eyes. Her fingertips ran across the waves at his temples and lingered on the boyish curls at the nape of his
neck.

Eventually she broke the silence. "You'll have to
handle Colton."

Standing tall again, he rested his chin on top of her
head. She couldn't see his face, but she could feel the
tension in him.

He tipped up her chin and kissed her again—much
slower this time and filled with promise—before he put
an arm around her shoulder and turned her toward home.

She hugged him as they walked. He unlatched the
gate and kissed her as she passed through. Closing it, she
kissed him. At her mailbox, they kissed again.

Reluctantly pulling away, she said, "I have a class to
teach."

He groaned.

"And I also promised to tutor a French woman."

"Of course, you did." He winked at her. "Off with
you, tease!"

಄಄಄

A knock on Kathryn's cottage door Tuesday morning
heralded New Year's Eve, but standing on her porch was
Colton not Joe. She was too astonished to speak.

"I don't have any scenes for two days," Colton announced and grabbed her in a bear hug.

Kathryn's head reeled. She stammered, "H—have
you talked to Joe?"

Colton's sandy brows bunched into a frown, and he
released her. "If you consider him biting off my head to
be talking."

"Wh—why?" Why indeed? Why was Colton at her door and not Joe?

Colton shrugged. "Y'know. One of his moods. Glad he was gone by the time I got here. Cardinal sin for me to leave a shoot."

"So—so you didn't really talk. Where'd he go?"

"I dunno." He planted a kiss on her forehead. "Let's me and you kick off the New Year by getting hitched."

Kathryn was too flustered for his silliness. She went to set up the coffee pot so he wouldn't read her confusion. Her cheeks burned, and she felt like a fool. After Joe got hot and bothered yesterday, had he run off to whoever he kept, wherever he kept her? Stifling an urge to scream or cry, Kathryn suddenly wanted to run away. She went back to Colton and gave him a mighty hug. "Let's take your convertible to the mountains, spend New Year's Eve with Dee and Tommy."

"Hey, that sounds great. But—" He patted his midsection. "—no mountain hikes for this fat boy. Howard knew what he was talking about, Kay. See? Thirty pounds does make a difference. I can feel the character, like I've stepped into his skin."

Kathryn couldn't help smiling. His unbridled self-absorption was quite dear.

e/oe/o

Dee stowed her collards and black-eyed peas as soon as she heard Colton was coming. Her cozy mountainside kitchen had morphed into an Italian eatery by the time he and Kathryn arrived.

"When that movie comes out," Dee declared, "I want credit for helping turn hunky monkey into chunky monkey."

"You got it, little mama." Colton gave her a smooch

and a once-over. "I'm not the only one getting big in the middle."

"She's cooking me up a little Matilda," Tommy said and laughed when Dee stuck out her tongue. He clapped Colton on the shoulder. "Come on, man. I've got the game on in the basement."

"Give him a beer," Dee called after them.

Over their noisy clomping down the stairs, the women heard Colton say, "Gimme two. I got the gut for it. That's for sure."

Dee turned to Kathryn in amazement. "He looks so different!"

"Isn't he funny? I've never seen anybody so happy about gaining weight."

"Here y'go, Gal Pal." Dee lobbed a bathing suit through the air. "Hot tub and wine time. Fancy Nancy won't allow me either, but I'll be out in a minute to keep you company."

"I'm glad you're having a girl, but if you don't stop calling her that, poor little thing is going to get stuck with it."

"Beats the heck out of Matilda." Dee laughed and went to check the lasagna in the oven.

Kathryn donned the suit and sank gratefully into the bubbling hot tub. "Ohhh, yesss." Sipping Pinot Grigio from a goblet, she wouldn't have been surprised to find her lips as bruised from Joe's fierce kisses as her feelings were. Remembering, she completely missed the soul-soothing view of the misty ridge beyond the hot tub alcove.

Dee came out and kicked off her shoes before flopping into a cushiony chair. "Gimme the scoop."

"What do you mean?"

"Duh? Am I making up one room or two tonight?"

"Two."

"One of these days—"

"Don't start, Dee. I'm not in the mood."

"I'm just saying…"

&

Joe eased out of Wrenn's bedroom and disconnected his laptop from the charger. He added a stick of gum to one he was already chewing and stewed over the previous night's aborted call to Colton. The first thing out of his cousin's mouth had been, "How's my Kay?" His stress on the pronoun gutted any intention Joe had of expressing his own feelings. He couldn't recall his comeback—something deliberately ugly and mean.

Admonishing himself to remain calm this time, he dialed Colton's phone. Daniel answered and hedged about putting Colton on. Joe said, "I'm not going to like it, am I?"

"No, but there was no stopping him. We're in Athens."

"So he's down The Lane?" Joe couldn't bring himself to say her name.

"More like up the road. In Blue Ridge with her and the Lyndon's."

Joe leapt to his feet. "Without his phone? Dammit to hell, Daniel!"

"No sweat," the big man rumbled. "I sent Eduardo up that way. He has good instincts and knows what to do if reporters show up. Hank is set to fly us back to Quebec first thing in the morning."

"Flying in and out of Athens is too damn easy."

"Yeah, but this trip gives me a chance to boot his coke-head wardrobe chick. I'm just glad he's after sex and not drugs."

"Sex *is* his drug."

Joe sat motionless for so long after he hung up that his laptop went into hibernation. Yes, he was thankful Colton didn't fool around with drugs. And if Daniel took care of the wardrobe girl, Joe wouldn't have to go to hell and back to buy his cousin out of his latest mess. But the philanderer's cozy sleepover at the Lyndon cabin was icing on a bitter cake.

Wrenn's illness had a way of taking her from bad to worse to better, like the flip of a switch. Joe was accustomed to Anna calling as she had last night. Wrenn appeared to be responding to treatment at home this time, but Joe didn't dare leave her. He didn't dare go back to Charlie's Corner, anyway.

Benny had staked a claim on Kathryn, but Joe suffered no illusion about what he would have done if she hadn't had that class yesterday. The way she responded to him, they were already linked, and on some level beyond biology. He knew it and so did she. Distance was his only defense.

Joe's marriage may have been a five-minute unconsummated courthouse deal, but it was his reality. Any hint of an annulment and Phoenix would turn vicious. Wrenn was not strong enough to take anything that witch was likely to dish out.

He'd spend this New Year's Eve the same way he'd spent many before, propped on the floor beside his little girl's bed, her hand warm against his neck as he poured himself into his writing.

He summoned a smile, fastening Wrenn's pink therapy vest. "Time to shake, rattle, and roll."

As he composed a scene for Kitty Quinn, much like the one he imagined Kathryn in at the moment, an unbidden thought washed darkly over him. He closed his eyes and kneaded his brow.

He constantly preached safe sex to Colton, but the

man was a pig. Kathryn was as fine and rare as Grand-mother Pet's pearls. If she succumbed to his cousin's overblown ardor, Joe prayed God would protect her.

Chapter 23

Satisfied at the way the group at the cabin devoured her lasagna masterpiece, Dee led the way into the sitting room for the New Year's count down. Colton propped his feet on the stone hearth and leaned back against the armchair where Kathryn had assumed her favorite comfy position, legs dangling over one overstuffed arm, head resting on the opposite wing.

"We caught you on *The Tonight Show* last week," Dee said, finding a comfortable spot on the sofa.

"Yeah?" Colton shifted his feet when Tommy came in and pitched another log on the fire. "Jimmy is always fun."

Tommy joined Dee on the sofa, saying, "Dee thinks your whole life is fun."

Colton turned to look at Kathryn. "See? That's what I've been trying to tell you."

"Y'all don't encourage him," Kathryn said. "He spent the whole drive up here pestering me about going to that premiere in LA."

"Come on, babe, let Hank fly you out. Give Lila Manning some competition. You'll love Bennetthurst.

Hey, I kept my side of the deal. I went to the Christmas Ball."

"I know, but—"

"*But* my hind foot," Dee squawked. "Get your Aunt Sass on that airplane, Matilda."

"Hollywood is your dream, Dee, not mine. Anyway, I can't go off and leave Goose."

"He mooches off Marleen all the time," Colton said. "He won't even know you're gone. You convince her, Dee, and I'll get that little surprise you asked for."

Dee went from lounging on the sofa with her husband to hopping all over the room like a pregnant cricket. She leaned down and kissed the top of Colton's head. "You dee-licious man, I knew you would!"

Tommy threw Kathryn a questioning look. "What?"

She shrugged. "No clue."

"Clue, clue. Here's a clue." Dee struck a Victorian pose and quoted: "It is a truth, universally acknowledged, that a single man in possession of a good fortune must be in want of a wife."

"*Pride and Prejudice*," Kathryn said.

Dee squealed. "Can you believe it? He's getting me an autographed picture!"

Tommy came off the sofa and grabbed his wife. "I should've known, Mr. Darcy again. Damn Colin Firth can't have my wife. She may be drooling over him, but she's having my little Matilda." Laughing and singing an off-key "Olde Lang Syne" they linked arms and withdrew to their bedroom.

Staring into the fire, Colton said, "A Bennett orphan can ruin his life being in want of a wife too soon."

Puzzled, Kathryn leaned toward him. "What does that mean?"

"Joey. Back when he was young and stupid."

"Oh." She caught her breath and frowned. "I didn't

know Joe had ever been married. When did he get divorced?"

"He's not."

"Not?"

Colton turned and pulled her out of the chair into his lap. "Let's me and you welcome the New Year."

Kathryn was in the habit of turning Colton's romantic overtures into brotherly bouts of play, but the news of Joe's marriage so stunned her that she had no resistance. She needed Colton to kiss away the memory of explosive, secretive, *married* Joe.

Colton hesitated as though waiting for her objection. When none came, he stretched out on the floor with her in his arms and kissed her. Long, deep, and, in Kathryn's opinion, sloppy. Kissing Joe had been exciting, passionate, but this—it completely turned her off.

"Mmmm." Colton trailed kisses down her neck and released the top button of her blouse.

With a bit of redirecting, she pulled him into another series of kisses.

His hands strayed again, and he flicked his tongue in her ear. "Come on, Kitty," he whispered.

Kathryn sat upright. "What did you call me?"

He reached for her. "Mmmm?"

"Stop it, Colton. We aren't doing this."

He sat up, looking confused. "For real?"

Leaving him, she went to her room. She knew what *real* felt like.

ເຂເ

Making a daybreak departure to get Colton back in the air, Kathryn tiptoed down the hall and tapped on his door. He opened it wide and beckoned her to examine the room. "See what you think about this."

Kathryn peered in and saw that he had put the room back exactly like he found it, as if no one had slept there at all.

"You think it'll fool Dee?" he asked.

She raised a finger to her lips and sneaked him out of the house before saying, "Is the famous Mr. Bennett worried about his image?"

"Cold showers aren't usually part of his shtick."

Once they were in the car, she put her hand on his arm. "Listen, I'm sorry about that."

He leaned over and kissed her cheek while she fastened her seatbelt. "Methinks one of these days it'll be different."

"Methinks we'd better hurry, or Daniel is gonna whip your big-ole butt."

☙❧

On a red-eye from Atlanta to Los Angeles, Joe glimpsed a text from Daniel—their highest priority code—just as a flight attendant insisted his phone be powered off for landing. He barely waited for wheels to touch tarmac before firing it up again and calling the big guard.

"Bit of a snag," Daniel said, "but I got my eyes on him."

"What snag?"

"Listen," Colton broke in, obviously commandeering Daniel's phone. "It's no big deal. We're on our way to the airport, Athens to Quebec, no prob."

"Big deal or not, exactly what's going on?"

"Porsche hit a little patch of ice, that's all."

"And…"

"Slid off the road, nothing but curves up there. Like a roller coaster. Yee-Haa! Not a scratch on me."

"What about your passenger?"

"Airbag hit her kinda funny. She's not very tall, y'know. She might have a little concussion."

"Give me Daniel."

"She's okay."

"You don't know that! Give the phone to Daniel."

Daniel came back on the line. "EMT's said she looked okay, but they took her to a local hospital for observation. Gainesville, I think."

"You just left her? By herself?"

"Eduardo's up there seeing to the car, and I called the Lyndon's."

"I'll talk to Eduardo. I don't want to hear from you again until you have my stupid-ass cousin back on set." Joe disconnected and called Eduardo. "You with Colton's car?"

Eduardo hesitated. "I am sorry, but I am not."

"Where are you?"

"The lady was alone. I followed the ambulance to the hospital."

Joe exhaled. The man did indeed have good instincts. "You did right."

"A tow truck will get the car."

"To hell with the car. Stay where you are and let me know what the doctor says."

Joe had arrived at Bennetthurst before he heard from Eduardo again.

"It is well," Eduardo said. "Miss Dee and Doctor Lyndon have taken Miss Kathryn to their house. She will stay the night there and go home tomorrow."

"No concussion then."

"Only a black eye."

Joe winced.

"But," Eduardo added, "it is very pretty on her."

ACT ON THE HEART

Joe smiled. "I bet it is. You on the way back to Athens?"

"After I arrange for the car."

"Sell it for scrap, fax me the paperwork. I need you at Charlie's Corner. You know that old gazebo at the service drive off The Lane?"

"Under the kudzu?"

"Yep. Clean it up and see if you can make a guardhouse out of it. It's a good location for you to keep an eye on things. Trouble follows Colton and I don't want Kathryn getting hurt again."

"She will not like being watched."

"Tough."

⋐⋑⋐⋑

"You didn't have to come help me pack, Dee. I've had all week to keel over if I was going to. You always said I was hard-headed."

"You are that. I don't know what changed your mind about the premiere, but aren't you glad you're going?"

"I probably shouldn't go. Colton probably ought not to go himself."

"Why not?"

"The movie he's shooting in Canada is behind schedule. Livelihoods depend on films coming in on time and within budget."

"Eww, don't make him all human and ruin it for me," Dee scoffed. "Let's eat. I can't stand smelling those omelets a minute longer."

"Since when is Covered and Smothered on a prenatal diet?"

"Gal Pal, I might eat mine and yours."

Kathryn picked up both their plates and brought them into her family room. "Oh, Dee, I can't believe we're going to have a little Fancy Nancy to take to the Waffle House."

"I know," Dee giggled. "How soon do you think we can start polishing her toenails? Let's watch *Devil May Care* while we eat."

"Again?" Kathryn started the DVD and sat down on the sofa next to Dee. "That must be your all-time favorite Colton movie."

"It definitely has the best love scene." Dee pressed pause and swooned back into the sofa. "Puh-lease! If that man isn't the hunkiest monkey ever, I'll pay for lying."

Kathryn involuntarily wrinkled her nose. "He is on screen."

"What's that about? What kind of kisser is he?" Dee suddenly reverted to an old girlhood game. "Describe it in one word."

Kathryn pursed her lips in thought before replying, "He's okay."

"Okay?" Dee screwed up her face. She took her dish to the kitchen for a second helping, then came back saying, "Well, ex-cu-use me for expecting a helluva lot more than just okay."

"Technically he's perfect, but I swear, Dee, it's all for show. He puts more feeling into thanking me for a sandwich. He wanted you to think he ravaged me at the cabin New Year's Eve."

Dee cut her eyes over at her friend. "He's gotta do more than spread up a bed to fool me, Matilda. I was hoping for a few fireworks for you, though."

"I'm almost thirty-three, Dee. My time for fireworks has passed."

"Gal Pal, have you ever had fireworks?"

Joe's image swam out of nowhere. Kathryn could almost smell him and feel the minty tingle of his tongue. He was everything Sam had been, plus something else.

Joe was pyrotechnic. She gave Dee a lopsided grin. "I have, actually."

"Then why would you settle for less? I'm the one who's star-struck. Not you."

"If you must know, my Mr. Fireworks is already married."

"Tell me it's not that jerk Steve Overby."

"Get real." Kathryn rolled her eyes. "It's that jerk Joe Butler."

"Joe? Married? Are you sure? Tommy would've told me if he knew."

"Joe is definitely married, whether he acts like it or not. Ever since he was young and stupid, Colton said."

"Well," Dee huffed, "old and wise could change that, if he wanted to."

"Yeah. Maybe."

Dee narrowed her eyes and crossed her arms. "All the time running off at the drop of a hat, that man can just take his painted toenails on out of here. We won't be thinking about him anymore."

Chapter 24

By the time Kathryn reached Los Angeles for Colton's January fourth movie premiere, she had gone from panic to calm and back a dozen times. She had dilly-dallied about going until Colton told her Joe wouldn't be there. Daniel took her from the airport straight to Bennetthurst. The lump in her throat subsided when the mansion at the end of the palm colonnade turned out to be less grand than she had imagined. Even with the fountain out front, the two-story stone structure with its three-story turret in the middle struck her as an overblown house of the seventies.

Once inside, she heard Colton's voice bouncing around the open foyer. Nailing his location to the second floor, she ascended the gently curved staircase. Yankee bounded up with Kathryn, and Colton met her with a hug on the top step.

"I've got a surprise in Pet's dressing room." He whisked her along the open balustrade into a suite at the end.

"Lord," she said, "I hope it's a fairy godmother."

"You got that right by half, Cinderella," a male voice floated out from behind a rack of evening gowns.

"This is Nicky Forrester, babe. He dresses me, has his own design house. You'll be red carpet ready in an hour."

Instead of shaking the hand Kathryn offered, Nicky lifted it above her head and walked around her in a circle. "Size six," he appraised and started shifting hangers up and down his rack of ball gowns. Apparently Kathryn's trusty green Chanel was not destined to leave the confines of its garment bag.

"Prepare to be amazed," Colton said. "He's a wizard."

Nicky double-snapped his fingers at Colton. "Out! Go dress your handsome bod. And take that canine with you." He motioned to an assistant. "Carole, get this adorable creature showered." Kathryn followed Carole toward an inner room while Nicky stepped to the door of the suite and shouted over the balcony, "Daniel! We need an energy drink up here."

Bound into a strapless bustier with a thigh-high slip attached, Kathryn was returned to the middle of the dressing room where Nicky had her step into one dress after another. "We must hit exactly the right note," he fretted. "And you must say 'I'm wearing Nicky Forrester' every time someone sticks a microphone in your face."

Daniel came to the door, deposited a silver tray on a tea table, and disappeared. Kathryn sipped from the tasty concoction he delivered and watched Nicky open a blue velvet box that was also on the tray. Nicky gasped. "Oh, yes! We will wear the opalescent A-line with these." Suddenly decisive, he snapped the box shut. "Sweep the hair off the neck, Carole, a chignon but loose, with movement. Keep the make-up fresh and light." He frowned and examined Kathryn's face. "You'll have to cover this bruise under her eye." He rolled his eyes at Kathryn. "How you got that, I don't even want to know!"

He switched out her shoes twice before settling on silver sandals with two-inch heels. "Sorry I don't have glass slippers for you." He removed pierced earrings from the velvet box and fastened them on her earlobes, then stepped back for her to admire his work in the three-way mirror.

Knee-length and uncomplicated, the dress was all about the fabric. "Ethereal" was the only word that came to Kathryn's mind. "How can I ever thank you?" she whispered—lest the spell be broken—and reached in wonderment to touch her hair.

Nicky slapped her hand playfully. "The woman wears the dress, *cherié*. It does not wear her." Leaning close, he lowered his voice, "Thank me by saying 'I'm wearing Nicky Forrester' every chance you get."

"I certainly will. I'm honored to wear a Nicky Forrester."

"And these," he touched the earrings reverently. "These are pure Harriette Bennett." A single natural pearl, a teardrop as big as the end of Kathryn's thumb, dangled from each earlobe on a slim chain of diamonds. Simple. Elegant. Before she could catch her breath, Nicky whirled her through the dressing room door onto the landing.

"Summon the pumpkin, Charming," he sang out over the railing. "She's ready." Ushering Kathryn to the stairs, he said, "My Cinderella, you may not be the most famous girl at the ball but you are definitely the luckiest."

Kathryn did not feel lucky when she peered down in-to the rotunda below. Both Colton and Joe, wearing Armani tuxedos and bemused expressions, were staring up at her. Kathryn didn't know which made her angrier—Colton for lying about Joe being there, or herself for believing him. She grabbed for the banister but found Nicky's steadying arm instead.

"Smile, *cherié*," he whispered. "They are in mortal fear of you."

Such a ridiculous notion indeed made her smile. Halfway down the stairs, Nicky called to the men, "I was going to say it's jaw-dropping time but I see you're way ahead of me."

Colton gave a thumbs-up and moved to a baroque wall mirror, fiddling with his cuffs.

Kathryn was aware of Joe's eyes on her. The energy drink churned in her belly, making her glad she had not finished it.

Nicky abandoned her beside Joe and ran to adjust Colton's sleeves.

Joe gave Kathryn a grim look of approval and bowed slightly. His unsmiling eyes were tense.

As much as she did not want his opinion to matter, there was no ignoring the beat her heart skipped.

Nicky dusted an imaginary speck off Joe's shoulder and air-kissed Kathryn at the front door. Daniel, looking star quality in a tuxedo custom-tailored for his hugeness, opened the limo doors. Seated between Colton and Joe, Kathryn felt bombarded by the double dose of testosterone. She wondered if they understood what an intimidating team they made.

Colton lifted her hand to his lips. "I'm not sure how I'll stand it, but everyone has to think you're Joey's date, not mine."

"Oh." Her bubble of safety burst. There was no safety with Joe. She glanced at him. His eyes remained steadfastly forward. She felt like a fool. Did he enjoy knowing how deeply he had touched her?

As the limo inched up to the red carpet, Colton ran the pad of his thumb over her knuckles. "Remember, this is Hollywood. All you have to do is act." The door was pulled open. He gave her hand a final squeeze, kissed her on the temple, and dove into his sea of fans.

She quelled an urge to throw herself into the cacophony with him. Daniel slid from the front passenger seat to shadow Colton, leaving Hank to drive Joe and Kathryn to another entrance of the theater. Joe seemed to suck the very air out of the car, preventing her from taking a deep breath. Kathryn felt light-headed as the limo halted the second time.

Joe popped a nicotine lozenge in his mouth and ducked his head at her. She frowned. What was that supposed to mean? The boyish nod, the meaningful look thrown from under his strong, square brow. Was he making fun of her? The car door on his side opened. He stepped out and reached back for her. His hand was not as cool and dry as she expected. Maybe he was nervous. Good.

Despite everything, the strength of his arm was comforting as spotlights blinded her. Without actually letting go, he posed her for a swarm of fashion photographers. She stammered Nicky Forrester's name as many times as possible before Joe drew her back to him and fastened her hand into the crook of his elbow. Feeling as if she could have been lost in the fray, she was grateful for him shortening his fluid gait and shielding her through the crowd.

As she took her seat beside him in the balcony, the fine cloth of his tuxedo jacket brushed her bare arm. Somehow it reminded her of working with him in the goofy flamingo glasses. He hadn't been faking enjoyment then. Or when he'd kissed her. Not unless he was a better actor than his cousin ever hoped to be.

During the lull while the theatre filled, Joe reached his arm around the back of Kathryn's seat and cleared his throat.

He leaned in close. "I need to tell you—I have complications."

Kathryn stiffened. How could he criticize Colton for telling lies when he lived one? Complications? Is that all marriage was to him?

"With you, I thought." His voice dropped to a low growl. "You know what I thought."

She pulled away from him, straightening her back, pretending to look at the crowd. "It doesn't matter," she said and slid to the edge of her seat to watch stars mingle into the auditorium below. Dee would have given her eye-teeth to witness such a spectacle. Kathryn felt beautiful, and miserable.

Her emotions arced when she caught sight of Colton making his way down the aisle. "There he is!" She joined the wave of applause, marveling at him in his element. Spotlights tracked him, and his face radiated from a huge screen on stage.

He greeted everyone with ease, nodding to studio execs, quick pecks that left women touching their cheeks as if they would never wash them again. "It's effortless for him," she murmured.

Joe noted Colton's arm around Lila Manning's waist and tried to will the bitterness out of his voice. "Yep. Grandfather personified." He stared at Colton's megawatt smile and then looked at Kathryn. The sway of Pet's pearls against the sweet curve of her neck dealt him a physical blow.

Colton meant to have her. Joe clenched his fist on the back of the seat where Kathryn's shoulder had been. Having her in his family and out of his reach was too painful to contemplate.

Before Colton took his seat, his eyes roamed the balcony. Joe saw him searching for Kathryn the same way he used to search for Pet. Playing to his private audience.

Joe had told Kathryn "what's his is mine," but in this case it wasn't true. His cousin, it seemed, was about to take the prize of their lives.

Chapter 25

Phoenix took no pleasure in Athens. A cold, drizzly Sunday morning was the pits. From her lousy student sub-let, she shuffled to the Five Points Waffle House to snag the entertainment sections from a stack of abandoned newspapers.

Colton's picture from last night's premiere beamed off the page. Ordering coffee, she lit a cigarette and transferred a fingertip kiss to his lips. Lila Manning clung to his arm, but Phoenix was used to seeing him with costars. They were nothing, this floozy less than nothing. She smirked. Colton wasn't even looking at smarmy Lila. Phoenix's grin gave way to a frown. He was definitely trying to find somebody. The camera had caught him, his sexy eyes scanning the balcony. The caption under the picture posed the question: Who is Golden Boy's Mystery Girl?

The paper shuddered in Phoenix's fists. She all but projected herself into the second shot, the one of him emerging from the limo. Did he kiss someone as he got out? The paparazzi said he did. Who? Phoenix was his mystery girl! If it weren't for the kid, she could have been in Hollywood last night instead of stuck in Athens, freaking Georgia. Coffee sloshed as she shuffled through the papers searching for more pictures.

"You want this *Hollywood Reporter*, too?" A waitress making the rounds with hot coffee stopped to wipe up Phoenix's spill and handed over the trade paper. "A lady comes in for breakfast on Sundays and leaves it here. She's an actress, used to be on Seinfeld or something."

Phoenix snatched up the paper and continued her frenzied search. In a fugue of fried onions, she came to a different photo, but it wasn't her beloved Colton. She narrowed her eyes. What was Joe up to? The press seemed to conclude he was escorting Colton's date. Pictured holding some woman at arm's length, Joe was showing off her dress and her figure, treating her like pure gold. Faced away from the camera, the woman wore her dark hair in an up-do to emphasize her slender neck and dangly earrings. Phoenix's ears roared. She felt as if a train bore down on her. Who the hell was that bitch?

Discovering the previous reader had left the front page of the paper folded to the back, Phoenix flipped the page over. A full-on head shot of the woman smacked her in the face. The press didn't recognize her, but Phoenix did. She glared at the picture of mystery girl for a full minute before soaking it with scalding coffee.

On the walk back to her apartment she decided to kill Kathryn. Phoenix grabbed her backpack and headed out, driving carefully at first, planning her moves. By the time she turned onto Morton Farm Lane, she had worked herself into a frenzy. Her van rounded the curve in Kathryn's driveway and fish-tailed to a stop. She clutched the steering wheel in a death grip and tried to bring the cottage into focus. More enraged by the moment, she slammed out of the van and stalked up the steps onto the porch.

Pounding her fist on the door, she screeched, "You aren't here, are you, bee-yatch?"

Utter silence deepened her fury. She picked up a pot of pansies and smashed it against the front window. Thick, old-fashioned panes held fast and the terracotta flower pot disintegrated. Emitting a piercing curse, she whirled back toward the door and snatched up the blue churn. She hoisted it overhead and crashed it down onto the brick steps.

In the distance a dog barked. She had forgotten about the mongrel. Mean, ugly SOB.

The dog cut off the curve in the driveway and raced toward Phoenix. She ran to the van and slammed its door shut just in time. "I'll show you!" she screamed and accelerated straight at him.

The beast side-stepped to the middle of the yard.

Phoenix cut the wheel and pursued him across the lawn. She rammed the concrete bird bath he dodged behind. When the basin sheered in two and fell on him, she laughed maniacally. By the time she backed up to make another run, he was nowhere to be seen. Screaming obscenities, she drove dizzying circles around the broken birdbath.

જ૦જ૦

Kathryn woke Sunday morning after the Saturday night premiere and became dreamily aware of her surroundings. Apparently unchanged from Pet Bennett's day, her bedroom was filled with classic French provincial furnishings. Gilded curly-cues were a tad pretentious, yet feminine and functional. Heirloom linens bore the Bennett monogram, white on stark white. Donning the spa robe she'd found draped across a boudoir chair, Kathryn studied an enormous watercolor centered on the wall across from the bed. The picture of Pet's boys at five or six years old, building a sandcastle, would have been the first thing she saw each morning. *And likely the last thing she beheld in this life.* Kathryn recalled Joe's solitary vigil at his grandmother's deathbed.

Drawn to the dressing table, Kathryn admired an array of small porcelain pots. African violets in variegated shades of amethyst against jade-colored leaves flanked a double picture frame. Surrounded in sterling, portraits of Grandfather and Grandmother Bennett shared knowing smiles. Phyllis had been correct: Colton was "the spitting image" of his grandfather. Blond forelocks waved across both men's brows with the same panache, and mischief danced in their lavender eyes.

Pet exuded a no-nonsense aura. Head cocked in an unyielding way, her expression was reserved and steady. Much like Joe's. The beautiful pearl earrings looked at home on the Bennett matriarch. Kathryn secured them into their box and wondered what the royal couple would have thought about her.

At last night's reception, Joe had introduced her only as "my friend" and given off a possessive vibe that quashed questions. He'd turned her away from a bald man who'd had the temerity to comment on her southern accent.

Colton had not come near her, but it wasn't for lack of trying. Whenever he seemed bored, he'd head almost teasingly for her, forcing Joe to move her across the concert hall. A wicked little game of keep away. With her as the ball.

Alex and Suze Whitlow kept her company for a glass of champagne. In their parallel universe they went easily from chatting with her to laughing with Sharon Osborne. Soon after the Whitlow's departed, Joe had escorted Kathryn back to the limo. Before she was settled, the rubber-necking crowd jostled him, and he fell into the car on top of her. Recoiling at lightning speed, he'd backed out, saying, "So sorry. I have a couple of people to see. Hank'll drive you home."

Kathryn sighed and snapped the earring box closed. Home! She was about as close to home as Dorothy in Oz. She brushed her hair and bound it into a low ponytail. Tuning in the rumble of masculine conversation outside, she crossed the room and pulled open the French doors to the balcony. Two wet heads, one glistening dark, the other golden as the sun, swiveled to look up at her from the pool area below.

Colton and Joe, both wearing swimming trunks, legs dangling in their heated pool, looked up at her. She felt as if she were Grandmother Pet from the first chapter of the Bennett biography, opening these doors to this same ocean view and opening her heart to these beautiful boys. Colton broke the spell by whooping the old boyhood challenge at Joe, "Last one to the balcony is a rotten egg!"

Joe reverted to a little hooligan along with Colton, and they scrambled across the pool deck into the house. Kathryn heard them yelling as they ran through the rotunda and elbowed their way up the stairs toward her. Yankee romped along, adding her racket to theirs. Joey cut through the dressing room, and Benny bounced across the bed, before they burst onto the balcony where she stood.

Kathryn held up her hands and yelled, "*Tie!*" before someone went straight over the railing. Laughing, both men collapsed into patio chairs.

Joe sobered first. "I haven't been on this balcony in ages."

"Me neither." Colton grabbed Kathryn and perched her on his knee, nodding toward the beach. "Pet used to watch the waves from up here. Hey, Joey, we gotta get those palms trimmed. So, Kay, what's your take on Bennetthurst?"

She moved off his lap and claimed a chair of her own. "It's lovely. When I saw your grandparents' portraits in the bedroom, I couldn't help wondering what they'd think of me."

"Ha!" Colton hooted. "Grandfather would've been all over you. Right, Joey?"

His cousin looked studiously toward the beach.

"I imagine your grandmother would have been possessive of her boys."

"Pet was fierce," Colton said, "but I could work her."

Kathryn eyed Joe. He met her gaze, a hard set to his mouth, but a soft light warmed his eyes. "She would have loved you."

Kathryn smiled wistfully.

"Y'know," Colton prattled on, "one of these days I'm gonna be up here watching over a whole pool full of kids."

"Children," Kathryn corrected. "Goats have kids."

Though not a muscle in Joe's face moved, she was somehow conscious of a thought silently shared. She was tempted to ask if he planned to populate his side of the house, or if he and his wife had already filled a pool of their own in Atlanta.

Daniel, his biceps bulging out of a sleeveless workout shirt, walked in and delivered a papaya shake to Kathryn for her breakfast. He handed the morning paper to Joe and tossed a towel at Colton. When a moment went by with no response from Colton, Daniel hooked his thumb toward the gym in the turret.

Colton groaned and got out of his chair.

"Benny, wait!"

Colton froze.

Joe leapt to his feet, scanning the front page, working his jaw angrily. "Look here." He shoved the paper under his cousin's nose. "Take a good look at what you've done!"

Colton raked his fingers through his hair and grimaced. "Uh-oh."

Kathryn looked at the paper and felt her face redden. There was a quarter-page enlargement of her from the premiere with the query—*WHO?*—superimposed across her forehead.

Appalled, she whispered, "That's horrible."

"Oh, that's just the beginning." Joe slapped the paper on the table and scowled at the horizon. His grip on the wrought iron railing rippled the muscles in his back.

Kathryn opened her mouth to speak, but Colton stopped her with a sharp shake of his head. The pall that descended on them grew worse with each passing second.

Joe turned to Daniel. "Tell Hank I want Kathryn in the air by lunchtime. Eduardo will meet her at the Athens airport and take her home."

Colton gave Kathryn a wry smile. "Welcome to my world."

"Go to the gym," Joe snapped.

Colton threw her a hasty kiss and left with Daniel.

Kathryn turned to Joe. "Don't I get a say?"

He shook his head. "You pack. I protect Benny, now you, too."

"Who protects me from you?" she asked, irritated by his brusqueness.

Myriad emotions played across Joe's face. "So you liked that little episode of being run off the road? Having your home stalked?"

She felt her face pale, the sip of breakfast shake heavy in her stomach.

"Are you ready to have photographers camped in

your yard? Want to run the gauntlet every time you step out the door?"

The way he spoke sounded as though he blamed her for this. Rising ire put a tremble in her voice. "I'm not afraid of your sharks. I don't want your protection."

"You don't always get to choose, Kathryn." He crossed his arms and jutted out his chin. "Are you never wrong?"

"Plenty. But I won't be reduced to a damsel in distress."

He whacked his fist down on the table. "I told Benny not to meddle in your life!"

"You're the one who meddled in my life," she spat. "What's he done?"

"He's courting the role of Kitty Quinn's husband as much as he's courting you. Don't you know that?"

"I—no." Confusion crossed her brow. What was he talking about?

"How's that make you feel?"

She reached back and tightened her ponytail. "I don't know."

Joe's gaze roved through the French doors into his grandmother's suite, then back to Kathryn. He tented his index fingers and thumped them against his top lip. With finality, he said, "Your world is perfect. You don't belong here."

☙☙☙

"Here's my suitcase," Kathryn told Daniel when he came for her things. "I don't know where my garment bag is."

"I got it. Nicky Forrester is sending his dress home with you, too."

"Wow. That's generous."

"You got him enough press to pay for a hundred."

"So when do I go?"

"Soon as Hank gives the word. Joe caught a flight out of LAX."

That was that, Kathryn thought. Joe was gone, and she was on her way home. "How does Eduardo Vasquez figure into all this?"

"He keeps an eye on things in Athens."

"Tell me, Daniel, am I one of those things?"

The big guard raised a cigar-sized forefinger to his lips and backed out of the suite.

Kathryn waited on the balcony, thoughts of Joe turning over in her mind. Either he melted her with a wink, his tanned face crinkled into that boyish grin, or he shut her out completely with an impenetrable mask. A married man had no right kissing her, certainly not in the unrestrained way Joe had. The mere remembrance brought an ache low in her stomach. She got up and paced around the table to the railing. Below a uniformed guard petted Yankee. Pool Kitty lay in the sunshine washing her paws. Kathryn could almost envy the cat having these powerful men to care for her, own her. But Kathryn wasn't the weakling Joe had met in New York. She'd worked hard to regain her strength and her sense of purpose. She wasn't afraid of his sharks, and he needn't spy on her.

Colton, all showered and dressed, cozied up behind her and nuzzled her neck. "Joey is pissed, but he'll come around. He always does."

Kathryn's voice was bleak. "He said you're more interested in learning how to play the part of Kitty Quinn's husband—my husband—than you are in me."

"Only at first, and I'm not proud of that." He spun her around to face him. "I don't want to play your husband anymore, babe. I want to *be* him."

"Joe says I don't belong at Bennetthurst." She looked

away as she spoke, but he tipped her head back toward him.

"Well, I say you do." Eyes sparkling in the sunshine, he smoothed a wrinkle from her brow with his thumb. "You have the distinction of being the only woman to ever sleep in Pet's bed."

"You have plenty of other beds."

"Don't believe the tabloids." He hugged her close. "Thank God I had Grandfather because I was born a bastard. A kid—excuse me, child—shouldn't grow up without a dad."

She pulled away. "What about Joe?"

Colton looked startled. "What do you mean?"

Eyes glistening, she whispered, "How does Joe feel—about us?"

Colton swung a jubilant arm around her shoulders. "Joey loves us. You can count on that. I admit to the Kitty Quinn husband thing, but that changed five minutes after I met you." Alerted by Daniel whistling up the stairs, Colton said, "Dang, Hank's ready."

"I'm ready, too," she said. "Ready to go home."

He planted a kiss on the tip of her nose. "Promise you'll think about us, me and you."

Nodding, she took the blue velvet box out of her pocket. "Put these earrings back in a safe somewhere."

He shook his head. "Those are yours."

"You can't give these to me. They were Pet's, and they're worth a fortune."

"I didn't." He shrugged. "Pet left those to Joey."

Chapter 26

Colton rambled around Bennetthurst after Kathryn left. Having both her and Joe there with him had been bliss. The balcony scene had ended on a sour note, but the weekend had been fun while it lasted. He ate a sandwich for supper, toying with a discarded cigarette lighter of Joe's he found in a kitchen drawer. Why had Joe gotten so bent out of shape about a few pictures of Kay? Could be things were worse in Atlanta. Colton tossed the lighter back in the drawer and went to find Daniel for a game of racquetball.

Colton didn't wait for Joe to call him that evening as he usually did but initiated the call himself.

"What?"

Colton frowned. Joe had an uncanny ability to lecture him in one word. "I get it that you're mad about the shark attack on Kay, but she has to get used to that sort of thing. I'm gonna marry her, y'know?"

"She might have something to say about that."

"She'll come around. It'll be the wedding of the year."

"That's the last thing Kathryn needs." Joe sighed

heavily. "Benny, right now I don't have time to talk about this, but can you just slow down."

The weariness in Joe's voice told Colton his suspicions were right. "You in Atlanta?"

"I will be in another fifteen minutes."

"Okay. I'll report in tomorrow when I'm back on set." Hanging up, Colton wondered why Joe had taken a commercial flight when Eduardo had his Lexus in Athens. Easier if he'd gone in the Gulfstream with Kathryn and then driven his car to Atlanta. Colton went into Joe's study and sat down in his chair. A pretty little girl on a pony smiled up from a desk photo that was only visible from that vantage point. Colton didn't have a clue how Joe would handle it if he lost her. Colton shrugged off the thought. He'd be married to Kay by then and she'd know what to do.

∽∂∽∂

Jetting back home, Kathryn hadn't been able to relax enough to sample the snacks set out for her in the luxury cabin of the Gulfstream. The Hollywood duo took turns invading her thoughts: Colton and Joe, Joe and Colton—Bennett and Butler, Butler and Bennett. Their lives were insane and she wanted no part of either. Hungry once she was back on familiar footing, she suggested Eduardo stop at the Waffle House on the way home from the airport. Neither a Covered and Smothered nor Eduardo's reports of Baby José lifted her mood.

It was almost dusk as they approached the sanctuary of her cottage. Eduardo sucked in his breath, causing her to look up. Her mailbox was dented and skewed sideways on its post. They rounded the curve in the drive to see the yard full of flattened shrubbery and chunks of broken birdbath. "Did we have a storm?" Kathryn asked.

"No storm." Scowling into the shadows, Eduardo switched off the motor. "There are tire tracks."

Goose limped out from under the porch.

"Oh, Goose! He's hurt!" Kathryn's hand flew to the door handle.

"No, no, you stay. I check. May you give me your house key?"

Kathryn handed it to him. A wave of sickness washed over her. She had been so cocky with Joe, so irritated. Suddenly she understood.

Although she was five hours from the nearest beach, she felt threatened by sharks.

"Keep the car locked," Eduardo said.

Getting out he unbuttoned his jacket and walked toward the house. Goose limped alongside him, stopping midway through the yard.

Kathryn came to the unsettling realization that the young Latino wore a gun in a shoulder holster. Holding her breath, she watched him go through her front door. Before he reappeared around the side of the house from the back yard, she was breathing again, counting each noisy breath.

"All well inside," he reported. "Outside not so lucky."

She climbed out of the car and hurried to examine Goose. He nestled up against her. "Nothing seems broken," she determined. "But something happened to him. If he isn't better by morning, I'll take him to the vet."

Goose already seemed better as he moved a little more freely beside her, limping only slightly toward the front porch.

"Tomorrow, I repair your mailbox and the grass," Eduardo said.

"Thanks, I'd appreciate you fixing the mailbox. Don't bother about the grass, though. It'll grow back."

Reaching the steps, she exclaimed, "Oh, no, not Aunt Tildy's churn!"

She picked up a piece of the broken crock.

Eduardo followed her. "I clean all this away."

Kathryn looked around and found a piece with her great-aunt's fingerprints frozen in the clay. It was all too much. Angry tears spilled out.

Eduardo touched her arm. "You have a long journey."

His kindness threatened to render her incapable of controlling her pent up emotions. Taking a shaky breath, she said, "Thanks for getting me home. And you can tell Joe he's right. I don't belong anywhere but here."

Eduardo glanced at the yard and then back at her. "You will be okay?"

Kathryn nodded and forced a weak smile. "Thank you, Eduardo."

She paused to pet Goose, who had made his way up the steps and was sniffing at pieces of the crock, before she hurried into the house, locked, and dead-bolted the door. Stepping out of her world had been a mistake she would not make again.

She looked out the window and saw Eduardo taking pictures of the damage with his cell phone. He gathered up the flower pot and churn debris before he left. Later, even though it was dark and Goose couldn't walk with her, she ventured out to collect her mail from the damaged mailbox. She was startled when her flashlight beam picked up a dark car parked at the end of her driveway.

Eduardo called out, "I am here if they return."

"Thanks," she said.

Perhaps Joe had told him to watch over her. Perhaps it was Eduardo's innate sense of responsibility. Whatever, she was grateful.

Maybe he would catch whoever had hurt her Goose

and destroyed Aunt Tildy's churn. She would like to personally give them an arse full of buckshot.

⌖⌖⌖

Colton went to bed without calling Kay, deliberately giving her a little space to miss him. That usually got him what he wanted with women. He awoke in the middle of the night with a disturbing thought. Why had Joe said Kay didn't need a big wedding? What the heck did Joe know about her needs? Colton got out of bed and wandered onto the patio. Shucking his sleep shorts, he slid into the pool. A world of blue illuminated from below. The warmed water caressed his skin like the touch of a maiden. He would have found that arousing if the maiden in question hadn't been Kay. He had built her into a sexual fantasy. He got that. What he didn't get was why she wouldn't play along.

He swam lengths of the pool until his arms were too heavy to drag his body. Floating onto his back, he homed in on Pet's balcony, shadowed beyond the lighted palms. Like dressing a movie set, he placed Kay up there, veiled in a filmy white negligee. He smiled lazily, imagining the lilt of her laughter. Could he actually be in love with her?

His feet found the bottom of the pool as he remembered her hesitant "what about Joe" when he was working the kid angle right before she left this morning. Her reaction had caught him off guard. He'd been so relieved it didn't mean she knew about the Atlanta stuff that he hadn't thought any more about it. Now, though, he remembered how she'd said it. With feeling, poignant, like her "oh" in the limo at discovering she was his cousin's date.

Bubbles streamed from Colton's nostrils as he sank down to sit on the bottom of the pool. He had spent months egging Joe on about Kitty Quinn, amused by his objections. It didn't seem funny now. When Colton bought perfume for Kay last summer, Joey had said, "She doesn't wear a scent. You don't know her at all." Colton replayed their last big argument. His cousin rarely cursed, but he had let loose a tirade and ended up shouting, "She's not *your* Kay." The very next night, New Year's Eve, Colton told her about Joe's wife. He had let Kay think the marriage was a big-ass deal. And then Colton had tried to sleep with her. Tried to make her his.

He exploded to the surface and staggered out of the water. Hitting cool air, he wrapped up in an oversized spa robe and huddled on a chaise longue. Now that he thought about it, Kay and Joey had barely spoken to one another the whole time they were at Bennetthurst. They had made very little eye contact and Joey sent her back to Athens much too soon.

Colton frowned. Maybe she wouldn't sleep with him because she had already slept with his cousin. That would explain Joey's over-the-top reaction to her picture in the paper. Having their Athens hideaway exposed should've been a mere blip on Joey's radar. Publicity usually offset inconvenience. Pool Kitty jumped onto the chaise and snuggled against Colton's feet.

He lay back and closed his eyes. Cuz closed ranks when sharks circled family. Obviously Kay had entered that category, but was she an extension of him or of Joe? Colton curled onto his side and pulled the purring cat up under his chin. "I got to her with the having kids bit," he murmured. "I'm sure of that."

Monday morning Daniel woke Colton on the chaise longue. "No gym today."

He yawned. "Maybe a run."

"No gym," Daniel repeated. "We gotta be out of here in an hour."

"I'll be on the treadmill," Colton snapped. "Leave me the hell alone."

೮ೞೞ

Dee read every tabloid account of the premiere she could get her hands on, but restrained herself from calling Kathryn until Tuesday. "Was the skinny chick with Harrison Ford? George Clooney doesn't really have bad breath like Clark Gable, does he? How close did you get to Jennifer Lopez? That woman just glows. Did you see Matt Damon? If Colin Firth was there, I'll just die!"

"Believe everything you read," Kathryn kidded. "If you see it at the grocery store, it has to be the gospel." She laughed off Dee's inquisition to avoid her own bittersweet memories, but the flurry of questions stirred sensations in her that she couldn't share even with Dee. Joe's eyes had smoldered as she descended the staircase, making her aware of power beyond the strength of his arm. Then there was his shyness, known only to her by those clammy palms.

Looking back, she saw his controlled emotion, unleashed at the hint of threat to her. Why did he have to be married?

"Say what you want, Matilda," Dee prattled on, "you were bee-you-tee-full. As soon as I have this baby, I'm stealing that Nicky Forester dress."

"Exactly where do you plan on wearing it?"

Dee hesitated only a moment. "To the Waffle House if I have to! Listen, I'm sorry somebody messed up your yard. Does hunky think it has anything to do with him?"

"I didn't tell him about it, but I can't think of any other explanation. Joe must think so. He doesn't have my driveway staked out anymore, but Eduardo has cleaned up the old gazebo at the estate and just about lives there."

"Good. He can watch The Lane and you can get back to your routine."

"Exactly—oops, Dee, gotta go. Marleen is at the door."

"Wait a minute. How do you know it's Marleen?"

"Three quick raps followed by four. And Goose didn't bark. Good-bye, Mother Hen."

Kathryn found Marleen half-hidden by an outlandishly decorated heart-shaped box. "Good grief," she said. "Valentine's is a month away."

Grinning, Marleen shook her head. "You know what I say 'bout Mr. Colt—anything worth doing is worth over-doing."

"Well, haul that thing in here and let's see what we've got."

"Reckon it'll fit through the door?"

Kathryn laughed. "Reckon I won't if I eat that much candy. Come on, let's divvy up the loot."

eⁿⁿⁿ

Kathryn lingered after Friday night's class to swap email addresses with some of the students. When they left, she reached for her purse, hung on the back of her chair by the shoulder strap, but the purse wasn't there. She looked around on the floor.

No purse.

Getting down on all fours, she searched beneath the pleated skirt of the table.

Phoenix, who'd signed up for her class this session, came back into the classroom from the hall. "Is there *problème*?"

Kathryn stood up. "My purse is gone!"

"*Non*, it was there when we broke."

"At break," Kathryn said. "Yes. I only stepped out

for a minute." She looked on the floor again. "Surely no one took it."

"A man go in, but he return out *rapidement.*"

Outraged at the thought of someone stealing her property, Kathryn stormed out of the room.

Phoenix kept pace with her down the corridor. "You will, perhaps, need a ride?"

"I'm going to report this to security."

"But then you need a ride home?"

"I guess so." Kathryn was flustered to be without her car keys, cell phone, and all the other accoutrements customarily at her fingertips. She was even more flustered to find herself stuck between bothering pregnant Dee or getting a ride from weird Phoenix. The woman wasn't serious about improving her English, and she was prone to spurts of anger. "Thanks anyway, Phoenix, but I can call a friend from the security office."

"But you help me so much. It will be my *plaisir.*"

Somewhere in Kathryn's head, Aunt Tildy chided, '*Beggars mustn't be choosers.*' "Okay, I'd appreciate a ride. But first I have to report my purse."

"I get my car and meet you in front," Phoenix said.

Dwarfed by her oversized backpack, she skipped awkwardly toward the parking deck.

Kathryn soon found herself in Phoenix's van resisting the urge to wrinkle her nose at an ashtray brimming with stale cigarette butts.

In the herky-jerky manner she did everything else, Phoenix drove down Lumpkin Street to Milledge Avenue and headed out of town.

"I live about six miles from here," Kathryn said. "I hope you don't mind going that far."

Phoenix braked sharply. "I am going the right direction, *oui?*"

"Yes, I'll tell you where to turn."

"Do you live in Athens for a long time?"

"All my life, except for five years."

"It is nice."

"I think so. I wouldn't want to live anywhere else."

After a few minutes of silent driving, Phoenix became chatty. "I have not found suitors plentiful here. Do you have that *problème*?"

"I suppose it depends on the type person you're looking for."

"I would hope for musician, but they are not, how you say, so reliable."

"Well, you don't want that, do you? What brought you to Athens?"

"*Amoré*," Phoenix said dreamily. "Love, it is what matters."

Kathryn felt a pang of sympathy for her. "Did your romance turn out like you planned?"

"*Oiu*, it will. The time has not yet been right."

As Kathryn directed Phoenix to turn onto The Lane she noticed the old wrought iron gazebo. Now that it had been glassed in, the green light of a computer made it resemble a gigantic lantern.

"What is that?" Phoenix asked.

"Gatehouse for my neighbor's estate. Do you mind stopping? The guard will want to know who you are."

"The street, it does not belong to him."

"Try telling him that." Kathryn rolled down her window to Eduardo already approaching. "It's just me. A classmate is giving me a ride home."

He scowled at the dirty van. "Something happen to your car?"

"I had to leave it at the Georgia Center. My purse was stolen."

"Stolen?"

"Yes. My own fault. It doesn't have anything to do

with—" She squared her back to Phoenix. "—that other stuff."

"You could call me."

"I thought of that, but the only place I have your number is in my cell phone, which is along with my car keys in my purse."

From an inner jacket pocket, he produced another business card for her. As the van rolled away, she saw his iPhone flash blue. Texting Daniel? Joe? She refused to care.

Goose heard the van turn in at the mailbox and accosted it halfway up the driveway.

"Your dog, he is mean," Phoenix said. "What is his name?"

"Goose," Kathryn said with her usual laugh. "It's silly, I know. Silly Goose." She was surprised to see him bare his menacing yellow teeth. "He's really sweet. I don't know why he's acting like that. I'll go ahead and get out here, calm him down. Thanks for the ride."

"How will you get into your house?"

"Goose has a key." Kathryn crossed through the beam of headlights and held the dog as Phoenix turned the van around and left. Tension rippled through the animal's meaty shoulders. "Yes, Goosey. I see. It's a light-colored van."

Phoenix lit a cigarette as soon as she was out of the driveway. She sighed with satisfaction. Tonight's goal was to meet the devil dog, get him used to her. Good to know he was all bluff since she would be back soon. According to Rusty, her expensive spy in Joe's camp, the kid was back in the hospital and might not make it this time. Phoenix pressed the ball piercing her tongue against the roof of her mouth. That had to be what Colton was waiting for. Everything had been fine between them until she got pregnant. With Joe camped out at the hospital in

Atlanta, all she had to do was get rid of Mystery Girl.

She couldn't see Joe's watchdog in the gazebo, but she smiled and waved as she passed by. Turning back onto the highway, she cackled raucously. Stashed inside her backpack, the cellphone inside Kathryn's purse began ringing.

Chapter 27

The arr-das-city of someone stealing your purse," Dee raged as she drove Kathryn to fetch her car on Wednesday morning. "Nowadays you have to be on guard all the ding-dang time."

"I will be from now on. I shouldn't have walked away from it."

"Don't blame yourself. It can happen to anyone. Good thing you have a service key for the Prius."

"Assuming the car is still there. They may have taken it. They have the key."

"They were probably after money. You've put a hold on your debit card and cancelled your credit cards, have you changed the locks on your house?"

"I probably should."

"Good grief, Kay, of course you should. Get the locksmith my office uses. We rekey houses all the time."

Kathryn frowned down at her hands. "Okay."

"What else is bothering you?"

"I'm kind of creeped out by that Phoenix woman. Her van looks sort of like the one that tried to run me off the road."

"You said she was nutty. Tell Eduardo."

Kathryn's frown deepened. Telling him would be tantamount to admitting to Joe that she couldn't take care of herself. "I might, but it's no big deal. Phoenix just gives off weird vibes. Anyway, Eduardo is supposed to go to Florida to see his mother and Lydia. I don't want to mess that up."

"Is Lydia settling in okay?"

"Yes. She's back in school. She sent me another picture of the baby. He's all roly-poly now." Kathryn smiled. "It's a real gift to be able to enjoy babies again."

"Good," Dee said, patting her baby bump that had swollen to the size of a soccer ball. "Fancy Nancy's gonna need a godmother."

"And soon," Kathryn said. She craned her neck looking for her car as Dee drove to the second level in the parking deck. "I see it over there. That's a relief."

Dee swung her BMW close to Kathryn's Prius. "Trust your gut, Kay, tell Eduardo about Phoenix when he gets back."

"I trust Goose to eat her up if she comes around. Thanks a bunch for the lift."

"Fix me a sandwich. I'm bringing my locksmith out at noon."

∂∽∂∽∂

Dee supervised Kathryn's individual lock changes while Goose supervised the operation as a whole. Dee handed Kathryn a new set of keys. "You're right about Goose. My guy wouldn't have set foot out of his truck if you hadn't been here."

Kathryn stood trance-like at the kitchen window.

Dee raised her voice, "Has he ever bitten anyone?"

Kathryn jumped. "Who? Goose? Not that I know

of." She trailed behind Dee through the lintel arch into the front room.

Dee spied the gaudy, heart-shaped candy box leaning against the wall, half-hidden behind the trash can. "Hunky is serious about marriage, isn't he?"

Kathryn nodded and expelled an exaggerated sigh.

"Don't act so put-upon. Marrying a movie star wouldn't be the end of the world."

"Yes it would, Dee. It'd be the end of this world. My life may be too simple for your tastes, but I like it. I'm healthy, and I'm happy, two things that really matter. I'm not in some holding pattern waiting to find a man, or waiting to be found by one."

"Don't go saying you'll never get married again."

"No. There aren't any absolutes in this life. I suppose there would be a lot of advantages to marrying Colton. He's not perfect, but who is? I wish I could be in love with him, but there's a presence hovering out there on the fringe that won't let me."

Dee stepped over to the desk and tapped a brightly polished fingernail on the glass of Sam's jovial picture. "Well, it's not him, Kay. This man is standing at the head of the Be-Happy Line." She gave a sudden yelp and snatched a velvet box off the corner of the desk. "Did hunky already give you a ring?"

Kathryn lunged for Pet Bennett's earrings and snapped the box closed, pinching Dee's finger in the process.

Dee sucked her wound and deflated onto the sofa. "What the hell-o is going on?"

"You'll think I'm crazy." Kathryn put her head in her hands. "I don't know. Maybe I am."

"Okay." Dee sat back, adjusting to accommodate her growing baby. "How crazy are you?"

Kathryn slumped down on the ottoman.

Dee reached out and took her hand. "It's okay if you don't want to marry him. You know that. Right?"

"It's just—I don't know." Kathryn shook her head. "It's all so confusing."

Dee took the box away from her and eyed the earrings critically. "What do these have to do with it?"

A tear slid from the corner of Kathryn's eye. "I wore them to the premiere and thought they'd come from Colton. But when I tried to give them back he said they weren't his. Their grandmother left them to Joe."

"How'd you get them?"

"From Nicky Forrester. Daniel delivered them while I was dressing. Nicky was the one who told me they were Pet's."

"I see."

"I don't."

"Think about it, Kay—by not giving them directly to you, Joe avoided rejection."

Kathryn brushed away a tear. "Why didn't he give them to his blasted wife?"

"Ah, yes, the secret Mrs. He didn't bring her to the soiree, either. Perhaps he's ashamed of her."

"I hope not. If he has to be married, at least he should have somebody worthy of him."

Dee raised an eyebrow and studied the earrings. "Maybe these are an endorsement, Cousin Fireworks saying welcome to the family."

"Please stop calling him that. Anyway I took them to your jeweler for an appraisal. Matched natural pearls this size are so rare even he couldn't put a price on them. They're museum quality. The jeweler said Joe's grandfather must've commissioned them."

"Whoa, Matilda!" Dee handed the box containing the earrings to Kathryn as if it was a hot potato. "The only reason a man gives a woman a pair of heirloom earrings that valuable is because he's in love with her—and in this case he can't give her a ring."

Kathryn hid her face in her hands and cried.

Dee embraced her. "Oh, my poor, poor baby."

യെയ

Joe hoped when Kathryn decided to marry Colton that they would elope. He couldn't stomach the best man bit. Colton apparently loved Kathryn as much as he could love anyone. With luck, he might stay true to her, at least for a while. They would have children, a life at Bennetthurst. Joe paced around his Atlanta condo. He could almost write it. He would watch their backs and make it work. He fantasized about giving life a wicked twist if he lost Wrenn. He'd live at Charlie's Corner and become an anathema like old Charlie.

He picked up his cowboy boots, gave them a glassy-eyed stare, and let them clatter back onto the parquet. They didn't matter today. He laced on running shoes, fished a cigarette from the back of a drawer, and took it out on the balcony. Thursday morning. Two days since his precious bird had been moved from a regular hospital room to pediatric ICU. Seemed more like two years. So far this lung infection had been drug resistant. He slumped against the railing and felt like a husk of himself. He ground the unlit cigarette into a flower pot and thought about last night's conversation with Colton.

Still on location in Canada, his cousin had a litany of complaints—too many promos, not enough perks, some petty rider request unmet. "I'm trying to get in character, and you've got me busier than a Kardashian brassiere."

Joe had ignored his cousin's fixation. He pinched the bridge of his nose and stuck to his practice of not mentioning Wrenn. "On the flip side, publicity sells."

"They're dicking around with set sketches up here. I oughta be in Athens turning my peach into a fiancée."

Joe's head pounded.

"I gotta send somebody to get her a ring." Colton had left the hint hanging in midair.

Joe couldn't have been quieter.

"Y'know, Pet's earrings are a damn impossible act to follow. Why'd you go and give 'em to Kay?"

"Because." Kathryn's being had enveloped Joe. Soft. Serene. Safe. He was an idiot not to have gotten rid of Phoenix. Wrenn could have had a mother, Kathryn a child, and he would have had them both. He'd spoken the unvarnished truth, "Because, they're real."

Chapter 28

Dee Lyndon wasn't keen on having her Thursday afternoon sales meeting interrupted. Her assistant eased open the conference room door and waggled a phone at her. "Somebody named Hunky Monkey insists on talking to you."

Twenty sets of eyes queried their pregnant powerhouse. She waved them all out of the room. "Go sell something, gang. Make Mama proud."

Closing the door behind the last realtor, Dee yelled into the phone, "I guess you know a living, breathing hunky monkey has never, and I do mean never, called me. Are you trying to make me drop this baby right here?"

"Don't go doing that," Colton said.

"Well, lemme sit down. This has to be about Kay."

"Yeah. Any chance you can come down to The Globe for a little pow-wow?"

"You're in Athens? By yourself?"

"That's me, El Skulko. Look for the ugly beard."

On the way downtown Dee drove past two billboards featuring Colton's bright and sunny visage. The contrast of him lurking in a gloomy back booth of a bar was not lost on her.

"You weren't kidding about dropping that baby," he said when he saw her. "Here, sit on this side with me." He shoved the table up against the other bench to give her ample room."

"How did you manage to get away from Daniel?"

"Dan's the man. He's cool. And what Joey doesn't know won't hurt him." Colton sat in a half-turn near the wall, one knee hiked up casually on the seat. "Kay tells you everything, right?"

Dee's cell phone rang. Without so much as a glance, she switched it off. "I'm sure she doesn't yet know if you have any hidden tattoos, if that's what you mean."

"What I really need to know," he paused and smiled, "and that's a good way of asking—does she know if Joe has any?"

Dee grew as silent as her phone. Equal to her animation was her poker face. She recalled Kathryn's lukewarm reaction to making out with Colton. Kathryn hadn't said she wanted to sleep with Cousin Fireworks, not in words, but her reaction had spoken eloquently. As had his gesture of the earrings. Dee carefully removed the paper sheath from a straw and took a slow sip of water. At length, she met Colton's gaze. "I'm sorry, hunky. I don't think we can talk about this."

"I know you're loyal to the teeth, Dee, but this is important."

"I can tell it is. Why do you ask?"

He surveyed the sparse crowd in the bar. After a moment, he said, "Except for Kay and Joey my whole life is scripted. They're my reality."

His last words came out raw, almost unbidden. Dee was sorry the truth would not comfort him, but it was all she could offer. "I have no idea what Kay does or doesn't know about Joe's tattoos. What I can tell you, is what you already know—Kay will never sleep with a man she doesn't love."

He took the brunt of her words. From his gloomy countenance, she gathered he'd also heard what was not said. He scratched his bearded chin.

Dee watched the consummate actor, famous for the range of emotion that played across his face. He wasn't acting. His eyes lost luster and gained resignation. He was still except for scritch-scratching his fake beard. "That must itch," she said.

"Yeah." He patted her hand. "I hate to ask you to get up, but can you excuse me a sec?"

She clambered to her feet and watched him disappear into the men's room. He was gone a long time, long enough for her to start getting concerned.

When he returned, she scooted over to give him the end of the bench and saw that he was wearing a wide, beardless grin. "You can't expose your face. People will recognize you."

He waggled his sandy brows and smiled bigger. His eyes were fairly dancing. "You're having a girl, right?" At her nod, he said, "Unky Hunky Monkey got her a little gift."

Dee opened the Tiffany's box he thrust in her hand and gawked at the sparkling solitaire he had obviously intended for Kathryn. "You can't—" she gasped.

"Oh, I'm not done." He tugged her up from the booth. "How many times have you sashayed your cutie patootie around town with a living, breathing hunky monkey?"

He led her to the front of the bar, tossed his ball cap in the trash, and stepped out onto the sidewalk.

A nearby couple did an instant double-take.

Colton proffered his arm to Dee. "Game?"

With a glance at the gathering crowd, she placed her hand in the crook of his elbow and giggled. "You bet your Aunt Sass I am."

ᏟᏅᏟᏅ

Phoenix frowned at the murky pond water and then scowled back toward Morton Farm Lane. She'd had a story ready for Joe's goon, but he wasn't in the gazebo. She planned to park her van down by the pond, out of sight. But after she had driven all the way across the pasture to the very brink of the water, she could still be seen from the blasted Lane. She lit her next cigarette with the ember of the last and drummed her fingers on the steering wheel. *Where else? Where else? Where else? Think*! *It's happening. It's happening. It's really happening.*

Last night, right after Rusty texted about the kid being in PICU, Colton had called. Phoenix pulled the stolen phone out of her backpack and listened to his sexy voice again, saying he would be in Athens today. *Today.* He would've sensed she had this phone, just like she sensed everything about him. And he called her "babe" just like he used to. She kissed the phone and let out a delighted squeal. "Together! Today!" As soon as she got rid of the teacher.

She jammed the van into reverse and stomped the accelerator. Retracing tracks she had made crossing the pasture in the first place, she backed over the same section of fence she flattened going in. Driving a mile farther down the Lane, over the hill toward the dead end, she pulled off the road and parked up near the tree line. "Nobody worries about a broken down van unless it's theirs," she snorted, leaving the hood up. Shouldering her backpack, Phoenix struck out through the woods, unmindful of briars snagging her orange leggings.

The dog alerted as soon as she set foot in Kathryn's yard. He charged but stopped short of biting her. "Looky what I got for you, Goosey boy." Phoenix produced a fast-food burger, hoping to bribe him.

Goose didn't even sniff it. A ridge of fur down his back stood at attention. His nerve-shattering barks were unrelenting, exposing a mouthful of weaponry, and blasting Phoenix with his hot breath.

She threw the burger on the ground in front of him, but he ignored it. Speaking in an even, friendly tone, she said, "Your mistress says you're really sweet. You don't want to prove her wrong, do you?" He made a lunge which she parried with her backpack. "You're just trying to scare me, Mr. Goose. And you're doing a very good job." She inched around the side of the house to the back door. "Looky here, Silly Goose." She took Kathryn's key ring out of her pocket and jangled it. "This belongs to your mommy."

He lowered his head and growled.

Phoenix inserted the key into the kitchen lock and confidently tried to turn it. The deadbolt didn't budge.

An unpleasant growl rumbled in the back of Goose's throat.

She held the key up to the sun and squinted at it. Spit on it, rubbed it dry on her cardigan sleeve, reinserted, and tried again. Nothing. Beyond fear of the dog, beyond fury, Phoenix screeched, "That bitch changed the locks!" She whirled and flung the key ring deep into a holly hedge along the far side of the yard.

Goose dashed after the keys, dodging thorny branches, tracking Kathryn's scent. His attention riveted back onto Phoenix when he heard her backpack crash through a window.

He disentangled from the hedge and raced back toward the house. She had scrambled halfway through a kitchen window when he clamped down on her calf.

Red pain seared through Phoenix. She screamed and kicked, punching him with her other leg. Shards of glass caught in the window frame viciously sliced her as she struggled. Finally freeing herself from the dog's grip, she thudded down onto the kitchen floor, plastering her palms and knees with splintered glass.

Goose's continuing wrath filled the air. He reared up against the back of the house, issuing vicious barks that vibrated straight through the wall. Phoenix felt her head would explode. She tried to gain her feet but slipped, falling down again. Hard.

"Shut up!" she barked back at the dog. "You're gonna be one dead Goose!" Leaning against the table, she climbed back to her feet and picked slivers of glass out of her palms. She twisted down to inspect the wound that burned like fire in her calf. "He wouldn't have bit the crap out of me if smartass hadn't made me break a window," she grumbled.

Digging a roll of duct tape out of her backpack, she stuck a piece over a gash in her forearm. She limped through the house to find the bathroom. When she pulled off her tights, blood-soaked specks of glass showered down onto the white tile floor. Gritting her teeth, she washed the dog bite in the old-fashioned claw-foot bathtub. A bloody trail arced toward the drain. Too much blood! The tape was dangling loosely from her arm. She flung it on the floor next to her tights and rummaged for a towel to wrap around her forearm. Pressing it tightly against her waist, she shuffled down the hall to Kathryn's bedroom.

"I saw your stupid car parked at that sucky little library," she muttered. "Bring your butt home and you'll be history by dinnertime." Yanking open the closet, she searched through Kathryn's clothes and snatched the

Nicky Forrester gown off its hanger. "You won't need this," she sneered. Her eyes landed on the shotgun. "Well, well, looky what else." She dragged it out and threw it down on the bed. "Too easy for you, smartass, but it'll take care of your devil dog."

Phoenix limped back to the front of the house, trailing the designer dress in her blood. Suddenly exhausted, she sat down at a desk. Under the house, beneath her feet, she heard Goose's incessant barking. "Shut Up! Shut Up! Shut Up!" She stomped the floor so hard that blood spattered onto a toy bear beside the hearth.

Kathryn's cell phone rang. Phoenix took it out of her pocket and stared at it while the caller left a message. She limped into the kitchen to get away from the dog's racket and played back the voice mail. Joe's third call of the afternoon wanting Kathryn to call him. "He sure is hot to trot to talk to you, smarty pants." She deleted the message.

Blood dripped down the back of her leg as she slouched against the kitchen counter and scrolled through calls she had saved during the past three days. The last call from Colton she listened to for about the thirtieth time. "Hey, babe, I'm on my way, don't make any plans without me." With an ecstatic sigh, she went about randomly opening kitchen drawers. She selected an ice pick and put it on the counter with the duct tape and a plastic trash bag. Carrying the kitchen shears to the desk she started methodically cutting the Nicky Forrester creation to shreds. She no longer heard the dog's barking, just Colton calling her babe.

Chapter 29

In dire need of a dose of gal pal silliness after closing the library, Kathryn decided to drive to Five Points and drop in on Dee at her real estate office. As she climbed out of her car, a distinctive, raspy voice hailed her from across the parking lot. "Hello, mystery girl."

"Oh, Alex, hi. What'd you think of my ridiculous splash at the premiere?"

He walked over and joined her beside the car. "You looked right at home on Joe's arm."

She gave the shaggy-haired musician a wan smile. Was he making fun of her?

He gestured toward the empty porte-cochère on the side of the building where Dee usually parked. "If you're looking for the little mama, she's not in."

"Okay. I thought she might stop by the library this afternoon, but when she didn't show up, I decided to come here."

"Tommy and I were golfing." Alex glanced around self-consciously and lowered his voice. "I'm playing hooky, supposed to have left on tour already. Tommy got called for a patient, and Dee didn't answer her phone, so I stopped by to give her a heads-up that he'd be late for dinner."

Kathryn shaded her eyes as the descending sun seemed balanced on the dormer above Dee's office. "She always answers her phone. I hope nothing's wrong."

"Her assistant said she went downtown, something about a hunky monkey."

Kathryn looked at him in surprise. "That's what she calls Colton. He's not supposed to be here."

"So, mystery girl's mystery thickens." Alex grinned salaciously.

"Cut that out. He needs friends just like everyone else. Real friends."

"Friends, huh? Is that all?"

"Not that it's any of your business, but yes."

He slanted a look at her. "And my man Joe?"

Kathryn flushed. She refused to be baited by Joe's crony. "Which Joe would that be, Alex? The Joe with the wife or the Joe that I—" Words failed her for a moment and then she blurted out, "I'm not stupid!"

Tears welled in her eyes, and she was furious at her shrill outburst.

Hard-core rocker on the outside, Alex Whitlow was an intuitive artist within. Kathryn's pain was palpable to him.

He considered the piece of paper he and Suze had witnessed a decade before. A document languishing in a California courthouse that legally hog-tied their friend Joe to a nut case. He considered that man now agonizing over his little girl.

Alex slung a wiry arm around Kathryn's shoulder. "Let's me and you walk over to Jittery Joe's and chill. If I'm gonna clue you in, I need some strong coffee."

∽↶∾

Anna tried to reason with Joe. "There's no need for you to be here all the time." Unlike him, she was good at waiting.

His eyes, red-rimmed from exhaustion and worry, were fixed on Wrenn. "I'm not leaving until we know for sure the new antibiotic is working."

Anna patted his arm. "I understand, but you wearing yourself out won't help."

He tucked Wrenn's small, limp hand back under the blanket. "Won't hurt."

Anna nodded solemnly. "Will you be okay while I go downstairs?"

"Sure." Joe didn't have to ask where. She would be in the chapel lighting another candle. Maybe she should light one for him this time. He picked up Anna's crochet basket and sat in her chair, holding it in his lap. The lace she was creating looked delicate. Delicate like Wrenn. But it felt strong as he ran it through his fingers, strong like he prayed his little bird would have a chance to become. He unraveled the last few stitches. Would Anna make something out of the lace or would it and her granddaughter's life both remain unfinished? Heaving a deep sigh, he leaned his head back and let his eyes close. Almost immediately, his phone jarred away the illusion of rest.

"Thought you should know," Daniel said. "I've been expecting Phoenix to show up on this Quebec location but accounting has tracked her to Athens."

Joe stood up and frowned out the hospital window. Phoenix didn't compute with Athens. "I thought she was in Chicago."

"Yeah, me too—"

"Dammit, Daniel!"

"The accountants showed a slew of charges from there—apartment, restaurants, concerts, all kinds of stuff.

Nothing indicated she'd been in Athens all this time. I'm particularly bothered by payments to the Georgia Center, fees going back as far as last fall."

"What kind of fees?"

"Classes. Some of them Kathryn's classes."

Joe scowled, pinching the bridge of his nose, trying to follow Phoenix's convoluted thinking. She hadn't gotten in his face for over a year. He'd fed Rusty hints about Chicago and kept him in the dark about Charlie's Corner. Joe couldn't control everything, though. Why'd she take Kathryn's classes? He thought about the van that rammed the Prius. Was Phoenix so warped she'd perceive the mere proximity of another woman to Colton as a threat? Joe clenched his fist. Damn those pictures from the premiere.

A nurse came in quietly and moved to Wrenn's bedside. Joe turned to watch as she recorded data from various machines. A rock dropped into the pit of his stomach. Eduardo had said the vandalism at the cottage looked personal. Another rock dropped. Phoenix had obliterated Matilda's churn. She could obliterate Kathryn, too. And he'd let Eduardo go to see his mother in Florida.

"Call Eduardo," Joe croaked, suddenly unable to swallow.

"I did. He's hauling ass from Miami, but he can't get there 'til morning. Marleen is in North Carolina."

"Okay. I'm on it." A tremor in Joe's hand caused him to overshoot Kathryn's number in his cell phone. Scrolling back, he located it and sent the call. Could he make her understand someone as twisted as Phoenix? He had to. She didn't answer, so he cleared the rasp out of his voice and left a message. "Kathryn, call me ASAP." Hesitating, he added, "Please don't ignore this. It's urgent."

He tried to reach Dee. Her cell rolled directly to

voice mail where he left the same plea.

Telling himself he would wait an hour, he prowled the room and called both Kathryn and Dee again before twenty minutes had passed. Again, neither answered. An involuntary shudder coursed through him. God willing, they were together.

ↄↄↄↄ

Anna returned and settled back into her chair to resume crocheting. Keeping her hands busy passed the time. She found comfort in simple things like brushing Wrenn's hair, but she could tell there was no relief for Joe. Every few minutes she saw him check his phone for messages. If anything, his despair seemed to have deepened. It etched his face and hollowed his eyes. Not for the first time, she wondered if Wrenn was as much his lifeline as the other way around.

Nurses nearing the end of their shifts, about to transition back into the normalcy of their lives outside the hospital, shared family stories with one another and gossiped about this and that as they went about their tasks. Over the years, Anna had come to look forward to the distraction of their chatter.

A bubbly blonde technician giggled her way into Wrenn's room. "Did you hear about Colton Bennett," she whispered to the RN at the bedside, a loud whisper Anna heard from across the room.

"Shush," the senior nurse said, initialing the patient chart.

Anna looked at Joe, but he was staring out the window as though he hadn't heard.

The young blonde was unable to contain herself. "He's making quite a stir with some pregnant girl. It's all over the news."

The older nurse rolled her eyes as the two women left the room. "All I can say is, lucky girl."

Reminders of Wrenn's biological father filled Anna with regret, but she had long ago released her anger toward him and Phoenix. Barely grown, they hadn't been aware of things such as gene mutation and cystic fibrosis. Joe was Wrenn's father in every significant and relevant way. Anna was not fooled by his apparent inattention. "Do you want me to turn on the television so you can see what's going on?"

He shook his head. "I don't care." Massaging his temples with the heels of his hands, he closed his eyes. "I just plain don't give a damn what Benny does anymore."

Anna went over and put her arm gently around Joe's waist. "Please, honey, go out for a little while."

He sighed wearily. "Okay. I won't be long."

Leaving the hospital building reminded Joe of leaving a movie theatre, blinking at the brightness outside. He jogged back and forth from one extremity of the hospital property to the other. Maybe he should get the Athens police to check on Kathryn. Already in a heightened state of anxiety over Wrenn, he didn't want to overreact to Daniel's news but, in the very core of his being, he sensed Kathryn was in danger. His need to hear her voice was overwhelming. He stopped in his tracks, called and left a third message.

He shuffled options. Alex was gone on tour, so he pressed Tommy's number. Maddeningly, the call rolled to the doctor's answering service. "No message," Joe said, "but can you give me the number of Overby Real Estate?" He jabbed in Steve Overby's number with stiff fingers. As much as he disliked Steve, the man spoke highly of Kathryn and he was big enough and mean enough to take on Phoenix.

"Yallow," the consummate good-ole-boy drawled.

"Hey, Steve, it's Joe Butler. I need somebody to get in touch with Kathryn Tribble. It's urgent, and I can't get her on the phone. Can you go out to her place?"

"Man, I'm at the damn bottom of Kay's list right now."

"Listen up. I'm serious. She doesn't know it, but there's a crazy woman stalking her. Go check on her, will you?"

"Well, I guess I could, if you say so."

"Soon as you can. And Steve…"

"Yeah?"

"…if you've got a gun, take it with you."

"Shit fire, I'm on the way."

Joe shoved his phone into his jeans pocket and picked up his pace for another lap around the parking lots. A light-headed feeling soon changed his mind. Running on an empty stomach was a bad idea. He couldn't remember if he'd eaten yesterday, but he knew he hadn't had anything today. He squatted down to let the dizziness pass and then went back into the hospital.

A big wall clock registering seven was his last image of the lobby through the slow-closing doors of the elevator. Time meant nothing in hospitals. Steadying himself against the side wall of the empty elevator, he discovered the vigil with Wrenn had not left him devoid of tears or prayers. The corners of his eyelids were wet as he squeezed them shut. "Please, God, take care of my little Wrenn. And please, please God, build a wall of protection around Kathryn and keep her safe."

Chapter 30

Kathryn drove slowly home, trying to comprehend what Alex had told her. Her head and throat hurt from holding back tears. She was heartsick. Joe had lived with unimaginable pain long before she'd ever met him. At this very moment he was waging a life and death battle for the precious daughter he had poured all his love into. Imagining such agony made it hard for Kathryn to breathe. How could he bear it?

On autopilot, she pulled up to her mailbox, took out the mail, and tossed it onto the passenger seat. From what Alex had described, Joe was the one with courage, not her. He acted on his heart every day of his life. He loved his cousin's child as his own. He'd restricted his life by marrying and providing for the no-account mother, whoever she was. All the while protecting Colton from one screw-up after another. He had protected Kathryn, too, even though she'd been an ungrateful wretch about it.

Goose confronted her in the mouth of the driveway. He dashed around the curve from the house, barking and dancing in front of her car. She stopped and got out to ruffle his fur. "What's up with you?" She ran her hands up over his face, and he closed his eyes. Beckoned to the solace of her cottage, just out of sight in the gathering dusk beyond the tree-lined curve, she smoothed his neck fur down and made a move back toward her car.

Goose whined and pushed against her legs.

She plopped down on the ground and hugged an arm around him, her thoughts still on Joe. Of course, he was dark and edgy. How could he be anything else? What torture, juggling Colton's public shenanigans while privately wrestling with problems big enough to take down Goliath. Joe had made a joke when she advised him not to let life get too heavy. How ridiculous that must have sounded to him. His life was already heavier than he could bear. What could possibly be sadder than knowing your child might not live to grow up?

Kathryn rested her head on Goose's neck and let go of her tears. "Please, God," she wept, "Wherever Joe is and whatever he's doing, please let him feel your presence and know your love."

Somewhere amidst the heartache came the thought that writing was what sustained Joe. He had created Kitty Quinn in Kathryn's image, and he was willing to sacrifice Kitty for her. That revelation caused her to raise her head and dry her eyes.

Sitting cross-legged in the grass, she shivered. She wore only a lightweight blouse and slacks, but her shiver had nothing to do with leaving her coat in the car. As far as she could see into the sunset beyond Charlie's Corner, con trails from jets heading to and from Hartsfield-Jackson laced the bruised horizon. All her life she had watched those tiny specks scribing fresh lines to far-flung places. She hadn't put any importance on their point of origin, but she had been drawn back to hers, drawn back home.

Quite unexpectedly she realized, in her heart of

hearts, that home wasn't here. Thanks to Alex, she now knew exactly where to find it.

She planted a kiss on the dog's grizzled head and stood up. "Love you, Goosey Loosey, but I don't have time for you right now." She pulled a takeout box from the car, opened the lid, and set it on the ground. "My compliments, sir, on your very own Covered & Smothered." She hopped back in the Prius, put the car in reverse, and sprayed gravel backing out of the driveway.

ოოო

Steve wondered how long since he'd been out Old Tildy's place. He and Kay'd had some mighty good times and he wasn't about to let some fool hurt her. A big dog snarfing the contents of a take-out box lit out after Steve's truck as soon as he turned in at the mail box. Barking for all he was worth, the ugly mutt chased his truck up the driveway.

Slowing, Steve let his window down and said, "Good puppy, good puppy." Like any realtor worth his salt at showing property, he had a way with dogs. "Good puppy. You're a good puppy." The dog kept barking, but gradually showed less teeth and more interest in him than the truck. When Steve parked, he opened the door and sat a spell so the ole defender could sniff him and realize he was friend not foe.

The dog shied away a few steps when the big man got out, and he kept a close eye as they both approached the cottage.

"Good puppy," Steve said. "You sure you belong here? I'd expect Kay to have a good-looking Collie or a Lab, not a big ole Sooner like you. But I guess I don't really know her anymore, do I? Good pupp—"

Steve fell to his knees with searing pain in his left shoulder.

The dog yelped and ran under the porch.

The blast had come from the house and Steve knew a shotgun when he heard it. His shoulder was on fire with buckshot. "Damn twelve gauge," he muttered, hunching beside the brick steps and peering over their buttress. Kay's wooden door was shredded. Joe's fool had fired straight through the front door.

Steve balanced momentarily on his all-fours and knew he had to get inside before she could reload. He bounded onto the porch and made a linebacker rush through the shattered door. He didn't see her at first, not until she stabbed him in the neck.

☙❧☙

When Joe reached the hospital room, Anna nodded her head to indicate an uptick in Wrenn's numbers. Pulsing with nervousness, he noticed Anna glance up from her needlework several times as he paced. He regulated his breathing to take the edge off his anxiety and held onto the window sill, forcing himself to stop moving. His body quivered with renewed urgency. As soon as his phone vibrated, he snatched it from his pocket and ran out into the hall.

Almost before the door closed, he said, "Did you get to Kathryn?"

"Beats all I've ever seen," Steve drawled.

Joe was used to Steve milking a story on the golf course, but he couldn't suffer the man's circuitous dialogue. "Tell me."

"Like I said, beats all I've ever seen."

Joe took a deep breath. "What?"

"That little woman is crazy as a bedbug."

"So she really was there. What about Kathryn?"

"Man, you almost got me killed. First, there was this big ole yard dog. Had to get friendly with him 'fore I could even get out of my truck. I'm used to that in real estate, but I ain't used to getting buckshot blasted at me through the front door."

"Phoenix shot at you?"

"Aw, the recoil hurt her worse'n she hurt me. I just took some pellets in the shoulder. She missed the dog altogether. But when I got in the house, damn if she didn't go and stab me in the neck with a pair of scissors."

Joe's lips went numb. "My God."

"That's what I'm saying. Close as catfish to my jugular."

"What'd you do?"

"What d'you think? I hauled her ass to the floor and hog-tied her. That's when I saw all the blood. Man, I've seen a lotta stuff, but I ain't never seen blood all over a pretty little house like this before."

"Is it—" *Please no.* "—Kathryn's blood?"

"Don't know yet. That's the thing. Ain't nobody found Kathryn. This woman here is going on about how she's killed her."

"Killed her!"

"That's what she says. She's all bloody herself. Broke a window to get in and cut herself up pretty good. They took her off to the hospital raving about, of all things, how Kathryn can't stop her from being with Colton Bennett." Steve let out a snort. "Like a movie star would have anything to do with either one of them."

Joe wanted to reach through the phone and strangle the man. "Kathryn's car? Is it there?"

"Don't think so—hey, lemme call you back. One of them deputies the sheriff sent out here just radioed the other one and he took off down the driveway. Reckon he's found something."

Steve disconnected so abruptly Joe felt dizzy again. He leaned against the corridor wall and tried not to hyperventilate. He willed the phone to ring, all the while dreading it.

Steve called back within minutes, devoid of any folksy tone, his words held a gritty edge. "Evidence says Kathryn and her car might be in the pond."

"The pond?" Joe thought his chest would burst wide open. "What kind of evidence?"

"Tire tracks running over a section of pasture fence, straight down the hill to the water. They can't do anything in the dark, so they'll wait and drag the bottom at dawn."

Anna was alarmed at how much more haggard Joe looked when he returned to the room. She set her basket on the floor as he pulled up a chair close in front of her. The new depth of pain in his eyes was frightening. "What is it? What's happened?"

He took both her hands in his and searched her face. "Anna—" he started, stopped for a hard swallow, and then said, "Phoenix has been arrested. Here in Georgia. She—she—I'm sorry, Anna. Whatever she is, she's still your child." He lowered his head, unable or unwilling to go on.

Anna sensed what she long feared had come true, but she didn't react as she had expected. The tears that sprang to her eyes weren't for Phoenix, not for the daughter she had known and loved. That person had been gone for a very long time. Anna's tears were for Joe. In the midst of his own personal torment, this kindhearted young man was worried about her.

Holding tight to his hands, she said, "There's only one thing to do. Like with her father, they'll have to put her where she can do no more harm. Who did she hurt? I would rather not know, but I must pray for them."

"A—it's—a woman." Joe's voice was barely audible and his eyes glistened with tears as he lifted his head. "She's—oh God, Anna—she's missing."

Anna's heart froze at the anguish in his voice. "Darling, is this somebody you know?"

He nodded. "Phoenix broke in her house—and she said—she said she'd killed her."

Anna whispered, "What's her name?"

Through ashen lips, he forced out, "Kathryn."

He laid his head on Anna's lap and she stroked his dark, tangled hair. His sobs were raw, convulsive, painful to hear. Anna closed her eyes and prayed.

෴

At the end of the hospital corridor, Joe stood looking out the plate-glass window that faced east toward Athens. In the morning, the sun would rise there with the promise of a new day, a hollow promise without Kathryn. Horror played in a loop in his head: *blood all over the place…no sign of Kathryn…tire tracks straight into the pond…deputies dragging the bottom.* He closed his eyes: *blood…no Kathryn…dragging the bottom.* Bile rose into his throat.

He was doing everything humanly possible to save Wrenn. Kathryn, he had failed. His heart felt like a balled fist punching him. He had been so focused on his pig of a cousin, he hadn't thought about Phoenix in context with anything except Colton's movie locations. How could he have put the man so close to Kathryn without seeing her as a perceived threat to Phoenix?

He pinched the bridge of his nose. How could he have been so self-absorbed? He was no better than Colton. Above all else, against all her objections, he should have kept her safe. Beautiful, precious, priceless woman. A low, guttural moan escaped him.

He yearned for her sweet, calm presence. He didn't just want her in his family. He wanted her in his arms. His—not Colton's. "God help me," he groaned. "I never stood up and said so. Now she's—Oh, God, I've lost it all."

℘ↄℰↄ

As Anna pressed the call button for the elevator, she turned and looked back toward the man Wrenn called Bapa. He appeared to be staring out the corridor window but was likely looking inward, fearing for his little girl, waiting for a doctor to come and officially pronounce the results of the new drug. Anna's eyes misted. Joe would fill her in later, but even if the news was as good as she suspected, he needed to hear it by himself. That's the way she'd known him to face things throughout the years. Alone. Before the elevator door opened completely, a young woman bolted out and plowed straight into Anna. Flinging an arm back to keep from falling, Anna dropped her crochet basket.

"Oh," the offender gasped. "I'm so sorry."

"It's okay." Anna stooped to pick up her belongings. "I wasn't looking," she said, but the woman was no longer aware of Anna.

Her pretty face flushed with pure joy when she caught sight of Joe. Making her way down the corridor toward him, she reached back to fix her ponytail, knocked askew in her collision with Anna. Checking a motion to tighten the band, instead she pulled it out of her hair and put it on her wrist like a bracelet. The loosed cascade of shiny brunette waves brought to Anna's mind an image of time-lapse photography, a bloom unfurling before her eyes. Transfixed, she ignored the arrival of another elevator.

The young woman stopped a few paces behind Joe and seemed to quietly drink him in.

Joe tilted his head and reached a hand around to massage the muscles at the base of his skull. Dark hair, overgrown and disheveled, curved between his fingers. His western shirt, sleeves rolled carelessly to the elbow, was half-tucked and rumpled. He hitched his shoulder in a gesture that might have looked careless had the motion not been so tense.

As though becoming aware of a presence, his posture stiffened. No doubt anticipating the doctor, he turned slowly. "Kathryn!" fairly exploded out of him, and he staggered forward. "You're safe!"

"Yes," she said, embracing him. "I am, with you."

The End

About the Author

Award-winning author Genie Bernstein began writing by falling out of the sky. After safely landing an airplane whose engine failed, she was unable to talk about the experience until capturing her emotions on paper. From that exercise came her ability to infuse writing with emotion and led her to the romance genre.

Originally from Eatonton, Georgia, Bernstein writes in an authentic southern voice. Swimming to keep fit she makes her home in Athens, Georgia, and shares with her husband their joyously combined family of six children and thirteen globe-trotting grandchildren.

Bernstein is a featured columnist for *Georgia Connector,* Georgia's premier regional quarterly magazine. Awarded South Carolina's "Carrie McCray Literary Award for Non-Fiction," her work was also selected to appear in four volumes of *O, Georgia!* anthologies of Georgia's newest and most promising writers.

CPSIA information can be obtained
at www.ICGtesting.com
Printed in the USA
FFOW01n1840301216
30889FF